PRAISE FOR M. L. BUCHMAN

Tom Clancy fans open t[illegible] strong female lead [illegible] clamor for more.

— *Drone*, Publishers Weekly

Superb! Miranda is utterly compelling!

— *Booklist*, starred review

Miranda Chase continues to astound and charm.

— Barb M.

Escape Rating: A. Five Stars! OMG just start with *Drone* and be prepared for a fantastic binge-read!

— Reading Reality

The best military thriller I've read in a very long time. Love the female characters.

— *Drone*, Sheldon McArthur, founder of The Mystery Bookstore, LA

A fabulous soaring thriller.

— *Take Over at Midnight*, Midwest Book Review

Meticulously researched, hard-hitting, and suspenseful.

— *Pure Heat,* Publishers Weekly, starred review

Expert technical details abound, as do realistic military missions with superb imagery that will have readers feeling as if they are right there in the midst and on the edges of their seats.

— *Light Up the Night,* RT Reviews, 4 1/2 stars

Buchman has catapulted his way to the top tier of my favorite authors.

— Fresh Fiction

Nonstop action that will keep readers on the edge of their seats.

— *Take Over at Midnight,* Library Journal

M L. Buchman's ability to keep the reader right in the middle of the action is amazing.

— Long and Short Reviews

The only thing you'll ask yourself is, "When does the next one come out?"

— *Wait Until Midnight,* RT Reviews, 4 stars

The first...of (a) stellar, long-running (military) romantic suspense series.

— *The Night is Mine*, Booklist, "The 20 Best Romantic Suspense Novels: Modern Masterpieces"

I knew the books would be good, but I didn't realize how good.

— Night Stalkers series, Kirkus Reviews

Buchman mixes adrenalin-spiking battles and brusque military jargon with a sensitive approach.

— Publishers Weekly

13 times "Top Pick of the Month"

— Night Owl Reviews

RAIDER

A MIRANDA CHASE ACTION-ADVENTURE TECHNOTHRILLER

M. L. BUCHMAN

Receive a free book and discover more by this author at: www.mlbuchman.com

Cover images:

Forest Fire, Pinus pilaster, Guadalajara, Spain © jalonsohu

Raider S-97 © DoD

SIGN UP FOR M. L. BUCHMAN'S NEWSLETTER TODAY

and receive:
Release News
Free Short Stories
a Free Book

Get your free book today. Do it now.
free-book.mlbuchman.com

Other works by M. L. Buchman: *(* - also in audio)*

Action-Adventure Thrillers

Dead Chef

One Chef!
Two Chef!

Miranda Chase

*Drone**
*Thunderbolt**
*Condor**
*Ghostrider**
*Raider**
*Chinook**
*Havoc**
*White Top**

Romantic Suspense

Delta Force

*Target Engaged**
*Heart Strike**
*Wild Justice**
*Midnight Trust**

Firehawks

MAIN FLIGHT

Pure Heat
Full Blaze
*Hot Point**
*Flash of Fire**
Wild Fire

SMOKEJUMPERS

*Wildfire at Dawn**
*Wildfire at Larch Creek**
*Wildfire on the Skagit**

The Night Stalkers

MAIN FLIGHT

The Night Is Mine
I Own the Dawn
Wait Until Dark
Take Over at Midnight
Light Up the Night
Bring On the Dusk
By Break of Day

AND THE NAVY

Christmas at Steel Beach
Christmas at Peleliu Cove

WHITE HOUSE HOLIDAY

*Daniel's Christmas**
*Frank's Independence Day**
*Peter's Christmas**
*Zachary's Christmas**
*Roy's Independence Day**
*Damien's Christmas**

5E

Target of the Heart
Target Lock on Love
Target of Mine
Target of One's Own

Shadow Force: Psi

*At the Slightest Sound**
*At the Quietest Word**
*At the Merest Glance**
*At the Clearest Sensation**

White House Protection Force

*Off the Leash**
*On Your Mark**
*In the Weeds**

Contemporary Romance

Eagle Cove

Return to Eagle Cove
Recipe for Eagle Cove
Longing for Eagle Cove
Keepsake for Eagle Cove

Henderson's Ranch

*Nathan's Big Sky**
*Big Sky, Loyal Heart**
*Big Sky Dog Whisperer**

Other works by M. L. Buchman:

Contemporary Romance (cont)

Love Abroad

Heart of the Cotswolds: England
Path of Love: Cinque Terre, Italy

Where Dreams

Where Dreams are Born
Where Dreams Reside
*Where Dreams Are of Christmas**
Where Dreams Unfold
Where Dreams Are Written

Science Fiction / Fantasy

Deities Anonymous

Cookbook from Hell: Reheated
Saviors 101

Single Titles

The Nara Reaction
Monk's Maze
the Me and Elsie Chronicles

Non-Fiction

Strategies for Success

Managing Your Inner Artist/Writer
*Estate Planning for Authors**
Character Voice
*Narrate and Record Your Own Audiobook**

Short Story Series by M. L. Buchman:

Romantic Suspense

Delta Force

Th Delta Force Shooters
The Delta Force Warriors

Firehawks

The Firehawks Lookouts
The Firehawks Hotshots
The Firebirds

The Night Stalkers

The Night Stalkers 5D Stories
The Night Stalkers 5E Stories
The Night Stalkers CSAR
The Night Stalkers Wedding Stories

US Coast Guard

White House Protection Force

Contemporary Romance

Eagle Cove

Henderson's Ranch*

Where Dreams

Action-Adventure Thrillers

Dead Chef

Miranda Chase Origin Stories

Science Fiction / Fantasy

Deities Anonymous

Other

The Future Night Stalkers
Single Titles

ABOUT THIS BOOK

A cyberattack penetrates US military systems. The woman to solve it? Miranda Chase.

The US Army's brand-new S-97 Raider reconnaissance helicopter goes down during final acceptance testing—hard. Cause: a failure, or the latest in a series of cyberattacks by Turkey?

***Miranda Chase,** the NTSB's autistic air-crash genius, and her team of sleuths spring into action. They must find the flaw, save the Vice President, and stop the US being forced into the next war in the Middle East. And they have to do it now!*

PROLOGUE

Ankara, Turkey
Siberkume – Cyber Security Cluster
Subbasement #2

METIN STRUGGLED AGAINST THE COLLAPSING CODE RACING UP HIS computer screen.

The American satellite's onboard software was self-correcting—constantly checking its synchronization and alignment.

His right-hand computer screen showed the geographic shift he'd managed to induce in seven of the thirty-three satellites in this single system. It wasn't systemic but, exactly as required, it was very localized.

On his central screen, the American code he had decrypted was about to rotate. Every hour, the encryption routine scrambled itself. He'd had one hour to decrypt and infiltrate his own code before the door closed again, and he'd have had to start over from scratch.

It had taken fifty-seven minutes for his program on the left screen to crack that code. That had left him only a three-minute window to alter the data broadcast that the satellites beamed downward.

After three months of trying, his first successful hack had finally told him which path he'd needed to pursue. A week to break down and rebuild his code had taken out the element of chance that had let him crack it the first time.

It still wasn't an easy task, but he'd done it! In under the required hour and targeted the exact location called for in the new mission profile.

But, between sixty minutes and sixty minutes-and-one second, the window into the American's code imploded once more into encrypted gibberish.

Metin collapsed back into his chair, drained as if he'd been on the attack for sixty hours, not sixty minutes.

The noises around him came back slowly, the same way Gaye Su Akyol eased into her Anatolian rock videos.

Siberkume was humming tonight, though with a very different tune.

In the big room's half-light that made it easier to stay focused on the screens, there sounded the harsh rattle of keys, soft-murmured conversations, and quiet curses of code gone wrong. It washed back and forth across the twenty stations crammed into the concrete bunker like a familiar tide. The sharp snap of an opening Red Bull can sounded like a gunshot. He liked that the Americans—all it took was watching the many eSports players Red Bull sponsored to know he belonged—were running on the same fuel he was, but still he'd beaten them.

He snapped his own Red Bull because he definitely needed something to fight back the shakes from the sustained code dive.

Siberkume might not have the vast banks of hackers like

the Russians or Chinese, but he was part of a lean, mean, fighting machine.

General Firat came striding up to his station like he owned the world. Since he ran Siberkume, he certainly owned Metin's world.

"I'm sorry, General. That was the best I could do this time." It was the Cyber Security Cluster's first real test of their abilities against a force like the Americans. *He* was the one who'd done it, but it was better to be cautious with the military. Their moods were more unpredictable than his sister's crazy cat.

"No, Metin. That was a very good start. Very good. You are *çacal*—'like the coyote'."

General Firat thumped him hard enough on the shoulder that his keyboarding would be ten percent below normal speed for at least an hour.

But "Metin the Coyote"?

He could get down with that. It was seriously high praise.

"I'll get the effective window wider, General. I don't know if I can beat the hourly reset. But now that I know how to get in, I can hone my code. I'll make it faster so we have more time." Though he had no idea how. He'd already streamlined it with every trick he knew to beat that one-hour limit.

Unless he could talk his way onto the Yildiz SVR supercomputer...

Wouldn't that be *hot shit?* (He loved American slang and ferreted it out whenever he could sneak online.)

"Yes, yes." Clearly the General hadn't understood a word of what he'd said about what could and couldn't be done.

Metin considered simplifying it, but he wasn't sure how. It didn't matter; General Firat didn't pause for a breath.

"Be ready. You have one week for the next level test. You are the very first one to make it through. Your skills have not gone unnoticed. Well done, *Çacal*. Bravo!" The general must mean it as he said the last loudly enough to be easily overheard by the ten closest programmers before striding off into the dim shadows of Siberkume.

Metin grinned across the aisle at Onur.

Onur groaned, but Metin didn't rub it in too much. Onur's sister Asli was the most lovely girl in the world, and his ability to visit with her, without appearing to visit with her, depended largely on Onur's continuing friendship.

But to rub it in a little, he rolled back his shoulders and pushed out his chest like Blackpink's Rosé being so nice and just a little nasty. They'd watched all of the group's K-pop videos over a totally illegal VPN to YouTube. It was one of the luxuries of working at Siberkume: access to the outside world —if you didn't get caught.

I've so got the stuff.

Onur snorted and gave him an Obi-Wan Kenobi, *Yeah, right!* look. Onur didn't look anything like Ewan McGregor, even with the expression. Of course, he himself didn't look much like the superhot Rosé.

1

MIKE MIGHT BE SITTING IN THE LUXURY OF HIS USUAL LEATHER armchair in the office, but he was definitely feeling crowded into a corner.

"I'm just saying that we didn't find anything mechanical," Jeremy Trahn waved at the big television screen on the wall. He was operating it from his workbench, which took up one whole end of the office.

He'd been adding to his toolset over the six months since Miranda had set up the team's high-security office, walled off in the back of her airplane hangar. Now there was little that the labs at the National Transportation Safety Board's Washington, DC, headquarters could analyze better. None of Miranda's team went into even the Seattle office anymore. Everything they needed was here.

What had started as a comfortable office space six months ago now looked well lived-in. Jeremy's cluttered tool bench at one end of the spectrum, and Miranda's meticulous rolltop antique desk at the other.

He'd expanded the kitchenette enough that he could cobble together a decent meal when they were working long hours and the airport restaurant was closed. Other than that, it was about comfortable seats arranged to face a lovely view.

Out the office's one-way windows lay a view of the quiet runway at Tacoma Narrows Airport and a stunning vista of the snow-capped Olympic mountains. Which reminded him all too much of their entire last week's investigation.

Between the windows hung a large monitor screen.

But he didn't want to look at that.

Jeremy had loaded a list of everything they'd been able to verify about the crash itself. For emphasis, Jeremy used a pen on his connected tablet to make a checkmark in front of each item on the long list of each system and structural test.

"Doesn't mean the cause isn't there. The debris field covered most of a mile." And it had been damned cold.

That was Mike's main memory of the site investigation. Eight August days at six thousand feet walking an Alaskan glacier on Denali's eastern slope. North America's tallest peak rose over twenty thousand feet above nearby Anchorage and created its own weather systems—none of them comfortable. There was gray with fierce winds driving horizontal ice needles into every exposed bit of skin, and there was an aching blue with a cold so biting that it kind of killed the wonder of it all.

They'd only left Alaska yesterday because an early storm dropped three feet of fresh powder over the investigation site. There wouldn't be anything to see until spring, if then, so they'd finally come back to the office in western Washington.

It had been past midnight last night when they'd crashed—no other word to describe their exhaustion—at the team house in Gig Harbor. Nobody had so much as moved before lunch. Now they'd come to the office to analyze what they'd learned.

Clarity? So not.

Mike still felt muddle-headed from the six-hour night flight down the coast. His joints still ached though they'd returned to the pleasant late summer of Puget Sound. If this was how old age felt, he was retiring to Hawaii before he hit thirty next year.

High on Denali hadn't been the cozy cold of Aspen. A quick one-hour jaunt in his company's little Beechcraft plane. Especially nice when he was dating someone. They'd carve up the slopes during the day and carve up the sheets in some firelit lodge each night. He'd loved that plane—the last business asset he'd had to forfeit shortly before he finally found a position with the NTSB.

The personal office that Miranda had built in her hangar at Tacoma Narrows Airport was physically both warm and comfortable. Except he *wasn't* getting a whole lot of comfort here. With Jeremy insisting that it wasn't his systems, and Holly claiming there was no sign of any structural failure, everyone was pointing at pilot error.

The atmosphere inside the warm office was just as chilly as a glacier on Denali.

He pulled out his phone, opened the fireplace app, and propped it where only he could see the cheerfully crackling flames. That felt a little better on the warm part. Now if he just had a little spray bottle for woodsmoke scent...

But Jeremy didn't let up for a second, arguing for the sanctity of his beloved mechanical systems.

To his right, Holly slumped on the couch with her feet on the coffee table. One of her socks had a hole in it so that her big toe stuck out. The other sock didn't match. Socks weren't the sort of thing that Holly Harper ever cared about. Her jeans, t-shirt, and polar fleece vest showed just how rough she was on her clothes.

Miranda was, as usual at this stage, keeping her thoughts to herself. She sat neatly upright in the padded armchair to his left. At a slight five-four, she could curl up and sleep in that chair—if she ever stopped moving.

She cared for her own looks about as much as Holly

cared about her socks. Her clothes were always neat and of the very best quality. But her longish brunette hair was always a slightly disorganized ruffle sometimes hiding half her face, or falling loose from where she'd tucked it behind an ear. She was wired so tightly that even sitting still she seemed to buzz. She was as near opposite Holly as could be found.

"You know, mate..."

He and Holly had both been on Miranda's team for a year—on-again off-again lovers for the last half of that—and still her smooth Australian Strine just slayed him. And that lovely long body. She'd chopped her gold-blonde hair at the jawline, probably with the big knife she habitually wore at her thigh. He suspected that she'd done it because he'd mentioned how much he'd liked it down past her shoulders. But that was Holly. It still looked perfect.

"This is a two-aircraft collision," Holly continued. "Those are almost always pilot error. In fact, it's usually both pilots in error. You know that, Mike."

He did know that. "But that doesn't mean it's right this time."

Two planes—a DHC-6 Series 100 Twin Otter, with a solo pilot and two thousand pounds of fresh-caught silver salmon out of Fairbanks, and a one-pilot-plus-seven-passenger sightseeing tour in a Piper Navajo out of Anchorage—had collided near the towering pinnacle of Denali.

And everybody was pointing the finger at him. Or at least his specialty of "human factors." But it felt personal.

"You want *my* list?" he nodded toward the offending screen.

Holly shrugged as if she didn't care.

Of them all, she'd been fairly well able to prove that the problem hadn't stemmed from her structural specialty. No wings had broken off from metal fatigue, and no engines had fallen out of the sky detached from their surviving chunk of wing. No part of the tail's empennage had failed on either plane—at least not from structural issues.

That left systems or human factors, and there was no convincing Jeremy that any systems failure could have caused the collision.

Flight recorders weren't required on planes carrying fewer than ten passengers. So no evidence there.

The collision had been bad enough that the Navajo had exploded in the air, as evidenced by the burn patterns on the metal that had barely melted into the glacier's surface when it landed, indicating that most of the burning had happened during the fall.

The body of the Twin Otter had impacted a quarter mile from one of its wings. But the ignition of the fuel in the one wing that had remained attached had ensured that the plane's destruction was complete. The deep divot in the glacier revealed that the second plane had exploded on impact and burned in place. The cargo of fish had scattered uniformly in every direction like a silver salmon fountain.

Thankfully, the *human* bodies had been removed by the pararescue folks of the 212th Rescue Squadron out of Elmendorf before their team reached Alaska. That was at least one memory he hadn't had to bring back to the hangar with him.

At least Miranda nodded for him to proceed, and that was all that mattered. She was always impartial and cared only about the facts.

The facts about people? Yeah, there was a good laugh. Capricious, demented, chaotic. How Miranda had avoided having any of those oh-so-normal tendencies was still beyond him. Maybe it was a part of her autism.

She might be challenged in so many ways, but she was *the* genius of air crashes—the very best in the entire National Transportation Safety Board. That he'd somehow lucked into being on her team was proof that there was a Fairy Godmother of Randomness at work in his life, a truth he'd always suspected before but never previously been able to confirm.

"First, both pilots were highly experienced. The Twin Otter pilot had made the Anchorage-Fairbanks roundtrip run roughly a hundred times a year for the last decade."

"Complacency."

He ignored Holly. "The tour operator had fewer hours but still over fifteen thousand, and you know that's more than many pilots retire with. He was also a certified flight instructor: multi-engine, commercial, and instruments."

"So he had some skills. He still smacked into another plane in broad daylight."

"Scattered clouds. Thick enough that they'd both filed IFR rather than VFR plans. So they were flying by instrument flight rules, not visual flight rules over very remote terrain."

"Then why were both planes off course?"

As to that? Mike didn't have an answer. By their flight plans, they should have passed a mile apart.

"Instrumentation errors?"

All that mattered was that he *knew* it wasn't pilot error. Both guys were mature career pilots, not Alaska bush-pilot boneheads.

Mike had uncovered nothing but glowing reports about both of them.

No depression.

No sleep deprivation.

No alcohol abuse.

One had left behind his high school sweetheart after twenty years together, the other a much younger but thoroughly pleasant second wife. The first wife had returned to the Lower 48 a decade before—the only one to not have nice things to say about him, most having to do with his choosing Alaska over her.

The meds between them included just one: a low-dose statin for the tour pilot's high cholesterol.

The only prior noteworthy incidents were an engine failure on the Twin Otter due to a load of bad fuel three years ago, and a destructive bird strike on the Navajo. Both had landed safely.

The Twin Otter pilot flying the load of salmon had drunk a single beer with his pizza at Moose's Tooth Pub & Pizzeria in Anchorage before his round-trip flight to Fairbanks. Mike had verified his wife's statement not only with the purchase receipt but with a waitress interview. He was a regular and easily remembered.

Two hours each way to Fairbanks, and the other was only a three-hour tour. So neither pilot should have been overtired.

One late thirties, the other early forties.

Both pilots had passed their FAA medicals within the last six months.

Malicious intent was about all that was left. But that hadn't fit either. The two pilots knew each other, but had few dealings.

He enumerated each point—again.

"Also, no survivors and no residents for thirty miles around, so no witnesses. No tourist's phones or cameras were in video mode at the moments leading up to impact, so no help there. No black boxes in such small aircraft, so no cockpit voice record to review. I did the rounds of air traffic controllers, fellow pilots, and the like, but there wasn't a single red flag."

Both their lives were such open books that he'd only escaped the investigation on the high glacier for a single day to complete all of the interviews. The other seven days he'd done little more than be grunt labor for the other three. Which meant little need for the team's human factors specialist —again.

Of all of their investigations over the last year, only two had traced to human factors—one stating it was his fault from the outset. It left his main role being little more than an intern for the other three team members.

The only definitive finding in the whole investigation had been an unending supply of frozen salmon scattered over a half mile of ice and snow. The pilots who ran them up to the site each day made a point of taking a couple coolers' worth back on each trip. He himself had a pair of massive twenty-five pounders tucked away in the freezer at the house for the next time he fired up the barbeque.

Nope, Mike just couldn't make the dual-error scenario fly. There were none of the telltale signs to indicate that was at all likely. The fault *had* to be with the planes.

"They shouldn't have collided," Miranda spoke for the first time since the whole review had begun.

"You didn't find even *one* thing wrong with the aircraft?"

Miranda shook her head, "All damage that we observed could be directly tied to the collision itself. A team will be performing analyses on what was recovered, but I do not anticipate metallurgy or deeper analysis to reveal anything else."

Mike sighed. Which left the Demon of Fickleness pointing directly at him. He'd take the Fairy Godmother of Randomness any day of the week.

2

MIRANDA HATED THIS.

There were accidents that were going to forever be classified as "No cause determined."

Sometimes the plane was never found. This only happened once every year or so, and was rarely dramatic enough to make the news. Thankfully, a loss like that of Malaysian Airlines Flight 370 was otherwise unheard of.

Occasionally an airplane was unrecoverable despite knowing its location. Early in her career, she'd investigated a flight that had ended up in the bottom of a deep Arctic lake. No question about the location, because of the few pieces that had floated to the cold surface. She still remembered the sharp scent of chilled pine that had pervaded the remote lake as a fishing guide had motored her back and forth across a surface so still and reflective that it looked like the sky continued down into the dark water. A seat cushion, a teenage girl's gym bag, a disposable coffee mug.

There'd been numerous pilot errors in weather judgment and load planning. The accumulated factors had so clearly indicated human error that no one had been willing to bear the expense of recovering the aircraft itself.

But to have the aircraft, both of the aircraft, available, and still have no clear direction of investigation was…

Miranda pulled out her personal notebook while the other three continued arguing. She flipped to the emotions page.

Negative category.

She began scanning the emojis pasted there and their labels.

Irritated? No. Too frowny.

Not angry. Too red-cheeked.

Irksome! She tried the expression herself, squinting with just one eye, and one cheek pulling a straight-line mouth to just one side.

Yes, irksome was a good word to describe what she was feeling.

She tucked the notebook away and contemplated Jeremy's list still on the screen. He'd done his usual, very thorough job.

"If I can't solve this…"

"If you can't solve it, no one else could, Miranda. You know that, don't you?" Mike was the only one sitting close enough to overhear her worry.

Did she know that?

Miranda tried to judge Mike's smile to see if he was joking.

No. He didn't appear to be.

To calm herself, she closed her eyes and did a round of "box" breathing. Four breaths. Count of four in. Hold for four. Count of four out.

The last exhale of the last breath was jarred out of her by the sudden ringing of her phone.

It was a special ring that she'd programmed for Jill at the NTSB.

It began as a low whine, a TF-39 jet engine winding up from pre-start. She'd made the recording herself quite close to a C-5B

Galaxy transport, the same model as her first ever military crash investigation. It rapidly grew to unnerving, a reminder to answer it quickly.

They all knew the sound of that ringtone. Mike's groan was emphatic. Jeremy's shoulders sagged. The team was exhausted and really deserved a break. She didn't feel much better.

"This is Miranda Chase speaking."

"Hello, Miranda Chase speaking," Jill always greeted her that way. Always cheerful and with a ready laugh, though Miranda occasionally thought that she herself might be the target of the latter more than others. Or maybe that upbeat attitude was the reason that Jill ran the NTSB's launch desk. "We have a launch for you."

Holly flopped sideways on the couch clutching her throat with both hands as if she was choking. Then she went so suddenly lax that Miranda was afraid she might have actually hurt herself.

Mike poked her in the ribs, at which point Holly flinched, then batted his hand aside. "Leave me alone. I'm dying here."

She wasn't dead. That was good.

"Are there any other teams available?"

The others looked at her in shock, she was fairly sure it was shock. Admittedly, it wasn't like her to turn down a launch for any reason.

"Sorry, Miranda. This is classified military. Rafe is the only other one with sufficient clearance and his team is presently in the Florida Everglades being chased by alligators."

"Why is he being chased by alligators?"

"Commuter flight went down there. Alligators have this thing about crash investigators; they think we're extra tasty."

"Oh," Miranda would have to be careful to watch out for that in the future, though she was unsure why an NTSB team member would be more, or less for that matter, tasty than a crash victim. She'd never known alligators were so discerning.

Was that a *Crocodilia* order-level trait, or was there a family-level taste differentiation between *Alligatoridae* and *Crocodylidae?*

"Besides, it was a by-name request for you and your team. That's all I have other than a destination."

When Jill told her where, Miranda could only sigh. Yes, it was a launch she couldn't turn down.

Even as she looked up, a sleek business jet swooped by the office windows to land on the runway. It was the first aircraft to use the runway since the rest of the team's arrival an hour ago. She did like the solitude of Tacoma Narrows Airport.

The touchdown was good. The pilot's timing was impeccable.

3

MIKE DRAGGED HIMSELF OUT OF THE OFFICE, THROUGH THE security door, and into the hangar. He really didn't feel up to flying. Miranda's Mooney was fast, but it was still a four-hour slog of a flight to Las Vegas. And the landing would be after dark.

Despite sleeping in and having lunch, he just didn't feel up to it.

Last night's flight from Alaska to Gig Harbor, Washington, had been a tricky six-hour haul, and he'd only recently earned his instrument rating. There hadn't even been a convenient road to follow from Anchorage to Juneau, for refueling, then southward to Washington State. Just a dark, jagged shoreline lost in low clouds for most of the route.

Still, he'd flown the Mooney a lot over the last year since Miranda had lent it to him. He'd come to love the tough little plane.

It was the height of cool after all.

The fastest single-engine, piston-powered production plane had spooked him at first. But as their investigation team had been launched time and again throughout the western US, he'd grown accustomed to its immense power.

The only other plane in the hangar was Miranda's 1958 Sabrejet. The old, solo-pilot fighter jet was her own usual form of transport, capable of briefly cracking Mach 1. At just under the speed of sound, it moved her around the country at three times the speed he could manage.

His six-hour flight last night had taken her barely two.

He'd envy her the extra four hours' sleep she'd gotten on her private island in northern Washington if he didn't know better. She'd probably gotten four hours *less* than anyone else. By the time the three of them managed to drag themselves into the hangar office, her jet had been neatly parked in the hangar beside the Mooney. The engine was fully cool when he'd come in. She'd probably arrived with the dawn and they found her working hard at her teak rolltop desk.

Her zippy jet always left him feeling a step behind.

The thing he really wasn't up for today was having Holly and Jeremy in the Mooney's tiny cabin for the next four hours badgering him to declare the cause of the Alaska collision as pilot error.

Miranda crossed to the Sabrejet. But rather than starting the preflight, she opened a small service hatch and withdrew her investigation field pack and her personal go-bag. Then she caressed the jet along the side of its smooth aluminum nose like she was petting it goodbye.

She might think it was a pet, but it had always looked a little vicious to him. The brushed aluminum plane looked like an artillery shell with wings and a tail—shining, even in the hangar's shadows. The jet engine's air intake made the nose a black hole rather than an arrow point. Six machine gun ports around the inlet, patched over with oval plates, were still a clear reminder that this had been a major weapon of war in both Korea and the early days of Vietnam.

But if she was petting it goodbye, maybe she was coming with them in the Mooney.

That would be awesome.

At a knock on the hangar's closed door, he turned and opened the personnel door beside the big slider.

"I have a delivery for a Ms. Miranda Chase." The man didn't look like a FedEx guy, but what did he know.

Miranda came over and signed some paperwork, then accepted a key.

She thanked him and the man was gone.

"New car?"

Miranda peeked outside through the door. "No."

Intrigued, he followed her when she stepped through carrying her gear.

And stopped dead in his tracks.

A Cessna Citation M2 business jet was parked immediately outside their main hangar door. A high T-tail with a jet engine low to either side. Low wing. Four windows ran along the cabin in addition to the sweeping cockpit windows. It looked like it was racing madly rather than sitting still. The long sleek aspect was emphasized by the red-and-gold racing stripes down the length of the charcoal fuselage. It even had those cute little upturned tips on its wings as if it was smiling at him.

"Miranda! What the hell?"

"What?" She opened a rear cargo door and placed her packs inside.

"You bought a new jet?"

"I was going to, because it would be more convenient if our whole team could move together. But Citation wanted me to consult on design and safety procedures for their next series of aircraft. They gave me this jet as a familiarization and test bed."

"Like a loan?"

She handed him the piece of paper from the delivery agent. It was a certificate of title, with her name as sole owner.

Mike grabbed her and gave her a big hug.

He kept it brief and wasn't surprised when Miranda didn't return it. Her autism didn't make that likely. A year ago he'd never even have been able to hug her at all. He did let her go quickly but he'd been unable to stop himself.

"What?" She looked up at him in surprise. She was the most unassuming woman. Miranda might barely weigh a hundred pounds and have the fashion sense of a field hand, but it didn't make her any less amazing.

"You are not only an absolutely brilliant boss but you absolutely have the best toys."

"It's not a toy. It's a jet," she answered with her perfect logic.

"Trust me, it's both."

When she squinted at him, he could only laugh. "Need a copilot?"

"No. It's certified for a single pilot. I have the CE-525 Type Rating, which covers the 525 series of Citation jets, including the M2."

"Okay," he often forgot to keep his questions very precise for Miranda. "Would it be okay if I flew in the right seat with you?"

"Of course."

"Wonderful. Thanks so much." Copilot seat on a jet was something he'd always wanted to try. As a complete—and major—bonus, it would spare him riding in the main cabin with Holly and Jeremy, and being harangued for the whole flight. He slipped his own pack in the rear cargo hold.

Holly was next out the door. It was hard to tell if she was unimpressed or just had chill down to a science.

"Nice," was her only comment before she moved to stow her pack and go-bag in the nose section's forward cargo hold.

While Jeremy went through a dozen stages of geeky enthusiasm, Mike followed Miranda around the plane, reading off the preflight checklist for her.

When they continued inside, it definitely had that new car smell.

Seriously amazing.

4

As copilot, Mike had been about as useful as a VW Beetle at a NASCAR race. Shuttling their NTSB team around in the Mooney, he'd recovered all of his latent piloting skills and then some.

Or so he'd convinced himself.

Miranda's new plane was in some other weird, science fiction category.

Instead of dials and a nice little LCD nav screen like the Mooney, *everything* here was electronic. Each pilot had a large central screen just packed with information about flight attitudes, engine performance, and flight paths. A central screen in the middle of the console between the pilots could be set to show terrain, weather, airport details, and probably the going price of jet fuel sorted by airport, along with any recent interstellar space launches.

Everything was controlled by a conveniently placed menu touchpad, one for each pilot, with more options than the little Mooney had controls—total. And most of those options had submenus.

Miranda only occasionally looked out the windshield. She

didn't need to. The jet was feeding her far better information than mere eyes could ever achieve. Even the radar screen fed information about each passing flight's altitude, course, and speed.

The twin-engine Citation M2 jet had rushed them up to forty-one thousand feet instead of his normal ten-thousand-foot cruise altitude. From up here there wasn't anything helpful to see anyway, just pretty blue sky and fluffy clouds far below. Even the horizon was just a suggestion from up here—the instruments were all the reference there was.

They flitted south so fast that he felt as if they were sitting still, and Miranda had somehow forced the Earth to spin beneath them.

Mike spent the whole trip down reading the manuals that Miranda had loaded onto his tablet. He didn't feel much smarter for all his effort. All he really understood by the end of the flight was how to control all the menu options on his screen.

They'd been to Groom Lake before, at the heart of the Nevada Test and Training Range. The airport, built on the dry lake's salt-pan bed, shimmered in the late afternoon heat.

They'd been here for their very first investigation as a team. His entire world had changed in the last year in too many ways to think about. He'd been—

His thoughts *definitely* needed a subject change.

He waited until they were down, off the runway, and taxiing toward the main terminal before he spoke. In a craft like this, you definitely didn't distract a pilot during landing.

"Is that what it's like flying your Sabrejet?" Mike also felt completely out of place due to the two-and-a-quarter-hour flash across so much of the country. It was so much more visceral from the cockpit.

Miranda blinked at him in surprise, as if she'd forgotten he was there.

"No. This aircraft is far slower, four hundred and four knots maximum cruise compared with six hundred and seventy when I'm riding the edge of the sound barrier in the F-86 Sabrejet. You barely have to be a pilot to fly this plane."

Mike was about to protest that you'd have to be more of a pilot than he was, but thought better of it. He liked being allowed to sit up here with her.

"The Sabrejet may have been the first fighter jet in history to have an autopilot, but its capabilities are quite simplistic. From the moment I line up this jet on the runway, I can literally program it to takeoff, fly, and autoland in zero-zero conditions —if the airfield is CAT IIIC equipped, which many now are. I barely feel as if I'm flying."

Zero-zero was when the cloud ceiling literally touched the ground and the visibility ahead was nonexistent, or so close to nonexistent that it would be impossible to react fast enough if there was a problem.

Mike tried to imagine letting a plane land itself—without being able to see the runway, perhaps even once you were on it. It was a very unnerving thought. Maybe it would be better if he just didn't know, instead riding in the four passenger seats with Holly and Jeremy in the future.

"However, there's more to why I wanted this plane than the convenience of being able to have the whole team with me from the start. I also felt that it would be good to have a more personal experience of modern avionics and flight systems. This Citation M2's design and avionics package *is* sixty-two years newer than my Sabrejet's—which was actually designed seventy-three years ago. A lot has happened in that time."

From anyone else, that would be a wry observation, even a joke. From Miranda Chase, it was simply a fact.

Mike almost asked what she'd learned, but knew that could well turn into a multi-hour explanation that he only had a moderate likelihood of understanding, and no chance of interrupting.

Besides, there was a crash. He'd learned not to sidetrack Miranda's focus with ill-timed idle questions. Still, he'd like to know, and made a mental note to ask her the next time they were just hanging around at the office in Tacoma, Washington. Not that they were doing much of that lately.

Their team maintained a slightly alarming launch rate, which left little time for just hanging out anywhere.

5

"EXCUSE ME, WHO ARE YOU?"

Andi had become a little immune to the question. A security guard had come by like clockwork, every fifteen minutes, to ask the question with some varying form of politeness and impatience.

Showing her ID and stating that she was waiting for a flight had always proved sufficient.

Too bad it was a total lie. Her itinerary had dead-ended here. After an hour, she still had no idea what to do next, and was well past caring. Standing out in the Nevada sunshine and watching the planes flitting in and out of the Las Vegas airport rated about as constructive as anything else she'd done since being thrown out of the Army.

She eyed the tall, sandy-haired man. His inquiry had landed on the polite side of the spectrum, but it was certainly the kind that fully expected to be answered. A military directness and tone she recognized just fine, even if she wasn't military anymore.

"Depends." Andi decided she was finally sick of answering that question.

"On what?" He had major's oak leaves on his uniform, but didn't push back about her sass. Oh right, she was a civilian now.

His words were muted by a United Airlines 787 ripping north along McCarran Field. They had a full load, judging by the length of runway they chewed up before lumbering aloft. Civilian jets looked so lazy compared with their military counterparts.

Easy excuse to pretend she hadn't heard him. Why should she waste time answering a military that didn't want her?

Not that she had anything better to do.

She rested her forehead on where her arms were crossed on the railing.

But she could still see his neat pant cuffs and shiny shoes. Except his shoes weren't shiny. He wore battered boots that no paper pusher would ever be caught dead in.

"Can't you go find someone else to bother? How about one of them?" Without bothering to look up, she waved toward the fifty or so people deplaning and heading out through the small AECOM terminal—which she'd never heard of.

Whoever AECOM was, they had serious perimeter security that had required US Government top secret clearance to pass through. No one had warned her about that ahead of time; her itinerary had just said to come here from the main passenger terminal on the other side of the airport—and had ended with that.

At the gate, for lack of any other ideas, she'd tried handing over her new ID.

Her Army CAC—Common Access Card, the pass to military places she was no longer allowed to go and to helicopters she was no longer allowed to fly—had been replaced with a "retired" CAC, which controlled which Vet services she could access.

A quick test showed that it no longer had any clearance

associated with it that AECOM cared about. Getting into the VA or a PX wasn't exactly top secret clearance material.

For lack of any better ideas, she tried her new CAC card. The one with the NTSB as the authorizing agency. They'd handed it to her along with today's itinerary and tickets, and she hadn't given it any further thought other than thinking it odd to have been given a Department of Defense CAC rather than an NTSB ID like she'd been given the first day.

Andi inspected it with some surprise when they gave it back to her and waved her inside. Other than the authorizing agency, it looked like any other CAC: her face, former rank and name, a bar code, and a chip. But the well-armed guards seemed to think that, despite her now being a lowly student investigator for the National Transportation Safety Board, she somehow still passed muster.

Damn but did she have them fooled.

And top secret muster at that. She'd thought that went away when she'd been tossed out of the military Special Operations.

Guess not.

No ticket counter. The terminal manager had looked at her askance and rescanned her ID carefully when she'd asked if any other directions had been left for her.

The place was sterile and more than a little shabby. No Starbucks or McDonald's either. She'd hit the vending machines for a Snickers-and-Coke dinner before coming out to lean on the walkway rail and watch the airshow for the last hour. No jetways here. Not a lot of baggage handling either. Mostly just planes and the old-style rolling stair sets.

Her ass was now parked in a strange land with no filed flight plan.

Major Sandy Hair was still hanging tough for his answer of who she was.

"What day is today?"

"Thursday," he answered her non sequitur with the sense of humor of a *major* rock.

"Then I have no idea who I am. I've never known who I was on Thursdays." Instead of facing him, she studied the pair of 737-600s that had landed in quick succession on the tarmac in front of the AECOM terminal rather than over at the main terminal.

People were streaming ashore and disappearing through the gates. Six in the evening, they could have been people streaming off the San Francisco streetcars back home in Chinatown.

The planes were white with a red stripe down the line of windows. Except for a tail number, there were no markings as to what airline they were. Up above, a long, lean Delta Airlines 757 came winging down from the south—the big blue "Delta" painted just behind the cockpit stood out just fine. But it was an easy bet that it wasn't headed for the AECOM terminal.

Half of this world was familiar. Planes shimmering in the desert heat of a late August afternoon. The smell of jet fuel and hot tarmac. Yet it was so...civilian. No sharp cordite of spent ammo. None of the tang of blood's iron that hammered in at the top of sinuses after a night gone bad. None of the ragged exhaustion of a four-hour mission suddenly taking fourteen.

She no longer belonged anywhere.

"Captain Andrea Wu?" Major Sandy Hair was still hangin' tough.

"Well, you got one out of three. Just a friendly tip? If that's your normal success average, don't ever gamble. It's Andi with an *i*. The captain part is ancient history. Last name *is* Wu. Because it's the ninth most common Chinese surname, it still doesn't get you a whole lot of points for getting it right. Who wants to know?"

"Major Jon Swift of the AIB."

"Seriously?"

He huffed out an impatient breath and handed over his ID.

The Air Force's Accident Investigation Board?

She looked back over at the growing crowd as a third red-marked 737 arrived and dumped its load of people.

Did she stand out that much?

The arrivals looked just like any other folks passing through an airport. Black, white, Latina, some other Asians besides herself. Though the crowd was heavily male. No kids either. Duh! She hadn't noticed either of those factors because they were so familiar—at least to her former military self.

This was a military crowd behind a top secret barrier flying on an unmarked airline.

So much for her vaunted soldier's skill at observation. Yep! She'd lost that along with everything else.

Worst of all? Every last one of them looked as if they were going somewhere, had a purpose.

So not her.

Who the hell cared?

Again, not her.

None of it mattered anymore.

She was civilian.

"Look, Major. Ten hours ago, I was sitting short and mostly bored in class at the NTSB Training Facility in Virginia: AS302 'Survival Factors in Aviation Accidents' in case you care. Then the director of the place, who I've never met before, pulled my ass out of class, told me I had a launch—because that shit happens to beginning students all the time—and hands a useless piece of shit itinerary that dumped me here, on the wrong side of a high-security barrier, with no clue what's next."

"NTSB Director Terence Graham gave me a call, asked me to escort you the rest of the way. Sorry I was delayed."

"Seriously?" Andi fought back on the reflexive need to add a "sir" when addressing a major. It wasn't typical for serving Air Force majors to escort discharged Army captains to places.

This being-a-civilian shit wasn't coming easy. After more than a decade in, she was completely adrift. Finding an apartment, shopping for groceries, utility bills—all kinds of craziness.

"Seriously." He shrugged. "Not a burden. We're headed to the same place and can share the flight. Come along." And he led the way through a gate and toward the planes, the opposite direction to everyone else still coming off the planes.

Decision time. She checked her watch. Taking a line from *The Hunt for Red October,* the sweep second hand was in the top half of the minute, between forty-five and fifteen seconds. So, that was a yes answer instead of a fuck-off answer if it had been the bottom half of the minute. It was the only reliable way she'd found to make decisions since her final catastrophic flight.

So, yes, Andi followed him through the gate. "Which flight are we on?"

He pointed off to the side. She hadn't even noticed the C-12 Huron parked there. No, this was civilian land, so it was a Beechcraft B200 King Air. Or was it? It still had the distinctive red stripe and no name.

"What airline is this?"

"It's called Janet Airlines."

"It's *called?* What the hell kind of airline is it?" Being out of the military also let her curse in the presence of a superior officer. She could get to like that. At least that one tiny piece of her new existence. The total gut-wrencher? That he still got to be on the inside and she didn't.

"It's an airline that exists to avoid questions like that." They were the only ones heading toward the ten-seat twin-prop plane.

Within seconds of them settling into their seats, the pilot had the door closed and they were on the move. At least the plane smelled military. No little meal service. Not even the leftover salt of too many bags of peanuts. Other than the comfortable bucket seats and a rack of water bottles, she took one, it was just as utilitarian as the C-130 Hercules transport that had dumped her ass back in Fort Campbell, Kentucky, for the final time barely four weeks ago.

"So, there's been a crash?" NTSB trainee and AIB major being all cozy on a top secret Janet Airlines plane made that an easy guess.

"You have a launch."

"And?"

"A friendly word of caution: she doesn't like it when people conjecture."

Hell of a slap-down for a simple question.

She who?

And that's when Andi remembered the sealed note that Director Graham had handed off along with her tickets and itinerary. It had been folded up in her back pocket since she'd left DC.

Give this to her.

The same her? Probably some rigid, lord-her-power-over-everyone bitch.

Andi had certainly seen enough of those in her time. The women who decided that the only way to prove they belonged in the heavily male military was to be even nastier than the worst of their male counterparts. Others went out of their way to be nicer, but a lot of them were steamrollered by people of either gender glad to walk right over such an easy target. She'd gotten a little frosty herself over the years. She was civilian now; definitely didn't need to put up with that garbage anymore. Whether or not she should let it go herself was way too tricky a question at this point.

With a loud buzz of twin turboprops, they rolled onto the runway and were headed aloft. As they turned for the northwest, Andi looked back at the field. They'd just jumped to the head of a line of six passenger jets at the runway's threshold.

Janet Airlines flew with a serious priority.

Who the hell are you people? was another question she knew would earn her no answer.

Northwest?

The only thing northwest of Vegas for a long way was the Nevada Test and Training Range. She'd flown training exercises in the NTTR, the center of America's most secret operations training.

Seven minutes later they flew past Creech Air Force Base and kept going. The only thing past that...

"Are we actually going to the lake?" At NTTR's heart lay the one airfield where nobody went—Area 51, Groom Lake. Except maybe Janet Airlines?

He just nodded and went back to studying his tablet. By the way he had it carefully tilted out of her line of sight, it was either top secret or it was her file.

Her hard-won paranoia voted for it being her service record.

Top half of the minute...*shit!*

6

While Miranda ticked her way through the on-screen shutdown checklist, Mike moved into the back of the plane.

Jeremy and Holly were fast asleep in the back pair of the four facing seats, so far out that even the landing hadn't fazed them.

Of course, the brunt of the Alaska investigation had landed on them and Miranda—though she, as usual, showed no hint of the long hours.

Holly looked atypically peaceful as she slept. Her straight fall of blonde hair comfortably tousled.

He leaned down and kissed her awake.

Pain sliced into his neck as she clamped his windpipe in a vise-strong grip.

He managed to squeak in alarm at being unable to breathe.

"Shit!" Holly let go and shoved him away to collapse into the opposite seat. "What the hell were you doing, Mike?"

"Kissing you awake." His voice sounded like a chipmunk who'd spent his entire life as a chain-smoking boozer.

"I'm not some goddamn Sleeping Beauty and you sure as

hell aren't Prince Charming," she glanced out the window to see where they were.

"I thought—" but that was all his damaged voice box would allow at the moment.

She turned back to him. "We're having sex, Mike. Doing the naughty. Having ourselves a nice old bangaroo. We're not 'lovers.' Just get that shit out of your head."

No wonder they fit together so well. It's a line he'd dropped a couple times—with a little more couth—when a ski-friend-with-frequent-benefits suddenly slipped the M-word into a conversation.

She punched a fist across the narrow aisle into Jeremy's shoulder where he still slept.

"Huh, what?" The force of her punch was enough to bonk his head against the plane's hull.

"We're here, Jeremy. Grab your gear."

"Oh, okay." He'd fallen asleep with his computer on the fold-out table and his tablet in his lap. He tucked them into the big pack he'd strapped down in the opposite seat.

"Move ass, Mike." The little plane's ceiling was only four-foot-nine high, so Holly hunched as she headed toward the door.

"You okay, Mike? You're looking a little pale," Jeremy squinted at him.

"Just stupid."

He'd forgotten two things.

One, Holly Harper was about as romantic as an Australian white shark, and, two, she'd been a sergeant in their SASR special operations regiment.

The woman was lethal when surprised. Or just in a bad mood. Or a good one. She was also gorgeous, amazing in bed, and had that sexy-smooth accent that was going to lead him to his doom. Yeah, his libido was in heaven; so what piece of idiocy thought for even a second that it went any deeper than that?

He risked a gentle swallow, which he instantly regretted, and deplaned after Jeremy with Miranda close behind him.

7

"Where did you get that?" Major Jon Swift couldn't look away from the sleek little bizjet that had landed hot on their tail. It had pulled up close while he and Captain Wu were still eating the dust of the departing Janet Airlines C-12 Huron.

"Nicked it, mate." Holly was first off the plane. "It was just sitting there at the airport, lonely as could be, so we decided to take her home. We're thinking of naming her Betsy."

"We are?" Jeremy trotted up beside her toting his monstrous field pack. "I never heard that. I think a better name would be like *The Millennium Falcon* or a Viper Mk II. You know, like in *Battlestar Galactica.* Oh wait, those are all gunships. But Betsy? Really? Oh, wait. *I Will Fear No Evil?* I guess that's kind of cool, though I don't get why anyone would name an airplane after an automated stenodesk from Heinlein's—" When Holly raised a single rigid finger as if to poke him sharply, Jeremy wisely shut up and scooted well clear of her reach.

Mike came next. Jon wished just once in his life he'd looked as smooth and together as Mike always did. His hair just a little too long, his clothes fine, but casual. Like he'd just walked out of some hip and modern store's display window.

He made a point of shaking Jon's hand and then introducing himself to Andi. Mr. Nice Guy on full display.

Instead, Jon had greeted her with an utterly unsmooth, "Who are you?" He'd sounded like an impolite jerk even to himself but hadn't figured out how to fix it.

Through the window, he could see Miranda clambering out of the pilot's seat.

The moment she was clear, a crew in ABUs—Airman Battle Uniforms—appeared out of one of the big hangars close beside the runway. With zero ceremony, they dropped the packs from the cargo holds onto the salt flats, then towed the jet into the shadowed depths. The big doors rattled closed again as if neither they nor the jet had ever been there.

Andi was having a first-timer's reaction to Groom Lake, gawking in every direction. Not that there was a damn thing to see midday. Groom Lake didn't even smell like an airport. Salt flat instead of baking asphalt. No odor of spilled Jet A. Not a single aircraft in sight—most of the aircraft here were only flown under the cover of darkness.

At a sudden high-whine of an air-ratchet tool sounding from inside the next hangar down, Andi jumped as if she was aiming for orbit.

That was a little strange. Usually Army captains, even retired ones, were steadier than that.

"Who the hell are you, mate?" Holly went toe to toe with her before she'd fully returned from orbit.

Andi pulled out Terence's letter, hesitated, then handed it to Miranda like an act of defiance. She could have spit in Holly's face with less ire.

Miranda opened the letter, read it over quickly, then handed it back.

Finally, she looked at Jon.

"Where's the crash?" was all she said.

Jon couldn't believe that—

Holly snatched the letter from Andi's fingers. When she went to grab it back, Holly placed a hand on top of Andi's head and pushed her out to arm's length as she opened it.

Andi slapped the arm aside.

Holly had anticipated that, momentarily catching the letter in her teeth as she put the other hand on Andi's forehead. Then she took the letter with her free hand as if nothing had happened.

Jon barely managed to jump clear as Andi dove to the ground and knocked Holly down with a sweep kick.

A kick that would have flattened him and left him on the hardpan to groan for a while did no such thing to Holly.

She did some kind of neat tuck-and-roll that he couldn't follow and returned to her feet suddenly close enough to Jeremy to lean an elbow casually on his shoulder as she read aloud.

"*This is Captain Andrea—*"

"Andi."

"*—Wu, formerly a pilot with the 160th Night Stalkers.*" Holly stopped reading and looked at Andi over the top of the letter. "Seriously hot shit, girl. Goodonya!" She held up her hand to receive a high five.

Andi didn't slap it.

Holly kept her smile and returned to reading. "*I heard your latest launch is for a rotorcraft, so I sent her along. She's about halfway through Academy training, and already knows far more than most of her instructors. Her skills remind me of you. Terence.*" Holly folded it up, then returned it to Andi. "From Terence Graham, that's a *seriously* off-tap recommendation."

Holly could play casual all she wanted, but Jon knew better.

Captain Andrea Wu was a former pilot for the best helicopter regiment fielded by any military. He had enough friends in special operations to know just what that meant. She hadn't been a good pilot, she'd been a superstar—because that was the only kind of pilot the 160th even considered inviting to try out. She was at least as elite as Holly's own entry into the SASR.

"I'm Holly Harper—structural. That's Jeremy Trahn—systems and team geek. This useless sack of shit is Mike Munroe—I mean he really *cares* about human factors. What kind of guy does that, anyway? He *is* great in bed, but he's mine for now, so stay away."

Jon hoped that Miranda didn't think of him that way.

"And her?" Holly finished the introductions with a hook of her thumb toward the approaching Miranda. "She's the boss lady."

Andi blinked in surprise. She must have thought Holly was in charge.

Of course she often acted that way to everyone except Miranda.

8

ANDI COULD FEEL THE GEARS GRINDING IN HER HEAD. SO THE Tall Blonde Bitch Australian wasn't the one in charge.

Andi had felt herself all poised to despise the team leader—except Holly wasn't. Holly, Jeremy, Mike. She repeated that a few times to drill their names in. And Major Jon Swift.

Andi focused once more on the pilot "boss lady." She had pulled on a pocketed vest, heavily filled with tools, and was tapping each one as if double-checking what was where. Everyone waited patiently even though it took a long thirty seconds.

Andi glanced aloft. Even the vultures circling high on the evening thermals baking off the salt pan airfield appeared to be waiting.

The last thing the pilot did was hang her badge around her neck, then make sure it was face out.

Miranda Chase, NTSB.

Jesus!

Something like every second case study they read in the Academy was written by one Miranda Chase. Her name was both a blessing and a curse among students.

The former because of the sheer amount of knowledge to be gained from close study of a Chase report, and the latter for their consistently long, highly detailed summaries.

Though none of the reports Andi had studied were of military incidents. Yet here was an entire team acting as if Groom Lake was old hat. A base she'd personally never had the clearance to stand on before, despite being a pilot for Special Operations Forces.

Miranda was standing silently looking up at Major Swift once more. Even though she didn't repeat her question, it was easy to hear it: *Now where's the stupid crash?*

"Hello, Miranda."

Miranda Chase didn't react.

"That's a nice new plane. Where did you borrow it?"

Still no reaction.

Now Holly and Mike were smiling, but Andi couldn't quite tell why. Amused?

"Haven't seen you in a while," Major Swift wasn't being so swift at reading the freeze out.

Andi knew from her own experience that being a woman, especially a small one—Miranda stood only two inches taller than Andi herself—in this man's army really pushed a girl toward being a ball buster.

"Twenty-two days and seven hours," Miranda finally replied without checking her watch. "Which isn't actually accurate. We've seen each other in video calls four times during that period, so it has been only three days and eleven hours since we last saw each other."

"I meant in person."

"That's not what you said." Then Miranda twitched away from Holly as if she'd just been pinched. "What? Oh. *Oh!* Yes. Hello, Jon. It *is* good to see you." Her speech sounded completely rote, then she stepped into Jon's arms.

Andi could only gape in surprise. Two seconds ago Miranda had acted as if she didn't care whether the major lived or died.

He embraced her. And even though she didn't embrace him back, she did look content to be there. He didn't appear surprised by the one-sided greeting; he'd just kept pushing until he got even that.

Andi checked in with Holly, but all she got back was a nod saying this weirdness was somehow normal.

"They just delivered my new plane," Miranda said as soon as Jon released her. She waved a hand toward the silent hangar where the plane had been tucked out of sight. "I was shopping for a plane that could move everyone quickly. Then—"

"You know that if you came over to AIB, they'd put a C-21A Learjet at your disposal."

Andi had always been proud of her ability to adapt quickly to changing situations. Another thing she'd lost along with the ability to serve. She checked her feet but they were acting like they were in balance.

Was it just her brain that was feeling so out of whack?

Her watch's second hand voted a clear *yes.*

Shit!

There was a grim silence. Didn't the guy even notice the instant scowl his statement had earned him from the others?

Majorly *not* swift.

Miranda didn't scowl. Instead, she once more became completely deadpan and waited him out.

When Major Swift didn't speak up, she picked up in midsentence as if there'd never been a break or the offer to use a nine-million-dollar jet as her own.

"—Textron Aviation offered me a trade. They asked me to consult on the design and all safety procedures for their next series of Cessna jet aircraft. They already have a superior safety record, but they're working on removing pilot error—the cause of all three incidents involving their jet aircraft since 2005."

"They *gave* you a four-and-a-half-million-dollar plane?" Major Swift sounded aghast.

"Five point three as outfitted—extended-range tanks, and the latest avionics suite. They offered to get me my choice of Thales or Collins helmets, but I wanted to fly it initially with the equipment any other Citation pilot would have."

Andi had always liked the Thales helmet and its inside-the-visor display. But the Collins Aerospace helmet was seriously next gen. She'd have loved the chance to use one again—not that she ever would. The helmet was four hundred thousand dollars of tech, had to be custom-built for each pilot, and was primarily used on the F-35 Lightning II fighter jets...and on the other aircraft she couldn't bear to think about. It should be strictly military issue, yet Textron Cessna had been willing to go through all the hoops to give Miranda Chase one?

Unsure what to think, Andi checked her watch.

Straight up Yes. Wild!

Miranda barely paused for a breath, as if she was in a hurry to not be interrupted again.

"And we've already discussed several times that I will never leave the NTSB for the AIB. I do not understand why you keep bringing it up. Besides, a C-21A Learjet is a wholly unacceptable solution. You already know that its takeoff roll is far longer than my runway."

"Oh, I didn't think about the ground roll. I guess so," Major Un-Swift had the wherewithal to wince.

"The C-21's is nearly half as long as my entire island."

"You own an island?" Andi couldn't imagine such a thing. Of course, she'd also never met anyone who'd "shopped" for a five-million-dollar plane...or been given one.

"She does, mate," Holly smiled at her. "Never, ever underestimate our Miranda." The last seemed aimed at Major Jon Swift even though Holly was still facing her.

Her wink confirmed that. Maybe Holly wasn't the holy terror that her first impression gave.

Andi glanced at her watch's second hand.

Bottom half of the minute.

No.

Holly was still a total bitch.

9

Miranda looked away from Jon. She enjoyed sleeping with him and working a crash together, but he was always so exhausting.

Despite careful study, she still didn't understand how his mental processes functioned. Not connecting the length of her runway and the C-21's minimum ground roll distance was just another example of the problem.

Did he expect her to clear her entire island and regrade it just for a plane she didn't want from an organization she had no intention of joining? That would require unwanted workers on her island from logging and grading companies. And the wild game that still inhabited Spieden Island left over from its brief time as a stocked, big-game hunting park would be horribly displaced. She'd never do such a thing to them and he should understand that without her having to explain it.

Or must she? The Sika and fallow deer, the mouflon sheep, and the dozens of remaining game bird varieties made her island unique in Washington State's San Juan Islands, perhaps anywhere.

She glanced at Holly, who tipped her wrist slightly as if to say, "Can we get a move on?"

She was right.

If Jon needed such basic responsibilities of habitat ownership explained, it would have to be done later. Even if such incomplete questions felt like steel wool being scrubbed across the inside of her forehead.

They'd been sexual partners for two hundred and fifty-two days, on the occasions when their schedules allowed.

But it didn't make him any less exhausting.

The flight had already been taxing. Short, just two and a half hours, but the plane was still unfamiliar. Earlier in the year, she'd managed two, nonconsecutive weeks' vacation from the NTSB to get certified. The first week was to obtain her type rating. The second week had been spent with Cessna's engineers and senior test pilots, discussing and flying each of their seven other current models for comparison—though there wasn't any point in certifying in those types.

She was a long way from fully integrating the knowledge of her own M2 plane, never mind the other models.

The new investigator, Andi, had been sent by Terence, which explained his earlier text message: *Sending you a present.* She never understood his sense of teasing.

She'd expected a manual of detailed specs on some Russian plane or a translated Chinese crash investigation. Instead he'd sent her a Night Stalker—a vastly superior asset.

But Miranda trusted Terence implicitly, so she felt no need to question Andi further—not that she'd know what to ask. That was Mike's department.

Terence had been her first trainer. He'd helped her figure out ways to advantageously leverage her Autism Spectrum Disorder for flight investigations. Finally, with a few adjustments, her ASD had been seen as an asset rather than a liability.

And she liked Andi's long, multi-colored hair. It gave Miranda something to focus on so that she didn't have to look at the woman's face. That was soothing.

Miranda heard it before she saw it: the distinct, two-blade *whoop-whoop* of a Huey UH-1 Iroquois. She waited for it to resolve into more than a dark dot approaching from the northeast before fully labeling it. Yes, it was a UH-1N Twin Huey in Air Force gray.

Since Jon wasn't being forthcoming regarding the crash, she hoped that whoever was approaching would be taking them to the site. Her vest was ready.

It was good to have the whole team present from the start. It saved repetition of information. Yes, the M2 would serve nicely.

The change of the pilot's mindset based on the plane model was an interesting set of variables.

Her F-86 Sabrejet was still sufficiently primitive that the pilot had to be highly trained. Instrument and night flights were terribly challenging due to the sheer volume of information that had to be processed. It was a single-pilot fighter jet designed for the daytime aerial dogfights of the Korean War. The escalation of information during aerial combat must have been overwhelming.

She appreciated Mike's earlier question regarding the piloting difference of the Sabrejet versus the Citation. It had enabled her to articulate that a modern passenger jet pilot was a technician first and foremost.

"Mike?"

"Yes, Miranda?"

"I have a theory based on your earlier question," she had to raise her voice and turn her back on the dust kicked up by the landing helo. "I'm thinking that one of Cessna's problems is that their flight controls are still designed by pilots. Despite the fact that the modern non-military pilot is much more of a technician now."

Mike looked up to study the sky.

She'd noted his habit of staring directionlessly aloft enough times in her personal notebook to understand that's what he did when he was thinking. She still couldn't help but look as well, though she was no longer surprised that there were no answers writ large across the section of sky he was inspecting.

"I think you're on to something. Maybe that's the problem I was having on the flight down. I'm a VFR pilot. I'm still at the level where I can fly IFR if I have to, but I'm *expecting* a Visual Flight Rules experience rather than an instrument rules one. The Citation M2 is closer to what Jeremy does for fun—a high-stakes video game—than the flying that I do. When you made a midcourse correction on the way here, you didn't touch the controls, instead you altered the setting on the autopilot's heading and it made the turn. But we still need pilots. Don't we?"

Miranda considered. "When systems fail? Yes. But we also need the technician to solve the problem. The piloting skills must be there for the unexpected, but the technician is all that's needed for the expected, and for most types of systems failures. There's a split in the thinking there that we'll need to pursue."

At Mike's nod of agreement, she pulled out her new, third, slim notebook "M2" and made a note of the concept. It was the only good way she'd found to switch topics. Otherwise she'd be worrying at that conundrum until—

"Hello, Miranda."

She closed her thoughts on the M2, tucked away the notebook, and turned.

"Thomas" stitched on the lapel. The bright star of a general on the collar points. Miranda looked a little higher for just a moment and recognized the face of Colonel Helen Thomas.

"You got older."

Helen grimaced a down-frown.

Miranda knew that emoji.

Maybe she shouldn't have said that. But it was true. In the year since they'd last met, Colonel Helen Thomas clearly had been promoted to General Helen Thomas, had deeper lines about her mouth, and a definite shift from brown to gray in her hair.

"It's been a hard year," Helen said softly.

"Yes," Miranda tried to be agreeable.

The last time she'd met a general in the NTTR, he'd pulled a gun on her and tried to have her arrested multiple times. Though the attempt to bomb her crew out of existence hadn't been his doing—it had only seemed that way.

"Being made general can be hard." She assessed that as being the most neutral topic.

General Thomas didn't look any happier.

Miranda kept an eye on her sidearm, but Helen didn't reach for it.

"I took over Groom Lake when General Harrington was arrested. I was going to resign, to go back to my family. But my children left for college and my husband, sick of my career, left me for a blackjack dealer at Circus Circus."

"I've never liked circuses." She could always feel the animals' sadness.

Helen smiled, "Me either."

"I didn't know circuses had blackjack."

"This one does."

"It can't be a very good circus then. Not if they also need blackjack to appease their audiences."

"It isn't."

Miranda debated briefly if that was worth noting down, but couldn't imagine any future relevance for the exception to the rule about circuses and blackjack—if it was a rule. No, she discarded the concept as truly irrelevant. Which she knew in itself was progress.

Using a lesson Mike had taught her, she reached over her

own shoulder and patted herself on the back, whispering to herself, *Good job.*

As she did, she felt the reflective six-inch letters NTSB stitched across the back of her vest.

The crash.

She had already introduced herself to Helen last year. Repeating her name and that she was the investigator-in-charge assigned to this project Miranda now recognized as redundant. Instead, she would keep it simple.

“We’re ready.”

Except she wasn’t.

10

There is no crash.

General Thomas' words still rang around inside Miranda's head but found no logical place to land.

"We asked you here to act as independent observers for a critical test flight."

Jon had wished them all luck. It turned out that whatever his duties were at Groom Lake, they didn't involve the non-crash NTSB launch that had brought the rest of her team here.

It would have helped if Jon had explained that he didn't know anything about the crash.

Other than the fact that there wasn't one.

He wanted to hug her goodbye, but it was one thing too many to deal with.

There is no crash.

But her job was to investigate crashes and prevent crashes. Not to watch a flight to see...

Miranda knew she was in churn but—as always—couldn't think of how to break out of the pattern when she was in it.

Then, just when she thought she might have a grasp on one corner of it...

"Let's just go down to Hangar 33B," General Thomas had waved toward the building standing all alone a mile down the field. "We're using that as an operations center for the test flights and support teams. The commander of the Night Stalkers is flying in. We already have three Sikorsky manufacturer reps in attendance. As well as nine other reps overseeing different aspects of the testing regimen."

Group dynamics.

No. No. No. No!

Each would insist that any problems during testing weren't their element—just as Holly, Jeremy, and Mike had been a few hours ago. So much noise with no sign of a possible rational solution.

If a problem arose, General Electric would say, "Not my engines."

"Not the weapons or navigation systems," Raytheon would be sure to insist.

Collins Aerospace would defend their helmets, and so on.

And Hangar 33B!

It hurt to even look at the building's outline in the descending darkness.

Yes, the disastrous MQ-45 Casper drone had been flown out of that hangar.

But it was also where she'd found out her parents were not who she'd thought they were. It made sense that they'd lied to her about their jobs—they had turned out to be in the CIA, after all—but even now, a year after the Casper mission and twenty-four years after their deaths, Hangar 33B was not a place she wished to revisit.

In Hangar 33B there would be reminders of—

Mike rested a hand lightly on her arm.

He knew she couldn't tolerate being lightly touched.

Intensely, horribly distracting.

Contact that was there but wasn't there.

Yet it was, impossibly, a relief from the former churning of her thoughts.

When he tightened his grip to something more tolerable, Miranda realized he'd prompted Holly to speak with the general.

"If we're supposed to be independent observers, then shouldn't we bloody well be independent? Not hanging out with that lot."

When Helen refused, Holly had begun demanding that they roll the M2 jet right back out of the hangar.

"No," Miranda managed to whisper to Mike. "I couldn't fly right now."

"Don't worry. You won't have to."

She didn't believe him at first, but she should have known better. Mike was never wrong about people.

Within minutes General Thomas agreed to let them use her office in the main administration building to monitor the tests.

Miranda wasn't sure if she'd ever been more grateful for Mike joining the team.

It was a more comfortable situation—marginally.

General Helen Thomas' office could have been any other slightly run-down governmental office, other than the light fading over the baking runway still hazy through the day's heat. An American flag, a photo of President Cole, and not much other décor. Helen's desk was military neat. The U-shaped conference table could seat ten and faced a set of large monitors mounted so that their inner corners were touching. Right now they were blank.

Except Holly's ploy hadn't worked completely.

Helen had decided to stay with them, adding a non-team member. Miranda had only met her briefly as General Harrington was arrested and she was given command of the Groom Lake complex last year. She was far from a familiar face.

Andi would have been equally unfamiliar, except she came

with Terence's recommendation. So her unfamiliarity was sufficiently familiar to not be disorienting.

Miranda wished she could think of any way to complain about Helen's presence in her own office but couldn't come up with one. While she decided that it would probably be rude to just ask her to leave, everyone got settled into chairs and she knew no one would be leaving.

But where was she supposed to sit? Across from General Thomas? In front of the blank monitors? Would it matter if she sat between Mike and Holly or beside them? Would Jeremy feel left out? She hadn't even spoken to Andi yet!

So instead, she remained standing.

"What do you mean there's no crash?"

Miranda knew she was repeating herself, a trait she had little tolerance for in others, but couldn't stem the tide of her disbelief.

She'd been launched by Jill at the NTSB. That meant there was a crash investigation.

Except there wasn't a crash to investigate.

This day had not gone well. Another round of box breathing left her pulse rate no lower or steadier than when she'd started.

This afternoon had begun with the unlikelihood of ever resolving the Alaska incident investigation.

Jon's presence was familiar enough, but it was always disruptive. It was a relief that he was now gone on a different assignment. Though seeing him so unexpectedly made it feel as if he was still here. Except he wasn't.

Andi and Helen made two additional people beyond the three members of her core team. A sixty-six-point-seven percent expansion of her normal sphere of people to deal with.

Even the three were often too much.

When the pressure of the Tacoma Narrows office built up to where she could no longer concentrate on anything for more than a few minutes at a time, she would climb into her Sabrejet and fly back to her island. The temptation to wrap her island about her and never leave had a very high potential energy.

So she'd learned to never allow herself more than forty-eight hours there when the pressures mounted or she might truly not leave again. Usually, after a day or two of listening to the chickadees at the feeder while a Steller's jay argued with the crows as she worked in her mother's garden, she could return to work without too much difficulty. The rainwater catchment system would keep the flowers and vegetables watered when she couldn't be there to tend them properly herself.

Today was testing that tenuous balance, and her current state of "peace" was mostly nonexistent.

"Tonight," Helen spoke in a serious tone that Miranda supposed was a "command" voice, "are the final acceptance test flights of the Army's newest rotorcraft, the S-97 Raider."

11

A HELICOPTER?

Miranda usually enjoyed a crash investigation.

She was fairly certain that was the correct emotion. Not the devastation, of course, but the puzzle. When something went wrong with an airplane, there was a chance to find a better solution for all future airplanes.

Airplanes.

Yes, the NTSB spread its four hundred personnel across five modes of transportation. She didn't care about highway, railroad, or pipeline mishaps. Maritime accidents were intriguing on a strictly intellectual basis.

Aviation was her area.

But there were at least as many subdivisions within that as there were lead investigators within the NTSB's aeronautics division: gliders, ultra-light, general aviation, commercial aviation, military, experimental, and rotorcraft.

She'd always felt unclear whether a hovercraft belonged in the maritime or aviation categories—perhaps dependent on its mode at the moment of the incident? She'd never worked on a hovercraft incident, so she wouldn't worry about the proper division assignment at this time.

Her preference had always been large-plane commercial aviation. Though she was also comfortable with the challenges of large-plane military aviation. Smaller aircraft were generally simpler merely due to fewer variables.

Rotorcraft.

Her last rotorcraft incident investigation had been the 2016 failure of the experimental Bell 525 Relentless. The eighteen-seat prototype had developed a severe low-frequency oscillation during an OEI—one engine inoperative—test.

The nose-up-then-tail-up swings had become severe twelve seconds into the test.

The pilot's grip on the collective control as he was subjected to an alternating force of plus and minus three g's exacerbated the problem. Each time he was slammed down into his seat by the rising nose, he had inadvertently slammed the control down. Each time the nose pitched abruptly down and he was jerked to a halt by the limits of his shoulder harness, he hauled the control up.

He had failed to exercise his only chance by not simply releasing the control and allowing the helicopter's tendency to autocorrect to neutral flight to have a chance.

Between twenty and twenty-one seconds into the test, the oscillation was so severe that the rotor blade was down-flexed sufficiently to slam into the side of the tail boom and chop it off. It had taken the same amount of time for the bits of the disintegrating helo to fall the two thousand feet as the failure itself.

Many design changes were made as a result of that flight, several by her recommendation.

The failure to require a cockpit voice recorder in test aircraft she had reported as a major oversight by the Flight Test

Safety Committee. She'd certainly insisted that Cessna install one in her M2.

She didn't know if her current team knew anything about rotorcraft.

She herself had never really understood rotorcraft. Not the way she did airplanes.

Jeremy now sat across from her, inhaling the files that General Thomas had provided. Becoming smarter every moment.

Miranda had tried. She could read the words but they didn't have any meaning. They must, but they didn't.

Holly was questioning Andi about her past, though eliciting few replies.

Mike sat beside her. He was smiling as he listened to Holly and Andi's sparring.

And Miranda herself was...

Trying not to freeze up.

As a child she'd rocked herself back and forth whenever she felt "the edge" come too close—and struck out every time Mother or Tante Daniels had tried to stop her. She never recalled Father being around for those episodes. She'd always thought that it was because he cut short her need for the self-soothing.

Tante Daniels had recently revealed that he made himself scarce when she was having problems.

She hated that second thought, but questioning the woman who had taken care of her for years—as therapist, then governess, and now friend—wasn't right either.

Over the years, Tante Daniels had taught Miranda to track her progress by the changes in her stimming.

Rocking had become finger drumming.

Drumming became hair twirling.

Then she'd watched *Top Gun.*

The Iceman twirled his pen between his fingers like magic.

It had taken her weeks to perfect it; the pen flipping end-over-end up and down her four fingers. Then she'd advanced to flipping both directions around the thumb and once more through the fingers. She could no longer watch the movie, not for the technical errors, which were surprisingly few, but because Iceman's simple finger pass now looked so slow and awkward.

Since then, in stressful meetings, she looked just like any other bored executive and let the smooth flow of the pen guide her nerves to calm.

But she couldn't do it here.

Her core team wouldn't mind, if they even noticed. She'd been careful to only rarely do it in their presence.

But she could feel Jon's presence even if he wasn't here. They'd spent frequent weekends together, just the two of them on her island as well as two brief vacations after a crash investigation. He caught her doing it enough to know it was a "thing" as he called it.

He would decide that she was stressing and...try to engage. She'd recorded that pattern in her notebook enough times. The last thing she needed at the moment was for him to engage or discuss, forcing her to *try* to give him the explanations he so needed.

Even if he wasn't here. But *they* were. Her team. She couldn't risk alerting them or she'd lose her hard-won method of relief.

She tried clicking her fingernails together next to her thigh, out of sight. But it just wasn't the same.

Rotorcraft.

An even narrower niche this time: experimental military rotorcraft.

The flight.

She'd just focus on the flight.

Even if it was a helicopter.

How could she make sure she didn't miss anything on a helicopter?

There was a feel to an airplane crash when it was resolved. She'd done fifty-two major investigations in the last seventeen years, more than *most* NTSB investigators did in an entire career.

Terence was the one who kept telling her that. Until she'd looked up his record and confronted him with it. Ninety-seven major investigations and untold smaller ones. He'd just smiled and told her that she'd better get her ass in gear if she was going to surpass his record.

Assuming that she was able to remain in the NTSB as long as he had, she should surpass his total by twenty-five investigations—theoretically surpassing his current record in fourteen-point-seven-two more years. That included the assumption that he remained at the academy and performed no more major launches, and that major crashes continued to occur at a consistent rate across time.

The Alaska crash was her smallest investigation in several years. Yet she couldn't even resolve that.

What good was she?

In desperation, she pulled out her notebook, flipped to the back, and stared down at the blank page.

Something should be here, *had* to be here.

But she couldn't think of what.

12

MIKE SAW THE PANIC SLAM IN.

Andi didn't just freeze. She looked as if she might puke, or just outright combust. Her jaw was clenched hard enough that the muscle in her cheek was jumping and sweat stood out on her forehead.

Holly and Jeremy were now engaging with Helen about the parameters of the upcoming test flight—paying no attention to what was happening to Andi.

Miranda had one of her notebooks out and was studying something closely.

Mike hooked Andi's arm, practically dragged her to her feet, and got her out of Helen's office. She offered all the resistance of a Raggedy Ann doll.

Helen's assistant moved to stop them for not having a security escort. But he got one look at Andi's now-greening face and pointed toward the ladies' room just down the hall.

There being so few women in the upper echelons of the military made that a good choice for privacy.

He led Andi in. A glance under the stall doors showed that they were alone.

"Uh," she needed to sit down before she fell down, but parking her in a toilet stall didn't seem the best choice. Lifting her up onto the counter like some child probably wasn't a good one either. He still couldn't believe that she'd managed to take down Holly for even a moment—she was incredibly fast. The sharp contrast of her easy compliance at the moment told him just how badly panicked she was.

The floor below the paper towel dispensers was military clean, he hoped, and he eased them both down onto it with their backs to the tiled wall.

Captain Andi Wu didn't sit, she crumpled. When she took on Holly, he'd decided that she had a spine of pure military steel. It had turned into a spine of Jell-O.

In fact, he wasn't even sure if she was a breathing.

"Andi?"

Nothing. Not even shaking her shoulder earned him a response.

Her eyes were saucer wide.

Mike remembered Holly looking just as freaked—once. It had been about survivor's guilt when her whole team went down on an operation gone bad. Whatever had triggered Andi, it was something at least as bad.

She might be staring directly at one of the toilets, but it was a good bet that wasn't what she was seeing.

He took the liberty of shoving her head forward between her knees so that she didn't faint.

"Breathe, Andi. It would really help if you would just breathe."

It was more of a stutter than a gasp, but she began moving air again.

"That's good," he kept his voice steady. "Try another breath."

She did. Shaky would be a kind description of it.

Would Holly know what to do? Or would it freak her out? It

was still hard to imagine anything pushing Holly to the edge, but he'd seen it. He considered going to fetch her, but didn't want to leave Andi.

Then he remembered how horrified Holly had been that he had even noticed. Better not to embarrass Andi further than she probably already was.

What was it with strong women who hated showing any weakness? Like they weren't human. Strangely, Miranda, the most messed up of them all, ended up being the most normal woman of the lot.

It took a few minutes, but Andi finally managed to sit up and lean against the wall on her own.

The way Mike saw it was, if Terence Graham had sent someone to Miranda, it meant that there were a whole lot of things right with her. Holly had sounded seriously impressed that she'd flown for the Night Stalkers. All Mike really knew about them was they were some ultra-secret helicopter group.

"Uh..." Andi made a soft noise.

He continued his own inspection of the opposite toilet to give her some space. Everything was blah beige right down to the tile and ceiling except for the white porcelain. It made him depressed just being here, aside from the fact that he was sitting on the floor of a ladies' bathroom. Could he sink much lower?

"Where..." but she didn't finish the question.

"Smells awful," she mumbled.

He sniffed. Bleach with that thin underlayment of piss that pervaded all public bathrooms. "Yep!"

"Ugh!" Her exclamation was just loud enough to echo a bit in the hard room.

Mike took that as permission to stop looking at the toilet.

Andi wore jeans and a black t-shirt. A light vest partially masked her slim figure, the pockets empty—except for her balled fists. He wondered how long that would last. Jeremy and

Miranda carried enough tools to take apart and rebuild a 747, or so it appeared. Maybe Andi wouldn't need any of her own. Who knew how long she was with them anyway.

Chinese and seriously cute. And, if he said that aloud, he'd wager that a US Army former captain would be glad to make him eat those words at her earliest convenience.

She blinked at him in surprise as if shocked to see where they were. Then she looked up at him. The darkness of her eyes was emphasized by the brilliant colors of her hair dye.

"Why the wild colors?" he indicated her hair. Always best to come at a problem by asking something completely normal.

She pulled a strand of it forward as if to inspect the color, even surprised by seeing it. " 'Girl who flies like her hair's on fire.' Too many grunts grew up in *The Hunger Games* era. Embracing it was easier than fighting it." The color slowly eased into her cheeks as she spoke.

"I was more the Batman *Dark Knight* trilogy era. Catwoman seriously rocked it. Anne Hathaway was hot."

"She was," Andi's voice was still rough.

"A beautiful and talented woman wrapped in head-to-toe black spandex, what's not to like, right?"

"Right." Andi had slipped back into the land of monosyllables.

"Anything you want to be talking about?"

13

"WAY NOT!" ANDI COULDN'T THINK OF ANYTHING SHE WANTED TO do less.

"Okay."

That surprised her enough to look up at Mike again. He didn't frown or push. Instead, his shrug said that he might actually be fine with her not explaining what had just happened.

As if she could.

All she remembered was...nothing. One moment she'd been sitting in General Thomas' office and the next she'd been inhaling bleach fumes.

Mike didn't appear to be trying to game her. What if Mr. Easy-going wasn't just an act and he actually was? If she was attracted to men, she could see how women could easily be attracted to him.

The last thing she really remembered was...

"The S-97 Raider."

"What is that anyway?"

Her breath caught in her chest and it couldn't escape.

"Oh, no you don't," Mike pushed her head down between

her knees again.

She shoved herself back upright, hard enough that she crunched his hand against the tile—hard. It was all that probably kept her from giving herself a concussion.

"Yikes! Okay, spine of steel is back in place." Mike shook his hand as if making sure it wasn't broken.

"Sorry." And she actually was. " 'The only way through is to beat the weakness to death.' My sixth-grade gym teacher had this slightly demented approach to how I should deal with all the teasing for being so small. It worked, I guess. I was top pick on most teams by the time I hit eighth grade."

"And on into the Night Stalkers." He massaged his hand but continued lightly, "That'll teach me to try and help."

Now she owed him. She hated debts. Could she trust Mike? Her instincts and her watch's second hand said yes. Andi suspected the two of colluding against her, but didn't argue.

"The S-97 Raider is America's newest helicopter. It's seriously hot shit."

"Why?"

"What's the top speed of a helicopter?"

Mike shrugged, making her rhetorical question less like rhetoric. She'd assumed he'd know since he was on an NTSB team called to evaluate a demo flight of the S-97.

"Okay, right now the fastest military helo in the world is the big twin-rotor MH-47G Chinook cargo helo. It can just hit two hundred miles an hour. My old MH-6M helo ran best at one-fifty. The S-97 can go two-eighty. It's also barely two meters bigger than my Little Bird, so it can still slip into tight little corners like I...used to."

Her throat constricted at the memory.

She could do this.

She could get through it.

The second hand was at the bottom half of the minute.

Shit!

"So, it's fast," Mike's simple statement snapped whatever was winding so tightly around her.

"It's more than fast," Andi managed to override the second hand's dire prediction. "It's stealthy. It has technology like you can't imagine and, well, I'd have thought I couldn't tell you except we are sitting on our bleached asses in a goddamn Groom Lake bathroom."

"Don't worry. Like Holly said, I wouldn't understand it. So, it's fast and cool. I can follow that much."

Maybe Holly had also been right that human factors really were all he cared about. He was here with her after all.

"Why does it freak you out?"

She opened her mouth but nothing came out.

"Wait a sec," Mike stared at the ceiling. "You know high security information about the newest helicopter. That means...that you were part of the development."

She flinched. Crap! There was an obvious giveaway that he was right on the mark.

"So, you *were* the test crew."

"All the first- and second-round tests. Down at Sikorsky Development in West Palm Beach, Florida." And those had been glorious days. Starting with basic hover, then hover and rotate, until she'd finally been cracking speed records. Sometimes two, three, four flights a day.

"Uh-huh. Except you got replaced by the two guys flying tonight. Two...Night Stalkers pilots. That means you were one of a two-pilot test team but now you're one and..." He looked down at her suddenly. "Oh, I'm so sorry, Andi."

And just that fast her secret was out there for all to see, as if Ken's blood was still splattered all over her. He'd been the best copilot she'd ever had. Right up until he died.

She could only nod. How to explain Ken or the guilt she had about his death? That he'd given his life and widowed his wife to save hers.

"My copilot died less than three feet from me while we were in an NOE—nap-of-Earth—flight, meaning really low, in someplace I can't mention. To even flinch as he died would have ended me in an instant."

She'd only wondered a few times if that might have been easier. The guilt would certainly have been more short-lived—unless the afterlife had guilt too. Maybe she should become a Buddhist, then she wouldn't remember any of this in the next life, at least not until she was a far more evolved person.

"I guess that you have every right to feel stressed."

Stressed. Such a simple word.

Captain Andi Wu is diagnosed as suffering from PTSD and may prove unreliable in any *flight situation.*

Or any other part of the service that she cared about. No TBI. Her brain was *physically* intact, just the rest of it was royally fucked up. Honorable medical discharge.

Only after she'd explained about why she'd been booted, let go, discharged like from a circus' human cannon out of the military, did it sink in what she was revealing.

"How did I just tell you all this? I've never said a word of it to anyone, never mind a total stranger."

Yet she had just dumped her guts out onto the ladies' bathroom floor.

14

MIKE DECIDED HE'D RATHER KEEP HER TALKING THAN TRY TO explain himself to himself, never mind anyone else.

"Were you close?"

"Not the way you mean," Andi's words came slowly. "He and his wife were my best friends. I can't even face her, though she's reached out several times. *Christ!*"

Andi twisted enough to glare up at him.

"Seriously, how do you get people to spill shit like that?"

Mike shrugged as if it was no big deal.

Andi huffed out a sigh and went to a sink to wash her face.

Sister Mary Pat had always loved telling him that he'd had the gift of the "secret superpower of gab" all the way back to when goo-goo and ga-ga were the extent of his vocabulary. She'd been a family friend. After the car wreck killed his parents when he was nine, he'd done the rest of his growing up in the St. Bernardine Catholic orphanage where Sister Mary Pat served. Bernardine, whatever the modern orphanage might be, had made himself popular for preaching against sorcery, witchcraft, homosexuality, and Jews.

Actually, Sister Mary Pat had been wrong.

His gift was getting *other* people to gab.

Looking back, he could see that it was a survival mechanism. It had earned him a disproportionate amount of Sister Mary Pat's attention in the crowded orphanage. Making himself her favorite had earned him a measure of safety and a lot of teasing. The latter had been easy to ignore because of the former.

Convincing other people that they wanted to tell him things made him important in their eyes, someone to protect. The priest had pushed hard for him to enter the clergy. As if.

At nine, when he'd arrived at the orphanage, he'd been a naive, lost little boy.

By the age of ten, he'd learned about leverage and had dirt on everyone, including the priest and a certain young lay sister who he'd convinced to take the "lay" part of her status very literally.

By the time Mike was fourteen—by the time he was five according to Sister Mary Pat—he'd learned that being a good and willing listener was a superpower around women as well.

Curiously, Holly never told him what she was thinking and feeling. Perhaps that's why he found her so fascinating.

Though *what* had brought him to kissing her awake he still didn't know. He knew women liked that, other women than Holly. If he'd thought for half a second, he'd have figured out that he'd gotten exactly what he would have expected.

That was what sent a shudder up his spine.

Since when had he stopped thinking about consequences when it came to women? That was a path to no end of pain. Sometimes literally.

Father Stevens had caught his favorite lay sister advancing Mike's education behind the altar in the chancel at Saint Bernardine's. In the very heart of the church, at Jesus' feet, Mike had been beaten senseless with a bible. Which had definitively completed his religious education.

Later, in his twenties, Violetta Celeste Giovanni had almost gotten his ass murdered by her mafia brothers as part of a scam to defraud them. That he'd gotten involved with her in the first place was a very pleasant accident. It had also been a dangerous one as he'd been a front for the FBI at the time—who had screwed him in a completely different and far less enjoyable way just two years ago.

Mike should thank Holly for the reminder, even if it still hurt to swallow.

Andi slid back down beside him. "How is it you know so little about planes but ended up in the NTSB?"

"I've always loved flying. Even if I'm only a private pilot, I love to talk about flying and planes. Usually that's all I need to get the conversation started. I've learned the types of information needed for an investigation. But as to what an S-97 Raider is or quite why Holly was so impressed that you were a Night Stalker? That's still out of my reach."

"That was Holly being impressed."

"Yep. She's—"

The bathroom door banged open hard.

"Hey, you two just gonna sit on your duffs all day?" Holly stood at the threshold with her fists on her hips.

"I don't know," Mike turned to Andi. "Are we?"

He could see Andi's relief that he kept it light. He knew better than to offer any hint of what they'd been discussing.

Ha! There was a laugh, he'd become a priest-confessor after all.

Andi tipped her head to the side as if thinking about it. "It depends. How mad will it make Holly if we just sit here?"

Holly rolled her eyes and strode into one of the stalls, slamming and locking the door.

Mike looked away when Holly's pants crumpled down over her boots.

Holly called out, “It’s not me you have to worry about—as long as you aren’t stupid enough to try waking me with a kiss.”

“Yeah, my bad. I already apologized once,” Mike shouted back.

“Actually you didn’t, but then neither did I,” Holly’s voice was surprisingly soft, and Mike didn’t think it was just the baffling of the door.

Andi used the cover of Holly flushing to whisper softly, “Thanks, Mike.”

He shrugged that it wasn’t even worth mentioning.

But what was he supposed to do now? What if she froze at the wrong moment? Well, Miranda did that too. Besides, it shouldn’t matter. How dangerous could a crash investigation be? And this time there wasn’t even a crash, just a flight.

Easy-peasy.

15

Miranda had found her way back by writing down a list of every major investigation she'd led, from memory. First she wrote them in date order, then again successively by aircraft model number, date of model introduction, date of frame manufacture (though she'd had to consult her tablet to look up two of those), and finally by tail number.

When she was done, everyone was sitting around the age-worn wooden conference table facing the display screens. The sun had gone down outside the windows and the buzz of fluorescents overhead now lit the room.

She'd never trusted fluorescents. They always appeared to flicker on the edge of her vision but were steady and constant when she stared at them directly. Her emotions page suggested that "smug" was the proper adjective. Smug lighting fixtures.

Jeremy and Helen were the only ones talking. He was asking very detailed questions about projects that forced Helen to keep saying, "That project is classified" over and over.

Miranda hadn't even heard of most of them, but Jeremy's curiosity didn't abate.

Holly was watching Mike and Andi closely, but Miranda couldn't see anything different that made them noteworthy.

Someone had delivered a cart laden with various dinners from the cafeteria. By the time they'd made their selections and returned to the table, the screens were lit.

Top left was a forward view from the front of the Raider, presently a hangar door opening wide. Bottom left was a view inside the cockpit, showing the two pilots, so encased in their flightsuits and helmets as to be indistinguishable if not for their names written across the brow of their helmets: Morales and Christianson.

Top right was a feed of the performance and engine instrumentation. Bottom right was all of the test instrumentation—accelerometers, strain gauges, even the pilots' pulse and blood pressure.

The only sound she heard was the pilot asking the control tower for departure clearance. Once it was given, they were gone into the night sky.

Finally, something to concentrate on.

16

"STABLE AT TWO-TWO-ZERO."

"Roger." Despite nineteen prior flights in the last seventeen days, Chief Warrant 3 Roberto Morales still couldn't believe this bird.

Small helicopters just didn't cruise at two hundred and twenty knots, two hundred and fifty miles per hour.

No helicopter did.

When it entered full service after this test, its Never Exceed speed of two-eighty would make it the fastest helicopter in the world by eighty miles per hour. It wasn't much slower than the MV-22 Osprey tiltrotor—when it was in airplane mode. Those guys at Sikorsky were superstars.

Normal cruise speed for his company's usual MH-6M Little Birds was a hundred and thirty knots. Jumping from one-thirty to two-twenty was freaking awesome.

The S-97 Raider was better than any wet dream, than any woman—except his Juana, of course. She always made it easy to keep his promise that she was Number One in his heart. Now she was pregnant with their daughter, as if he needed another reason to love her.

But between the unborn kid and the S-97 Raider?

At least until her birth, second place was still too close to call.

It was time to rip this awesome bird out of the test pilots' hands and get it certified for combat. Every test in the acceptance suite had been blazed through with flying colors. All that remained was this final free-for-all stress-test. Their instructions were simple: "Go and really wring it out."

Right now everyone would be watching over their shoulders, but he shrugged that off easily. Night Stalkers only flew one way—never giving less than a hundred percent.

The first several batches of Raiders would be deeply customized for the 160th Night Stalkers Special Operations Aviation Regiment. And he blessed whatever saint on high had decided that it was the 1st Battalion A Company's job to run the acceptance tests.

Hard luck for Andi when Ken was killed. They'd done most of the early testing, and had been sent back to active duty time after time during the long waits while fixes and upgrades were incorporated.

But he and Christianson were now the lead team, the final test pilots, and he was going to ride that high for a long time. They would be the first Night Stalkers certified in the military's newest rotorcraft.

The night desert rushed by invisibly twenty-five feet below them.

The console had only minimal displays. The information he needed was all projected on the inside of his Collins Aerospace helmet—a direct cousin of the ones used by the F-35 Lightning II pilots.

The helmet muffled all sounds until he could hear little other than his heartbeat—steady at fifty a minute no matter what was going down.

They'd created something incredibly new in the Raider.

The GE YT706 turboshaft engine was fifteen percent more powerful and twenty percent more efficient than its predecessor T700. That had provided a brilliant improvement in the difficult high-and-hot operations tests.

The two sets of coaxially mounted, counter-rotating four-blade rotors looked unusual. Stacked one set above the other, they looked as if they shouldn't work. The change from a single rotor allowed a sixty percent faster speed, with full control.

And to reach that speed, the six-bladed rear pusher propeller *drove* the Raider forward at thirty-seven percent the speed of sound. The bird of the future, as the replacements for the Black Hawk, Apache, and Cobra were all going to be a scaled-up version of the Raider.

Best of all, he and Christianson would forever be the first pilots to fly this wave of the military future into the battlefield—delivered courtesy of the US military. Even when the other countries inevitably stole the plans, they still wouldn't have the key factor, Night Stalker pilots.

Yet all of those differences were easily ignored. The ride was so smooth it was hard to believe he was even aloft.

Everything had been done to reduce distractions so that all of his attention was focused on the feel of the controls and what the helmet showed him. Yes, it had engine data, course plans, even radio frequencies.

But the helmet's magic was in the terrain that rolled by him in a three-layered view.

First was the pre-programmed map of the terrain. It was generally accurate to within one meter—worldwide. He could safely slalom through the concrete canyons of New York City, the heart of the Kremlin, or the Khyber Pass without looking out the windshield once.

The second was the radar image of the terrain ahead.

And the trippy one, the one that always chapped his ass, was the DAS. The Distributed Aperture System was fed by an array of six external cameras mounted on the outside of the Raider. The seamless day- or night-vision image it produced let him see the world outside the helo as if the bird wasn't even there.

As long as he kept his flight profile above all three layers of the terrain display inside his helmet, he'd be safe.

"Take it down to three meters, one-zero feet?" On a mission, even a practice one, Night Stalkers of the 160th SOAR didn't waste words, but Morales wanted to be absolutely clear with his commanding officer.

"Cleared to three," Christianson confirmed from the right seat.

Morales slashed south away from Groom Lake.

At three meters, he had to climb to avoid rocks and the rare struggling tree. Hugging the valley floor, he swooped through the Pintwater Range around the south flank of Quartz Peak's two-thousand-meter pinnacle.

As they slid out of the mountain pass, the threat sensors auto-recognized a vehicle's profile parked at the head of Dog Bone Lake—*tank*—and flashed a warning.

Without hesitating, Christianson swung his helmet to center the target on his visor's crosshairs. Magnetic sensors in the seatback read the exact position of his helmet and fed that information into the selected warhead when Christianson hit the fire button.

After three seconds of supersonic flight, forty-two inches of Hydra 70 missile punched into the old M60A1 "Patton" tank that had been left in the desert as a practice target. The Hydra had a low-charge head, just enough to show up as a clean hit without shattering the remains of the tank.

They raced past and plunged into the rough terrain of the Desert Range on their way to Tikaboo Valley, where three more targets were waiting—though he wasn't supposed to know that. Morales had flown there during a massive Red Flag war game two years before. He remembered that trio of old Sheridan tanks clearly because he'd nearly been burned by one of them.

The Raider was light on the controls. Her ride was roller-coaster wild mixed with Corvette smooth.

She weighed three times more than his Little Bird (or his Vette), but she was only two feet longer and her rotors just seven feet wider. All the rest of the weight was speed and capability.

"Can you imagine what we could have done with this bird back in Mosul?" Major Christianson was feeling it enough to speak.

"Roger that." Morales was debating whether to take them down to two meters when the digital terrain overlay didn't line up with the imaging—the cliff suddenly flickering two meters closer to their starboard side.

That never happened.

Sometimes there was a truck parked somewhere that the pre-programmed map didn't know about, then it was time to watch the other two systems.

But there was probably no better-mapped—or less likely to change—terrain anywhere than the Nevada Test and Training Range.

"Did you see that?"

17

MUCH TO METIN'S SURPRISE, WHEN HE'D SUGGESTED ACCESSING the SVR supercomputer at the Yildiz Technopark, General Firat had made it happen within minutes.

"It is time we stop fooling around with Greece," Firat had declared. "NATO is no threat; we know how to manage them. Some argue that it is the Americans we must learn to manage now. They are wrong. It is *they* who must learn to *survive* us."

The SVR might not be anywhere near the power of the TOP500 supercomputers; in fact, it was barely a tenth as powerful as the five-hundredth ranked machine. Despite being five years older, it was still over a thousand times faster than even his overclocked desktop—terraflops instead of gigaflops of speed.

Metin had asked Onur for help. He would have preferred to own this triumph himself, but there was too much information to manage.

By recruiting Onur he'd not only grabbed the second-best programmer at Siberkume (he'd already proven who was best, at least for today), he'd also secured his inside track to Asli. This might be the twenty-first century, but it was still Turkey.

Not that he'd seen her even once this week.

After they'd been moved into their own office, it had taken them three days and nights to figure out how to port his programs onto a secure sector of the SVR. It wasn't perfect; even with the SVR, it still took twenty-three minutes to grind his way into the satellite's code. A lot of that time was lost due to uplink / downlink speeds, but some was non-optimized code that they didn't have time to fix.

Once aboard, he'd found the next hurdle, cracking the M-Code. The "military code" was locked down tight on the latest-generation American GPS satellites—supposedly unhackable.

It was Onur who'd suggested the trick, though Metin still had bragging rights because he was the one who figured out how to use Onur's idea.

There was no need to actually unravel the M-Code signal, it was merely a matter of retiming it. He couldn't alter the onboard atomic clock. But he *had* looped its output through extra cycles within the transmitter's main processor before its delivery as a GPS signal.

Rather than breaking the signal, it simply delayed it for a few crucial milliseconds.

By the time General Firat said they must be ready, he could alter the signal within a very specific locale for up to a hundred-and-ten seconds.

He and Onur might not command the American's GPS satellite network, but locally warping it? They had that down.

It was now five in the morning.

They'd been up all night, but they'd been ready when the general had walked in.

18

"WHAT?" CHRISTIANSON HAD MISSED THE TERRAIN ANOMALY, though he had other duties for the flight than following Morales' incoming data flow: course, systems status, weapons, to name just a few. He was the flight commander; all Morales had to do was fly.

They were still solid at three meters and full-on hustle.

Maybe he'd imagined—

Again!

The programmed terrain map didn't match radar or the DAS. A rock was two feet north on the map of where the other two systems showed it. Landslide? But it was just two meters on a flat section of the canyon's floor.

"Saw that," Christianson reported.

Not his imagination.

Staying barely above all three layers of the map and superimposed views was always a challenge. That task was made doubly difficult by the sheer speed the S-97 Raider was delivering. Change happened faster than his reflexes had been used to, though they'd mostly shifted over now. If he ever had to fly it again, his MH-6 Little Bird was going to feel as ungainly as a VW Beetle—an old one.

A Night Stalkers pilot of the 160th flew as much by instinct as conscious control—thousands of flight hours honing it to a perfect melding with the machine.

But when there was a disjunct, it was like a slap in the face.

He could feel himself slam out of the instinctual zone.

No longer part of the machine, he was in his seat and back to the much slower process of thinking about his flying. Please don't let it be some glitch that was going to delay aircraft acceptance.

They were in a sixty-degree bank around the base of some no-name mountain when he decided he'd better gain more altitude. Had to be a software glitch, but he'd been trained that arriving intact—to infiltrate or extract his Special Operations customers—was far more important than the ego boost of a hot flight.

19

"What did they see?"

Miranda didn't know how to answer Mike's question.

She'd spotted no anomalies on any of the readouts. The cameras showed nothing unusual ahead. The pilot-focused cameras showed nothing either.

"Something they saw inside their helmets?" Andi reached the obvious conclusion at the same moment she did.

It was the only remaining possibility as that information wasn't on any of their display screens.

Whatever it was didn't matter.

It was already too late.

20

Neither the S-97 Raider's radar nor the view from the DAS cameras could show what lay hidden around the last jagged abutment to the mountain. The automated map, if still correctly aligned with the GPS, would have. It wasn't.

Chief Warrant Roberto Morales rounded the final steep cliff, which dropped from the flanks of the easternmost mountain of the Desert Range. The twisting canyon cut between a resistant knob of Eureka Quartzite and the comparatively softer stone of the Ely Springs Dolomite.

Except for a lone pillar of the quartzite sandstone that remained close by the dolomite cliff.

According to the GPS-driven terrain map, Morales would be over ten meters clear of the tall, wind-carved pinnacle as he rounded the cliff's final abutment.

He wasn't.

It lay barely fifty meters—zero point four-three seconds —ahead.

The right-side gap between the pillar and the cliff—too narrow.

The open space to the left of the pinnacle—wrong bank angle.

The S-97 Raider achieved straight-and-level flight before it rammed into the face of the sandstone pillar, seven meters above the terrain at two hundred and forty-nine miles per hour.

The dual sets of counter-rotating rigid rotor blades shattered against the rock.

The composite shell of the airframe accordioned like an empty aluminum beer can being stomped on by an Army boot.

The crash-proof fuel tanks were shattered, spraying fountains of fuel to either side of the pillar like firehoses. At least the helicopter wouldn't burn—much.

The six-bladed rear pusher propeller, driving the helicopter hard into the cliff face, was the last thing to slam into the rock.

The Raider didn't have far to fall to reach the canyon floor, not that there was much recognizable left to fall.

Neither Morales nor Christianson had sufficient time for any final thoughts.

21

Six hundred and eighty-six kilometers above the Nevada desert, the Göktürk-2 earth observation satellite captured images of the flight's final moments and complete destruction.

The signal was delayed by over three hundred milliseconds as it was relayed through two RASAT communications satellites before being beamed to the ground, eleven thousand kilometers away.

There was an additional hundred-and-twenty-millisecond delay as the signal was processed at the Gölbaşi Ground Station south of Ankara, Turkey, rerouted, delivered, and finally decrypted.

Nineteen milliseconds later, the image reached an office in subbasement two of the Siberkume building.

22

IT HAD HAPPENED SO FAST THAT METIN COULD ONLY STARE AT THE image on the screen.

Onur, beside him, didn't appear to even be breathing.

"Excellent! Excellent!" General Firat was not at a loss for words. "That is simply exceptional, gentlemen. Bravo!"

He shook both their hands as if they were his contemporaries and peers rather than a pair of kid hackers he wouldn't have deigned to wipe his boots on two weeks before. Then he hurried off to effuse about his great personal success to some military or government leader who would elevate his career.

"Think we'll get an invitation to *Ak Saray,* the White Palace?" Onur was the first to recover the power of speech.

"*Kaç-Ak Saray,*" Metin barely managed to whisper. The "Illegal Palace" had been built by the President at incredible expense despite the nation's highest court forbidding its construction. The thousand-room complex had cost four trillion Turkish lira, a half trillion US—nearly a year of the entire country's GDP.

Metin couldn't look away from the screen.

He wouldn't turn nineteen for another week and he'd just killed two Americans on the other side of the world.

Onur's sister Asli was a staunch progressive and spoke vehemently, and dangerously, against Turkey's "heinous dictatorship." She spoke English often, wore modern clothes, and had strong opinions.

He loved the rebel in her, the passion that took no prisoners.

"We can never tell Asli we did this," he whispered to Onur.

Onur agreed quickly, "Never."

23

"Now we have a crash."

Andi couldn't believe that Miranda actually looked pleased as she rose to her feet and tucked away the notebook she'd had open.

Though considering how angry Miranda had sounded when she'd found out it was just a test flight, Andi supposed that it made a certain amount of sense.

"It could just be a loss of signal," Jeremy suggested.

She ignored him and turned to General Thomas. "I'm Miranda Chase. Investigator-in-Charge for the NTSB. We're ready to begin."

"Wait, Miranda. Your Jeremy could be right."

"Didn't you hear their words?" Miranda spoke to a brigadier general as if she was a schoolgirl who needed help to learn their next lesson.

Andi had heard.

Did you see that?

What?

I saw that.

And the words sent a chill up her spine.

Miranda turned away, as if she was done making her point, and faced Mike.

A moment before she'd been an insignificant woman watching the screen with the rest of them. Now she commanded the room and didn't need to speak her question—her *demand* for concurrence—aloud.

Only *some* military officers could do that—she herself certainly never had.

They simply commanded a room with their presence. Perhaps their presence *and* their rank, but even the air seemed to snap to attention around them.

Suddenly Miranda had that. With her simple statement, she'd taken absolute command of the room.

And her team had shifted from a random group of experts. Each, even Holly, was now sitting upright and turning their full attention to Miranda. No side remarks. Nothing now except the business at hand.

Mike was nodding slowly. "The timing of the gaps in their conversation implies that they are facing something unexpected. Their tone doesn't indicate any sense of panic, nor does it indicate any problem, but I do find it indicative that they spoke only two other times since the start of the test. That would imply something going very wrong."

Mike turned to *her.*

Andi then glanced to Miranda, but despite her suddenly formidable demeanor, she was waiting patiently for Andi to collect her thoughts.

Her years of training and flying with the 160th SOAR had drilled in that the mission was the only priority. Feelings came later.

She'd been "flying with them," imagining each moment of the flight as if it was hers. Morales' hand on the flight controls was as smooth as she'd expect from a pilot of such high caliber.

There'd been a "bump." Nothing big, but the moment before he'd spoken the first time he'd—

"Please, give us the process aloud," Mike prompted her.

Andi nodded and repeated what she'd been thinking.

"The moment before he spoke, there was an unexpected control correction on the cyclic," she indicated the minute motion with her hand. "A tiny shift to the right. Not up, but to the right. Perhaps surprised by an unexpected obstacle. Then they had to wait an additional two seconds to both see it, whatever *it* was. Whatever they saw was at least seven hundred feet apart at the speed they were traveling. This implies that what they were seeing was onboard, not external."

Nobody was stopping her, so she kept following the only logical chain.

"Flying at three meters NOE, they were only a few tenths of a second from impact with the ground. Far too fast to recover."

"Actually two-point-seven hundredths of a second," Miranda said in a dead flat voice.

Andi had flown NOE missions for years. There was so little margin for error that they were the ultimate challenge for any helo pilot. She'd never actually done the math to understand that the margin for error was effectively nonexistent. She had faster than average reaction time to visual stimuli, barely a tenth of a second compared with the quarter-second average person. But three thousandths? Not a chance. She felt nerves all over again even though she'd never fly another mission like that one.

Miranda continued, "Helen, you will want to scramble your search-and-rescue team to their last known position. Be sure to keep everyone else away from the site; I don't want any evidence moved by Sikorsky, GE, or any of the others. Arrange transport for my team at dawn."

While Helen did as she had been told, Miranda turned to face the rest of them.

"First light here is at 6:01 a.m. Be ready to board at 0530 hours."

24

Mike stayed close by her side as they were escorted to a visitors' dorm.

"You okay?"

Andi nodded. She was still on internal lockdown, and the safety pin on her "inner grenade" was holding.

"I'm fine. And for future reference, Mike, we're trained to focus solely on the mission at hand—solely! No 160th pilot would inflect their tone even if a bomb had gone off in the cockpit."

And there it was.

The thought she swore she'd never revisit was there, yet again.

She managed to make it inside and close the door in his face—before the internal pin let go and she collapsed to the floor.

The psychs had kinda said, without quite saying it, "Welcome to your new standard life." They *had* stated it would become more manageable with time but had made it sound as if the apocalypse might happen first.

Which sucked big time.

Her...panic response, (that's what she'd call it today), was definitely on her list of things that needed changing. She just didn't know how to go about it. Going fetal wasn't helping much, but it was all she had in her. She couldn't even roll toward the still dark room to avoid the painful brightness slipping under the door.

The *blinding* light.

In between testing cycles of the S-97 Raider, she and Ken had been deployed to typical hellholes that US Special Operations always deployed to.

Their final mission had flown deep into the Syrian Desert. They'd taken their Little Bird in-country to place a four-man team close by the Tiyas Airbase. A massive Russian air base (that of course Russia said was Syrian) lay in the very center of the harsh *badhi* terrain. Someone wanted eyes on the ground—whether to set up air strikes or a factual report to the UN wasn't her business—at least not until they called for an extraction.

What *was* her business was the grenade that had been fired at them as they raced back to the relative safety of the American-held DCZ—the Deconfliction Zone—at al-Tanf in Syria's south. Nothing more than a flat area of red sand and dust, but the Americans had made a fifty-five kilometer stretch of desert their own.

She hadn't been flying hard nap of earth—instead holding a solid five meters above Syria's central desert with the doors off. It wasn't in a Night Stalker to not turn any flight into a training session.

In the dead of night with no navigation lights, they were near enough invisible.

But not *quite* near enough.

It had been a thousand-to-one chance shot—probably by one of the Syrian government troops who always lurked along the edge of the DCZ. Or one of the Russian Spetsnaz they'd heard rumors of patrolling the area.

It didn't matter.

One moment she and Ken had been racing low and fast, nearing the DCZ's edge and the relative safety of the American zone.

Then Ken had grunted in pain.

"Grenade," he'd scrabbled at his Kevlar vest. "Went in the side seam. Busted some ribs."

Andi had automatically begun counting seconds.

One, the shot and a second of travel.

Two, Ken reacting.

Three and Four, Ken's struggles to recover the grenade.

Five, her shout of protest was drowned out by the grenade exploding.

By its blinding flash of light, she'd been able to see that he'd wrapped his arms around his chest, turned away, and curled up around the grenade to protect her and the helicopter. He'd been splattered across her and the inside of the windscreen.

The funeral had been with a closed coffin.

25

Mike continued down the hall to the room he'd seen Holly enter.

He knocked, then tried the door handle.

Locked. It had been a while since she'd done that to him. Woman was pricklier than one of her Tasmanian echidnas.

He looked back toward Andi's room, then thought about Holly walking in on them "just chatting" in the ladies' bathroom. Andi had forced herself to act normally so quickly that she clearly didn't want her panic attack made public.

Had Holly assumed...?

"Oh, give me a break, Holly," he thumped the side of a fist on the door. "I was just helping her out." But he couldn't say why.

No response.

The team's escort was gone. Even the escort had assumed he was bedding down with Andi.

Perfect.

The hall was just a long, off-white corridor of closed doors and well-spaced fluorescent tubes.

The numbers on the doors told him nothing.

At a loss for what else to do, he tried knocking on the door across the hall. He was in luck; Jeremy answered in his jockey shorts.

"Too much information, buddy," Mike made a show of covering his eyes. "Does your room have a second bed?"

"No, but it has a couch."

Mike could see it over Jeremy's shoulder. A short couch. Sagging with too many years of service.

Fine.

Just fine.

26

Andi appreciated the rhythm that Miranda set at the crash site. It had the same feel as her masterful reports.

It also let Andi not have to look at the crash.

The bodies of Morales and Christianson had been removed in the night, but otherwise General Thomas had followed Miranda's request and kept the site completely isolated. Their arrival in the general's UH-1N Huey helicopter had woken two very grumpy security guards, snoozing in their Chevy Suburban.

The area had a stark clarity in the dawn light. The brick-brown rock rose in steep and jagged thrusts above the sand-patched desert. The grit was coarse and crunched beneath her boots.

Even purposely not looking at the crash, it was impossible to ignore the pillar of rock that rose above it like a ten-story tombstone. Soot marks from burned fuel had blackened its flanks without scorching the front. The unburned rock face looked like...

"Eye of Sauron," Jeremy said as he passed close beside her. "The great eye of the Necromancer. The evil that glares down and devours all." He looked to be very pleased with the analogy. It was hard to argue. The sun was rising directly behind it and streaming around both blackened sides. It was simultaneously blinding to look at, and shading the crash in darkness.

Andi mirrored Miranda, turning her back to the crash. Miranda again went through her vest ritual, then said softly enough that only Andi could overhear: "I'm Miranda Chase. Investigator-in-charge for the NTSB."

Extracting a pocket recorder, she turned it on and then tucked it away again so that only the microphone showed above the fabric. A small notebook from another pocket was marked in clear block letters: S-97 Raider and the date.

She pulled out a weather multi-tool and recorded the wind speed, humidity, temperature, and GPS elevation. A brief narration describing the crystalline blue sky was then recorded.

Miranda handed Mike a high-resolution topo map of the area.

"I want you and Andi to verify the canyon's profile back along the flight path."

Then she'd turned away as if she'd already forgotten them.

"Wait! What?"

Mike shushed her until they'd rounded the corner, out of sight of the crash. No complaints from her about the change of scene; again an excuse to delay facing the wreckage. But...

Once alone, Andi flapped the map at Mike, "Really? She doesn't trust a topo map? Gee," she held it up and looked along the valley, "the canyon's landforms look just like the map. I'm so shocked." She did let her eyes slide along the lines just like a helo's flight.

"She has her ways. It's better not to question them too much because she always has her reasons and they're usually right."

"Actually," Andi double-checked, then pulled a pen from Mike's shirt pocket, "there's a slump there on the right, about three hundred meters along, that must have happened since the map was made. The debris can't have shifted by more than ten meters, but it is different even if it's well off the flight path." She marked the correction.

Mike was looking back and forth between the landscape and the map. "Wow, you certainly saw that fast."

"Terrain is remarkably important to those of us trained to nap-of-Earth flight."

"Would have taken me forever to notice that, if I had at all. Thank you so much for marginalizing my purposefulness even more."

"Anything I can do to help, just let me know," Andi tried to make it a joke, but Mike looked tired and humorless this morning.

Probably best to simply ignore that. Especially because she suspected that it had something to do with her.

"Why are we doing this anyway? She doesn't act like some anal dictatorial bitch. Why doesn't anyone dare ask her questions?"

"You're right, she isn't. And I try to ask only *pertinent* questions because anything else may confuse her."

"Confuse her? She doesn't appear to be stupid."

Mike waved her toward a pair of rocks and waited until they sat opposite each other. "We'll give her a few minutes to think that we're being thorough, because if it was just me, a terrain review *would* take a while."

"So what's her deal?"

Mike stared at her long enough for her to shift uncomfortably on her rock. If he wasn't already with Holly, she'd think it was one of those I'm-such-an-open-guy come-ons. Except he was...and it didn't feel that way.

"I don't know you," Mike said softly.

Andi didn't know whether to laugh or cry. "You know more about me than pretty much anyone now that Ken's dead."

"Sure, I know that you're a good pilot, feel totally lost

without your flying partner and your career, and you're a good person."

"*Way* more than I know...or believe."

Mike ignored her. "That doesn't tell me much about how you feel about other people."

Andi could only shrug. At this point in her life, she was too busy trying to keep one person from totally coming apart to think about anyone else.

All she'd told her family was that she'd been honorably discharged from the military and was going to DC to investigate helicopter accidents. The main reason she'd decided to do that was DC was about as far from her parents and brother in San Francisco as she could get and still be in the same country. The only places further away were northern Alaska and Maine. Maybe after this.

"Miranda is..." Mike hesitated for a long moment, then started over. "Have you ever met someone with ASD?"

"What? Like Automatic Smile Disease, spread by the Joker in Batman?" Mike didn't even acknowledge what Andi felt was a pretty decent comeback on no notice.

"Like Autism Spectrum Disorder."

"Oh...no." Yeah, she'd heard of that one, but never had any reason to think about it.

"Imagine..." Mike stared at the wide slot of blue that was the brightening sky above the canyon. "You're a pilot."

"Past tense."

Mike focused on her, eye-to-eye. "You *are* a pilot. You may not be flying at the moment but— Never mind. That's a discussion for another time. Okay, imagine that you're on a flight. Engine sputtering, stall warning goes off, master alarm slams on, the stick shaker is trying to get your attention about the stall while you're talking to a control tower, except six other flights are all talking over you."

"Eight kinds of ugly," Andi nodded. She'd been in similar

situations a few too many times for comfort. "It's what a mission into a battlefield sometimes feels like. You simply can't think fast enough. You have to trust your instincts to get through it."

"Right, exactly," Mike pointed at her. "Just like that. Except no one ever issued you any instincts. That makes your life one continuous sensory overload."

"What does that have to do with Miranda?"

"That," he leaned forward and flicked a finger against Andi's forehead hard enough to sting.

She batted at his hand, too little too late. It seemed that her reaction time had followed wherever her flaky brain had gone to. Rubbing her forehead, she could still feel where he'd zapped her.

"That is what is going on inside Miranda's head twenty-four seven. Nothing is instinct, everything is learned—usually the hard way. How she happens to be a genius crash investigator and a nice person despite that is a lot of what makes her so miraculous. We neurotypicals have it easy."

"Seriously?" Andi couldn't equate that with the woman she'd met. "She just seems a little odd."

"A little odd, yes. But I'm starting to think that she's also the best and smartest person I've ever known."

Andi chewed on that. "So...what? Like with Jon yesterday?"

"Right. A perfect example. They're in a relationship, except she has no idea what that *means,* and no instincts about how to handle it. If Holly hadn't given her a nudge, Jon could have tipped Miranda off the edge. Not likely, as she's getting steadier even just in the year that I've known her, but he certainly wasn't helping by trying to force her somewhere closer to being normal. Whatever the hell that is—don't be asking me."

Mike shuddered as if it must be something nasty, actually forcing a laugh out of her.

"*My* theory is that part of how she gets through it all is by having a team around her. The reference points we create in her world just by consistently doing what we do is what lets her not only do what *she* does, but maybe it also helps her to know *who* she is. If you, Captain Andi Wu, are the kind of person I'd like to think you are, you won't do anything to make her question that. That includes asking irrelevant questions in the middle of an investigation."

"Like why she doesn't trust a topo map."

"Right. But I do know the answer to that one. Short version —which you wouldn't have gotten if you'd asked her—she'd most likely have given you a step-by-step full breakdown on how she got through the two months of work to explain a crash back in 2009. There was an aberration in the topo map that had been mirrored on the Sectional Chart. A hot-dogger beginner pilot, not even licensed yet, decided he should do an instruments only flight without an IFR chart or training. He was well below flight minimums, but for all that was doing it correctly. Right up until he slammed into a mountain that the chart had said was a hundred feet lower. The trees saved his life, barely; he'll never walk again. And he killed his girlfriend, who wasn't legally on the flight."

"That's why she doesn't trust topo maps."

"Exactly. Don't be messing with Miranda's internal topo map." Mike pushed to his feet. "That should be long enough. Let's go back."

As they came back around the bend in the canyon, Holly was the first one to notice them. She offered a glare that would make Superman proud. Andi double-checked that there were no heat-ray burn holes through her chest. But she could feel the scorch marks like skin prickles.

Still a cast-iron bitch.

Then Mike's words sank in.

However, while *Mike* might seem as Holly described him, the "touchy-feely" Human Factors Specialist that didn't have any real skills, that wasn't right. While appearing to be very kind, he'd actually just put her on notice more effectively than any drill sergeant or Special Operations flight instructor. She was either an asset to Miranda—or she was toast. And he'd done it using a pilot's metaphor specifically for her, which only made it all the clearer.

27

"Seriously, Holly. Get a grip."

"Around your throat? Should have crushed it while I had the chance."

Mike should have had this conversation on the ground. Instead, he and Holly were roped up and exploring the face of the stone pillar. Miranda had wanted them to inspect all of the ledges for possible debris, study the point of impact, and collect rock samples from the rock face for hardness analysis back in the lab.

The rest were walking the debris perimeter several stories below and far enough away that he and Holly wouldn't be overheard without shouting. Which was fine, because her voice was low and dangerous.

"I was just trying to help her."

"By fucking her instead of me. Fine. We never made any vows or anything. But for going after her ass on her first day, you're just a total shit despite being Mr. Touchy-feely All-aware New-Age-creep!"

Mike sighed and hammered another piton into the hard rock. He clipped in, then tested the hold before climbing higher. Climbing was a trust exercise. At the moment he wasn't so sure that Holly wouldn't just let him plummet to the rocks below if he fell. She might not do that if it would kill him, but they were only high enough that it would merely break him in many places, so all bets were off.

When Holly was good, which was most of the time, she was amazing.

When she was pissed? Not so much.

What did he owe to Andi? He wasn't some priest confessor, but she had told him things in confidence.

He free-climbed another five meters, being especially careful not to slip, before spiking in another piton in the hard quartzite.

Mike belayed Holly up to his position, but kept the belay tight before she could head farther up the rock face, trapping her face-to-face with him on the bare rock.

"Holly?"

"*What?*"

"Do you honestly think that my role is as useless as you told Andi?"

"Yes," but she said it with a snap of anger that he'd learned to ignore. Her first reaction was rarely the true one.

Mike waited her out as she stared up the cliff—anywhere other than looking at him. They were just a few meters below the impact marks carved by the rotor blades. She rested her forehead against the rock and he could barely hear her mumble.

"I'm really sorry about your throat."

Mike laughed right in her face. "You think that's what this is about?"

"Isn't it?"

"No, it isn't." How much shit did he have to put up with? "I kissed you awake because I wanted to. I *wanted* to. I, me, the guy who never cares about women past the morning after.

You're pretty much the most lovely, fascinating, and utterly ornery woman I've ever been with. I'm with you because I *want to be*. You better figure out why *you're* with *me*."

At that, he called out, "Belay!" and didn't wait for an answer, instead leading the final section himself.

He could inspect a few scrapes in the rock pillar's hard exterior just as well as the next person. And maybe somewhere in there, he'd figure out why, of all craziness, he himself actually wanted to be with Holly Harper.

28

THE DEBRIS PERIMETER ITSELF WAS LESS THAN A HUNDRED meters across; it felt as if Andi could wrap her arms around it. It was hard to imagine that such a small space of rough stone and sand could contain the remains of an entire helicopter and two lives.

Yet despite the clear outline, she, Jeremy, and Miranda walked it in a well-spaced perpendicular line to make sure they didn't miss a thing. From the cliff face ahead of the crash, through the canyon, and back to the cliff face.

The practice launches that Andi and her classmates had made at the academy hadn't followed this methodology. Yet now that she was doing it, she could see how neatly it mirrored the style of Miranda's reports. Or rather the reports mirrored her method.

Also, if Miranda was actually as Mike had described her, the method fit the woman herself.

Neat, thorough, and a laser focus on one element at a time.

No need to think of the crash. Yet.

Instead...

Three steps.

Stop.

Scan the ground.

Turn and scan behind for anything that might have been hidden by a twisted tuft of creosote bush or withered clump of grass.

Mark the outer extent of the debris with a little green flag.

Three more steps.

She wondered what Mike and Holly were discussing. They were doing as much talking as climbing on the rock face.

Andi herself was the obvious topic.

Holly's occasional laser-glares left little question about that.

Yet she knew Mike was somehow to be trusted with what she'd told him in confidence.

Her watch concurred with a hard yes at straight-up twelve.

They were both tall, beautiful, and athletic—a seriously striking couple. So why had Holly throttled Mike for kissing her awake? Be nice to have someone do that for her.

All the way around the debris field, she managed not to look even once at the crash itself. Ignoring the flight path was harder because it was plenty obvious, but she managed.

"Hey!" Andi spun to look back up the canyon where she and Mike had walked.

"Hey?" Miranda answered. She was standing close beside her as they waited for Jeremy to photograph the complete flag-marked debris perimeter from several angles.

"There's more."

"You mean the crash," Miranda turned to face it for the first time.

"No," Andi still wasn't ready for that. She took Miranda's shoulders and turned her the other way. "This way."

Miranda didn't question, she simply waited.

Andi flexed her hands. Miranda, *the* Miranda Chase, had felt surprisingly normal. Andi didn't know what she'd been expecting: Batman's crazy body armor or something. Instead

Miranda's normalcy itself was unexpected. Did autistic people feel different than…what had Mike called them… neurotypicals? Stupid idea. Just like her, their challenges were inside their heads, not out in the world for all to see.

She hoped her idea didn't break Mike's rules about not distracting Miranda with trivial matters.

Andi led back along her own earlier tracks with Mike, careful to place her feet where she'd walked before.

Mike must have matched his stride to her own as Miranda was able to follow her in his footsteps. Instead of two women of an age, they were two women of a size—short.

As they rounded the curve of the cliff, Andi pointed down at the sand.

Before she could even say what she was thinking, Miranda was squatting down and inspecting their footprints.

No hints required. Mike was right, Miranda was that sharp.

When Andi had looked down at the tracks she and Mike had made leaving and then returning to the crash site—the sand ripples on the surface lined up with their feet.

They ran in long, sinuous lines along the canyon's floor. They should have flowed longitudinally across the canyon, perpendicular to the wind's natural path sluicing through the narrow gap. No rain ripples in these achingly dry hills.

Is that what had killed the helo? A crosswind between two steep cliff faces? It shouldn't be possible. In fact, in ten years aloft, she had never flown into or heard of a canyon crosswind. Eddy currents when someone flew too close to canyon walls? Yes. Helo killing ones? No.

"This had to be created by the downwash from the rotor." It had blasted the sand sideways.

Even as Andi reached her conclusion, Miranda was already pulling out rulers and a notebook. The page wasn't ruled, but was rather graph paper.

In a matter of minutes they had staked and measured the

varying sizes of the ripples across the width of the canyon, Miranda recording all of the data with a draftsman's precision. They tracked down three other sandy patches around the curve of the cliff face from beyond the sitting rocks and the crash site, and staked those as well.

By the time they were done, they had an audience. The others were gathered and watching them.

"What does this tell you about the helicopter's flight path?" Miranda asked her.

Great! No pressure! Just her first test by the boss in front of the entire team.

Andi let her eyes follow the line of stakes, not just side to side, but also linearly along the canyon.

There was no sand build-up or rippling along the inside of the curve around the cliff. The ripples began well out from the cliff as mere centimeter-high suggestions. By the far side of the canyon—some forty meters away, they were roughly hand high.

The line of flow was consistent.

She scooped up a handful of the lame excuse for soil out here. Fine and powdery, it would blow easily, and a coarse under-grain that had held the overall form across the width.

She looked up at the flight path, or rather where the flight path would have been—less than two meters over her head.

"They were hugging the inside of the turn in the canyon. They didn't vary their distance from the cliff face throughout the turn. To create this sand pattern..." she held up a hand palm down. Tilting it sideways, Andi kept one eye on the angle of her palm and the other on the sand. It felt...right, when she reached an angle of about forty-five degrees. She tried raising and lowering her hand, picturing the aircraft's height.

"Forty, maybe forty-five degrees bank angle and flying at—Oh, wait. It was an S-97 Raider." The pair of four-bladed coaxial rotors had a decreased downdraft compared to the six-bladed single rotor of the MH-6M, which would have been nice in the

Southwest Asia dustbowl wars of Iraq and Afghanistan. Dust brownouts had caused a lot of hard landings even among the Night Stalkers.

She tilted her hand a little more to compensate for the coaxial rotor. "Fifty-five, maybe even sixty degrees of bank. Under twenty feet AGL. They were carving this corner hard."

Then it sank in.

If Ken hadn't been killed—and her brain hadn't turned into total shit—this could have been their flight.

Whatever had surprised Morales and Christianson could have killed them just as dead.

Her life over in this crash?

In some parallel reality, that was *her* smeared against the rock face.

Snuffed out just like—

Miranda didn't say a word about Andi's estimation of the flight.

Instead, she silently pulled out her notebook and made a notation. When she was done, she turned to Jeremy, "Make sure you photograph this. Plus a set of half-kilo soil samples taken every two meters laterally across the canyon. We'll want to create a wind-tunnel simulation to confirm Andi's estimation."

Which told Andi the level of precision that Miranda brought to her investigations.

Jeremy scowled at her. Not Miranda, but her.

S-97 Raider had been the complete extent of their communication—oh, and his comment about the Eye of Sauron.

"What?" she whispered to him.

"Huh?" The expression cleared from his face as if he'd been unaware of it. He didn't seem like the cliched inscrutable Asian.

"Never mind."

"Okay." Jeremy offered an easy shrug that maybe wasn't so

casual, then began recording the lines of stakes with close-ups of the sand ripples next to a ruler for scale. He might *appear* to be the overeager-puppy-dog type but there was something else going on there. She just hoped it wasn't malicious.

Her Chinese family was all about appearances, a lesson she knew by the time she was three, and being the perfect daughter. Major laugh. If she'd been a perfect daughter, she'd be a partner in the family law firm instead of a half-trained, one-quarter-functional NTSB investigator.

Miranda headed back to the crash without another word.

"What was that? Did I fuck up?"

Holly punched her arm.

"Ow! Hey!" Andi punched her back—harder.

Holly merely grinned as if she'd barely been brushed by a feather.

"That's top marks from our Miranda. When she doesn't say anything, you either aren't worth noticing or you nailed it. You can bet fair barter on the second one...this time," she then followed in Miranda's wake.

Andi didn't want to move.

The only thing left around the corner was the wreck itself.

Morales and Christianson had never had a chance.

Which felt all too familiar.

29

"The GPS system was hacked," Wizard Boy spoke first, which didn't happen often. Harry Tallman was far more likely to let Heidi the Witchy Lady do his talking for him.

"And the reason I could possibly give a damn?" CIA Director Clarissa Reese continued studying the latest analysis of the unfolding situation in Mali.

Couldn't those people hold their country together for ten minutes in a row? Not so much.

Briefing this to the President wasn't going to be any fun. The human rights violations were fast headed for the category of "atrocity," which meant "genocide" wouldn't be far off. It wasn't the sort of word that any president wanted in the news on his watch.

"We depend on those satellites for far more than positioning. They're used all over the world for precision timing of any number of services," Witchy Lady kept pushing.

"Fine. Fix it. That's why I brought you two aboard anyway." She tried waving them away without looking up.

"The system already did. It auto-annealed the breach after *each* hack."

At their continued silence but continued presence, she forced herself to switch her attention away from the Mali report.

Neither one had sat down.

She left them hanging. It was best to remind people just who had outmaneuvered everyone else to become CIA Director.

They stood in front of her glass desk. She'd finally dumped Clark's cherrywood monstrosity, all of the dark leather, and the matching bookcases thick with citations, awards, and pictures with presidents past. She'd had enough of taking on the predominantly male division directors on their own level. Instead of an old boy's club feel, the glass-and-chrome CIA Director's office now said only one thing: Here lies the power.

Everything was muted. Even her brushed-silver laptop blended in.

She wore strong colors herself, the only color in the room.

They waited stock-still, like the Tweedle Twins—might as well be twins for her purposes.

Actually, it was very unusual for them to leave their basement cloister. Wizard Boy headed the Cyber Attack Division and Witchy Lady led Cyber Security. Out and inbound. She wondered if that's what they thought about when they had geek sex.

Clarissa rocked back in her chair.

There was little point in playing power games with these two.

If only she could browbeat her division directors into equal submission. Even the ones she had hard-and-fast blackmail over still felt the urge in their jockey shorts to try and fuck her out of the CIA's directorship. Not a chance of one of those dweebs getting it up outside their mistress' boudoir. Yet somehow they didn't get that if they tried, she'd cut their balls off at the throat.

The three female directors were at least subtle in their machinations to displace her. Being Senate-approved and married to the country's new Vice President was going to make that damned difficult but she wished one would try—she needed a good sacrificial slaughter demonstration to make the others behave.

The twins were among the few she didn't understand. At least they had skills that were useful enough even if they hated her with a consuming passion. She couldn't give a rat's ass about that.

Yet they *had* left their underground hideaway…

"Okay. Explain it to me." This time they took the chairs when she waved at them.

Clarissa tossed her twenty-five-hundred-dollar Louis Vuitton fountain pen on top of the report she'd been reading. Clark was very good at selecting unexpected presents. Of course, it had cost her some money too—when she'd seen the new Gucci platform boots that went so well with the pen's alligator leather barrel. She propped her boots on the corner of the desk.

For Clark's "birthday week" she'd purchased a set of La Perla bodysuits and camisoles in all of the colors of the rainbow —all but one. For the last night, she opted for a red silk floor-length nightgown that actually felt as amazing as it looked. The collection had set her back over five grand, but he'd been most appreciative when she'd revealed them on the seven successive nights.

She'd made herself his obvious successor to the CIA directorship through hard work—and enough background dirt on the Senate committee to bury all of them. But it never hurt to remind the former director, who she'd made Vice President though he'd never know that, exactly why he'd married her.

The Tweedle Twins, on the other hand, were both wearing

t-shirts of something called *Babylon 5,* which was apparently about fin-headed bald female aliens. All the fashion sense of a pair of toads. But very smart toads, she reminded herself.

"Our GPS satellite system is what's called a single point of failure," Heidi started out.

"I thought there were fifteen of them up there. Or was it twenty?"

"Thirty-one. Twenty-seven active and four spares. More spares if you count some of the older birds."

"How hard are they to hack?" She wasn't going to fall into some trap by asking how so many satellites could be called a single point of failure.

Actually she could have. It wouldn't have mattered to these two. It was hard to remember that they didn't think about one-upmanship the way everyone else at the top levels of the CIA did.

"Not very."

Clarissa sighed. "Again, why do I care?" Getting either of them to come to the point was never easy. Both of them together? It was a fast trip to the mental ward.

"Because they didn't hack or spoof the easy, civilian part of the GPS system," Harry this time. She wasn't sure if it mattered which one spoke. Maybe their new wedding rings were neurotransmitters that linked their brains. She wouldn't be surprised if they were.

Heidi continued without a missed breath. "There's a layer in the new series III satellites called the M-Code, short for Military Code."

"Which just might be the first time that the military had ever made a sensible acronym," Harry just couldn't seem to help inserting that utterly useless factoid. True though.

"It's high security, deeply protected, and is supposed to be unhackable."

"So, tell the Air Force to fix it."

"Actually, the GPS satellites are run by the US Space Force now," Harry blushed at correcting her. Christ, she hadn't been that innocent at twelve. Well, maybe she had. By the time she was thirteen her father had cured that.

The US Space Force definitely snagged her attention. The newest branch of the military had been launched with a paltry forty-million-dollar budget, probably what the Air Force spent on paperclips. But in their first full year of operation, they'd been given fifteen *billion*—matching the CIA's entire hard-won budget. Their *first* year!

That was incredibly annoying.

"So, tell the Space Force. Who did it? Some fourteen-year-old in mom's Kansas basement?" She picked up her pen, unscrewed the cap, and dragged the Mali report from her desk to her lap to keep marking it up. It definitely needed a redraft before she could take it to the White House, including a trending that should have been there to begin with. It was following the same buildup patterns as the Hutu slaughter in Rwanda, the Rohingya by Myanmar, and the Uyghurs incarcerations in China. She definitely had to put one of her Gucci boots up the Africa Desk's ass for missing that.

The Tweedle Twins glanced at each other, so maybe they weren't wired together and just had some weird mental powers.

In unison, they said, "Turkey."

Heidi continued, "At least that was the first satellite we traced it to before we lost track of the signal."

Clarissa dropped her pen to the pewter-gray wool carpet where it blurted out a blot of blue ink that would never come out. The Mali report fluttered out of her lap and covered it.

"I thought they spent all their time attacking Greece, like a child with a smartphone couldn't do that. It must have been Russia, merely using their satellite."

"The core code didn't look Russian."

"It looked...Turkish?"

At her hesitation, they both nodded uncertainly.

"Since when did Turkey have a hacker capable of attacking our military assets?"

Again the double look, though only Heidi spoke this time.

"Since now."

30

If General Helen Thomas was here, Miranda might have taken her sidearm herself and started shooting people. Or at least asked her to do so.

They had barely completed the first pass through the wreckage when all of the industry specialists had shown up at the crash site. In the name of assistance, they had already moved and displaced hundreds of fragments.

The ultimate crime was when one inspector had used a rotor blade to roll over the remains of his engine, damaging the blade past inspection and destroying one of the infrared sensors lying beside, now under, the engine.

Unable to proceed, the rest of her team had gathered around her. Holly's efforts to stop them had been overrun by the very same security guards that had protected the site overnight.

After safely extracting Holly before she took on two armed guards with her bare hands, Mike went and talked to them for a bit, then came back to report.

"They said that orders had come down from on high to let

these people in. Some contractor must have leveraged some high-ranking general to countermand Helen's security order."

"How am I supposed to do my job?" Miranda felt as if she was in a bubble floating somewhere beside the wreckage but unable to reach it.

Mike's answer was to pluck her satellite phone from her vest, select a number, dial it, and hand it to her.

"Hello?" A man answered on the second ring.

"Who is this?"

"I believe that's my line. Miranda?"

"Yes, it's me. Who is this?" The voice was familiar. Maybe...

"Drake," they said in unison.

"And you called me," he continued.

"Actually, Mike called you. I didn't."

"Which means you need help."

Miranda considered and decided that *was* an accurate assessment.

By the time she'd finished explaining the problem, Mike had brought over a man she didn't know. He wore Army camouflage, had a colonel's birds on his collar points, 'Stimson' above his shirt pocket, and an airborne patch on his arm.

"Hand him the phone, Miranda," Mike might trust him but his down-frown made her less certain.

Unsure if he'd do to her phone what the people were doing to her site, she kept it in her hand and turned on the speaker.

"There's a Colonel Stimson here now. You're on speaker."

"Hello, Colonel. Commander of the 160th SOAR, am I right?" Drake didn't sound surprised.

"Who the hell are you and who's on the phone?" He was glaring at her. Severe down-frown. No red cheeks, so not angry, just...

Rather than reaching for her reference notebook, Miranda kept her attention on his sidearm to ascertain that he wasn't reaching for it.

His hand was resting on it, but he'd had it there as he'd walked over as if that was just a comfortable position. She tried it herself, pulling a screwdriver out of her vest and tucking one end into a pants pocket so that the shaft simulated the butt of a handgun. No, it was *not* comfortable.

Then she recalled that she should have made introductions, but Drake was already taking care of that.

"This is the Chairman of the Joint Chiefs of Staff, General Drake Nason. Colonel, I would *highly* recommend that you take the next sixty seconds to get every one of the people off your site, excepting Miranda's team. She's NTSB's on-site lead on a crash. That gives her absolute command. Are we clear?"

"Uh," the colonel hesitated.

"What is it, colonel?"

"I have a quite different set of instructions...from the Pentagon."

"Give me their names. I'll rip off their stars and jam them up their asses. Jesus, I begin to understand why JJ had that colonel at his side."

"JJ? General JJ Martinez?" Colonel Stimson grimaced, "Jesus no, sir! Colonel Taser Cortez was a lethal bitch."

"Was not!" Jeremy, who'd been standing between her and Andi, knocked aside Miranda's phone arm as he moved forward. Jeremy was suddenly toe-to-toe with the colonel, who towered half a foot over his five-seven.

Miranda had never seen Jeremy angry. But now his fists were clenched, his face suffused with a bright red (that had been lacking from the colonel's cheeks), and his eyes were narrowed. Miranda didn't have to consult her emoji emotion chart to be sure of his fury. He looked ready to take on a battle-hardened colonel barehanded, despite his sidearm.

Mike rested a hand on his shoulder. "Easy, Jeremy. He didn't know her the way we did."

"*Your* team knew her? Please tell me she's dead."

31

ANDI HAD BEEN FROZEN IN PLACE FROM THE MOMENT COLONEL Stimson had walked up. She hadn't seen him arrive at the site with all of the other invaders.

She'd seen him often enough, he was a very involved commander for the Night Stalker regiment, but being a lowly captain she'd never actually spoken to him.

He returned her automatic salute without recognition, which was fine with her. Coming to the attention of regimental commanders was almost universally a bad career move. Even if she no longer had a career, the desire to be invisible was far from gone.

Her plan to lie low lasted until the moment Jeremy swung a fist at Colonel Stimson's face.

It was an untrained civilian punch. He broadcast it clearly, but Stimson was turning back toward the man on the phone.

The Chairman of the Joint Chiefs was Miranda's "go to" for help?

No time to think about that, but—What the *hell?*

Andi took a shuffle step forward and managed to snag Jeremy's arm.

But he was so strong with his fury that he dragged her forward. She'd slowed the punch, but probably not enough. The colonel might need some new teeth, and the way Jeremy's fist was clenched wrong, it would put his hand in a cast for a month.

Andi's feet were dragging in the soft sand—when Holly abruptly body-checked the colonel, sending him tumbling to the dirt.

With no impact, Jeremy's haymaker punch twisted him half around until his fist nearly caught Miranda in the ear.

She yelped in surprise.

"What the hell's going on?" The Chairman shouted as the phone flipped out of Miranda's hand and spun away to land in the sand not far from where the colonel lay swearing.

"Next time, mate," Holly offered the colonel a hand to haul him back to his feet but was looking at Andi herself.

Her Australian accent was thicker than it had been a moment before.

"'Stead of a shuffle step, make it a hop step. Get yourself some extra good traction on your landing foot, but get the other foot up on his hip for leverage to knock him clear. Look."

The colonel was dusting off his clothes, his face was a red as livid as Jeremy's had been a moment before.

"You stand where Jeremy was and start feeding our friendly colonel a knuckle sandwich," Holly pushed Jeremy aside and shoved her into his place.

At a loss of what else to do, Andi followed Holly's instruction and threw a very slow punch in exactly the form Jeremy had.

Holly took a hop step, grabbed her arm just as Andi had grabbed Jeremy's. But instead of planting both feet, she landed on one and planted the other firmly on the colonel's hip—then shoved hard.

The colonel tumbled back to the dirt.

But at the same time, Andi was thrown backward and would have landed hard herself if Holly hadn't kept her grip. Yes, she could have stopped Jeremy's punch herself using that trick.

"See?" Holly turned to help the colonel up again, but he scrambled clear as he rose, then turned to glare at her.

"Consider yourself under arrest, lady," he snarled out.

"Don't chuck a wobbly, cobber." Holly grabbed his hand and shook it cheerily.

Her accent was so thick it was on the verge of totally incomprehensible. Maybe kicking Andi's former commander into the dirt, twice, was Holly's idea of fun.

"I'll get you for—"

"Buckley's chance of that, but you're welcome to try, mate. Staff Sergeant Holly Harper of the Australian SAS Regiment, retired of course, at your service."

SAS! A female SAS operative? Jesus! That explained a thousand things and brought as many more into question.

"Presently on long-term loan to the NTSB from our Aussie ATSB chaps. If you can unwind that chain of who can charge this girl with what, you're a better man than I am. Of course, I'm a woman so I'm automatically better, right?"

She gave Andi a friendly hip check that almost sent *her* into the dirt.

"But who's counting. Personally, I'd have let our little Jeremy take a poke at you, but I didn't want him messing up his hand." She turned to Jeremy and cuffed him soundly on the side of his head.

"Ow! Hey!"

"Seriously, young padawan, I need to give you some learning on how to throw a king-hit better than that."

Jeremy was still steaming. "He shouldn't have said what he said about Taz. She was...amazing!"

Well, it was clear what he thought of whoever Taz Cortez was.

Was!

Past tense.

Oh shit! He too had lost someone that had ripped out his heart.

Andi could only hope for his sake that it hadn't also ripped away some chunk of his mind.

32

"You okay, Miranda?" Mike slipped an arm around her shoulder.

When he tried to return the phone to her hand, her grip didn't appear to be working very well, so he held it for her and whispered for her ears alone, "Just...breathe, okay?"

She nodded but winced again when General Nason shouted from the phone.

"What the hell is—"

"Sorry for the delay, sir," Mike cut him off. "There was a difference of opinion being expressed here." There was a crash and a banging from the wreckage. "We really need to get these vendor people under control here. I thought they were supposed to assist the NTSB, not usurp it."

"Colonel?" Drake's tone sounded ready to grind the colonel into the dust.

"General Kavanaugh ordered us onto the site, General Nason. We were told to specifically displace the NTSB team."

"And do you still think that's advisable?"

The colonel glared at each of them in turn. "Damned if I know what to think, sir."

"Would that be Major General Arkin Kavanaugh?" Mike really hoped that it wasn't.

"Yes," the colonel said it so carefully that each letter was a separate delivery.

Mike sighed and held Miranda's shoulder a little tighter before he continued. "General Nason. It's personal. He recently promoted a Colonel Arturo Campos, formerly in command of Davis-Monthan Air Base, to Brigadier General as one of his key advisors. General Campos has a significant grudge against several of our team dating back to the two prior classified operations that involved his command." Mike had felt it was a good idea to keep tabs on Campos. He just wished it hadn't paid off.

Miranda looked up at him in shock.

"I actually think he's angrier at Jeremy for taking over that boneyard C-5 Galaxy, than you refusing to date him."

Miranda didn't look very reassured.

But the colonel was doing exactly as Mike had hoped, hesitating.

"General Nason?" Mike handed control of the conversation back to Washington, DC.

"Colonel Stimson. You are the officer on site. But I will tell you that Ms. Chase and her team have the highest confidence of myself and both the President and Vice President. If you want to know what happened to your S-97, put her in charge and shoot anyone who gets in her way."

"Yes sir," the colonel was remaining thoughtful.

"And if you don't, Colonel Stimson..."

"Sir?"

"You're an idiot who shouldn't be in charge of the 160th for another goddamn day. Are we clear now?"

"Sir!" Stimson's reply had a snap to it.

"Is that okay, Miranda?" Drake asked in a much kinder voice.

Mike could feel her hesitate, then take a deep breath before managing to answer. "Yes, thank you, Drake."

"Anytime, Miranda," and he hung up.

Mike returned the phone to her vest pocket. As he did, he leaned in close and whispered, "Good job, Miranda. You should congratulate yourself for that one."

He wasn't fast enough.

As she reached over her shoulder to pat herself on the back, just as he'd often suggested to her, the back of her hand smacked him hard on the nose.

33

"What the hell am I doing here?"

Drake had thought to have a friendly chat with two-star Major General Arkin Kavanaugh. But when he'd brought Campos along, despite Drake telling him to leave all of his sycophants and aides out of this meeting, he decided he was feeling far less friendly.

As Drake himself had climbed to the highest levels of the Pentagon, he'd landed in those exact same chairs more and more often. Frankly, of the four, he preferred the one on the right that neither man had taken. It had let him face his predecessor more directly—General Thomas Tadman had always faced toward that seat.

Drake looked down at his own feet and now realized why the former chairman had sat that way. He'd always propped his feet on the same drawer that Drake did. That was a comforting thought.

There was a continuity, a legacy, to the Office of the Chairman that was sorely missing in most of the Pentagon.

He stared at Campos. The man didn't fuss, he'd give him that much credit.

Had he himself been so self-assured on his first time across from the "Old Man"? Perhaps on the outside, definitely not on the inside. Now? There was a whole new breed in the military that had learned all of the wrong lessons. Instead of fear and respect, they now radiated arrogance. These younger officers, flag or not, always thought they knew so goddamn much. Humility had been completely lost.

Vietnam had taught humility. Iraq and Afghanistan should have done the same, but for some reason they hadn't.

President Cole had convinced Drake to stay in the military and take on the chairman's role by giving him permission to fix the problem.

Sadly, he wasn't having a lot of luck.

Drake was going to start taking heads if he couldn't slice through the petty infighting that ruled so much of the Pentagon, now more than ever before.

"Well, Arkin. You're in charge of US Air Force weapon systems acquisitions. I don't see your name on the Army's S-97 project. Why the sudden interest in it?"

"I don't know what you're referring to."

Drake had been waiting for Arkin's gaze to flicker even momentarily toward Campos. He was too old a hand at playing power broker to reveal anything.

Campos' glance, however, *did* slide toward Arkin.

Not surprise at his boss' denial, but instead a cautious glance when Drake asked his question.

Drake hated this game. Hated it even more than when he'd had to play it to fight for his own place.

Enough!

He dropped his feet to the floor, kicked the drawer shut and faced them both squarely.

Thankfully, his own assistant had done his homework. Drake tapped a key to wake up his computer and he flashed the first document up onto his monitor wall.

He didn't look at it. Instead he watched the two of them.

"Who's this Miranda Chase?" Arkin glanced over at him.

"Check out your signature, Arkin."

"What the hell? Did you do this, Drake? If so, why? I'm a CAS man. Close-air Support is all I ever cared about. Started in the A-1 Skyraider before jumping to the A-10 Thunderbolt. I still can't believe Congress cut the future-CAS program. I've been meaning to talk to you about the work SOCOM is taking on in this area. I want in on that project, even if it's no longer USAF. The S-97, that's one of the new vertical lift programs, right?"

Drake turned to Campos. Arkin didn't take long to catch on and stared at his new assistant in surprise.

"Arturo? Are you issuing orders in my name? That's a goddamn court-martial offense whether or not you're dating my daughter."

Nepotism! Another dagger in Drake's heart.

Campos shook his head. "You need to talk to your boss, sir. I was ordered to issue that."

"To Barry? The head of US military weapons systems acquisition told one of *my* assistants to issue an order in my name?"

Drake sighed and punched the intercom to his assistant. "Find General Barry Sizemore and get his ass to my office. Pronto. If he protests, tell him we're about to be at war and I'm going to blame him." Which Drake could well be in minutes.

At war with his own Pentagon.

34

"What tipped you in Miranda's favor, sir?" Andi couldn't quite believe she was talking to the 160th's regimental commander. But they'd landed side-by-side when lunch was delivered to the crash site. At midday, the crash site was deep in the canyon's shadow, and they'd both sat on a soft patch of sand.

"Other than General Nason threatening my career?" Stimson actually smiled.

"Other than."

"You did, Captain Wu." He handed her a roast beef sandwich from the cooler before taking one himself. Jeremy circulated, handing out sodas and extra water bottles.

Andi had taken a bite of her sandwich, but couldn't remember how to chew. She hadn't even known that he knew her name.

"When my best Little Bird pilot gets knocked off the FARA team, I might take some notice. The Future Assault Reconnaissance Aircraft program was at the top of my mandate when I took command of the regiment. I'm very sorry for what happened to Ken, but losing you *both* from the team was a harsh blow."

Andi cowered and choked when she tried to swallow her half-chewed bite.

PTSD. The acronym hung there in the air between them, just waiting for a chance to crush her spirit even further, as if that was possible.

"I was no longer...reliable, sir. I'm sorry."

"We still miss you from the program. Especially with this," he waved his hand at the wreckage spread before the stone pillar.

"All I ever cared about was flying, sir."

"Which is why I want you on FARA."

Wanted. But she knew that's what he meant. "I just can't sit by and watch others fly in my place, like I'm some broken toy. 'Oh, didn't she used to be good?' I could never stand that, sir."

"So, you're going to become an expert in other things that are broken?"

A shrug was the best that she could manage. Once she was out of the Army, she'd searched online for rotorcraft jobs. She wasn't a mechanic or crew chief; she was a pilot who couldn't be trusted to fly.

Only one opportunity had matched that, the NTSB. Her watch had voted a very tentative forty-five seconds, but she'd applied anyway. If it had been on the downswing from fifteen, she probably wouldn't have.

"Well, Captain Wu, why do you think this one broke?"

"Not the pilots, sir."

At his raised eyebrows, she took another bite of her sandwich to buy a moment and check her watch, but she already knew the answer.

"I've flown over fifty missions beside Morales and Christianson. They were both meticulous and exceptional to the highest Night Stalkers' standard."

"I don't need past loyalties clouding—"

"They're not. If I'd have been...functioning," God help her, "at the time, I certainly would have recommended them to take over the S-97 testing. Whatever happened, sir, I can *guarantee* that it wasn't the pilots."

"That's jumping to conclusions before we've completed an investigation," Miranda sat on the sand opposite them, clutching a small bag of chips. Right, Major Sandy Hair Swift had said "she doesn't like it when we conjecture."

"Don't you ever cross factors off the list as you proceed through an investigation?"

Miranda actually looked as if that was a new concept. She considered it, then shook her head. "No, I don't."

"Well, you can cross the pilots off your list this time. And remember the audio feed, they *saw* something. Something surprising to both men."

"I don't know how we'll ever figure out what," Jeremy set down the shattered remains of a pair of bright-orange black boxes.

Holly and Mike soon joined their circle. None of the industry specialists had willingly come near either Miranda or Colonel Stimson since he'd told them that he'd make them walk back to base if they touched a single thing without asking Miranda's team first—Groom Lake lay twenty miles away across rough hills and arid desert.

"When the propeller's driveshaft sheared, it pithed the flight data recorder. The data module didn't survive. No record of what the instruments were displaying." He pulled a baggie from his vest pocket. A few carbonized scraps of electronics were all that remained. Then he held up a second baggie that looked only marginally better. "I checked it out. The core from the voice data recorder is fully recoverable."

During the NTSB Academy orientation tour, she'd been informed that CVR and FDR—cockpit voice and flight data recorders—were never opened outside of the NTSB lab. A rule that Jeremy had clearly ignored.

No one commented. Apparently Miranda's team ran by other rules.

This was a military crash, but the labbies had all had high security clearances so that they could handle such things. That meant Miranda's entire team must have top secret or better clearance. They'd need it to be at Groom Lake. This team became stranger the longer she looked at it.

"Okay, Captain," Stimson was looking at her again, "then what caused this crash?"

Miranda started to speak, but Mike rested a hand lightly on her arm to stop her. Then he nodded for Andi to proceed. Miranda's breathing was accelerating as she stared at Mike's hand.

He glanced down, then wrapped his hand firmly around her arm. "Sorry, Miranda. I wasn't thinking."

Were autistics touch sensitive? Light-touch sensitive? Andi had no idea.

Mike nodded for her to continue without removing his hand. He was one of those touchy-feely guys, but again it didn't appear to be offensive. Like he used that bit of connection.

"I..." Andi looked at Miranda again. How had she created those amazing reports that she'd read so many of in class? By assuming nothing.

But she couldn't ignore that Colonel Stimson was still awaiting her response, as was everyone else. The colonel wanted an answer, but she suspected that the rest of the team was waiting to see *how* she answered.

This team had unwritten rules and she had no idea what they were. There were a thousand rules drilled into a Night Stalkers' head, after the thousand drilled in by being a pilot, and the thousand more by joining the military to begin with.

So, she was supposed to sit here, with no goddamned flight plan telling her where to turn, and answer anyway.

Perfect!

No pressure.

She used to thrive on pressure, but was less sure now. The pressure felt like the need to fly perfectly while her best friend was blown up close beside her.

Did she care what they all thought of her?

Her watch said she did. Huh! That was a surprise.

"Okay," she closed her eyes and pictured the flight.

35

Mike watched Andi closely. He had no measure of her flexibility of thinking.

Major Jon Swift was a good guy. Nice to Miranda. Even good for her. But he wasn't the most flexible of thinkers.

Andi was... He wasn't sure what she was yet.

"They were coming down the canyon's curve in a hard bank, wrapping close to the cliff." Andi wasn't pointing.

Instead, she'd propped her feet in the sand in front of her as if working the flight controls with those and both hands.

"Early in the run, Morales requested permission to fly lower—"

"*Take it down to three meters, one-zero feet?*" Jeremy spoke up, repeating the transmission they'd heard during the flight. "*Cleared to three.*" He even had the timing and intonation down.

"Morales was being very careful in his communication with Christianson. But it also illustrates a great confidence in the aircraft. Christianson shared that confidence or he wouldn't have authorized the descent."

"But they blasted into the pillar two stories up the rock. That's *seven* meters up," Mike had measured it himself.

Andi's hands moved through a series of motions. Then she repeated them. No. They were slightly different. And again. And again.

"At what angle did they strike the wall?"

Because of his argument with Holly, that had also been Mike's to estimate when he'd topped out the climb. "Hard to tell exactly, but the rotor blades were roughly parallel to the ground. Not banked."

Andi manipulated the phantom controls again.

Then her eyes snapped open and she stared straight at Miranda.

Damn it! Mike hadn't been ready for Andi to push an agenda on Miranda.

"I—" was all he got out before Andi overran him.

"We need to look at the pillar again," Andi pointed.

Mike relaxed. She wasn't pulling a Jon. Major Swift always jumped to conclusions, then set out to disprove them. Completely anathema to the way Miranda functioned. There were whole stages of the investigations they shared where Mike made sure to stay close to translate between the two of them.

Andi made slicing motions with the edge of her hand. "Scratches will show a climb and rollout. He had half a second max, but Morales rolled from a sixty-degree bank at three meters to straight-and-climbing flight at seven meters." Andi swung her hand around her body as if carving a turn with her fingertips in the lead. Then she rolled it flat and tipped it upward as she jabbed it toward the pillar's face.

"Actually," Miranda didn't even blink. "That is unlikely."

"What? No, Miranda. It's the only flight path that fits the pilot's abilities and reaction time."

"The problem," Miranda spoke calmly, "isn't your suggestion. The challenge is that the Eureka Quartzite impacted by the Raider is a very hard stone, a seven of ten on the Mohs hardness scale. Much of the S-97 Raider is built up from composites that have a hardness near two. Even the aluminum frame is only two-point-seven-five. Neither would leave much of a mark. We're more likely to see a shift in how fragments of the crash were back-scattered after the event in order to judge the precise angle of impact."

Andi looked down. "Oh. I didn't think of that."

"We'll look for both," Miranda nodded, "but the evidence will be on the ground."

"So, he saw the pillar?" Colonel Stimson asked.

"Yes," Andi confirmed. "But too late."

"But—" then the colonel glanced at the rest of them and snapped his mouth shut.

Well, she was no longer a Night Stalker.

And the smile that Mike was giving her said she'd done good. She hadn't seen that in a long time, not even from Ken. He'd been a Night Stalker—the height of praise among the teams was a firm nod at the end of a mission.

"The problem...Jeremy—"

Mike shared a smile with Holly when Jeremy twitched in surprise as Andi singled him out.

"—we need to find out what they were seeing. A nap-of-Earth flight has nothing to do with looking out the windscreen, even in broad daylight. I guarantee that whatever they saw was inside the cockpit. And it was a recurring problem because there was a long pause before Christianson confirmed seeing it, whatever *it* was."

"There was a six-point-two second gap between Morales' *Did you see that?* Christianson saying, *What?* And Christianson finally saying, *Saw that.*" Jeremy should be nodding in agreement, but he was more abrupt than the usual Jeremy.

Mike hadn't a clue why.

"Exactly," Andi agreed, but Jeremy didn't appear mollified. "There's a system installed on our helos—"

"Captain," Colonel Stimson's voice was a warning growl.

"Sorry, sir, but do you want a solution or not? I mean, we're all sitting in the dirt at Groom freakin' Lake, sir."

Mike hadn't been wrong when he figured she had a spine of steel. Maybe it was more like adamantine.

Which was more tactful than what Holly would have—

"She's normal people now, mate," Holly could never resist baiting people, and the colonel was her newest target. "No longer under your orders. Dag it up, Andi."

"Dag?"

"You're nerding it, girl. On a roll. Don't stop now."

The colonel grumbled, but didn't stop her.

"When we're terrain following, we have a four-layer display. A look-ahead / look-down radar. Also a new direct-vision system called DAS—Direct Aperture System—which is an all-around seamless day-or-night view of the outside world. There's an inertial guidance system, but it has a significant drift rate, so we don't watch it much unless someone starts spoofing GPS signals, which gets pretty obvious pretty fast. We also have a world map accurate to one meter underlaying it all. Except for little aberrations like a truck or a cow, the four are always in sync unless..."

Her gasp of horror was the last sound she made.

Captain Andi Wu's eyes shot wide open, but whatever she was seeing, it wasn't local.

Then she went fetal.

Mike was barely in time to catch her before she face-planted in the colonel's lap.

36

"DRAKE."

"Barry. Kick your entourage out." Three-star generals went nowhere without a buffering entourage, prefiltering everything that stood a rat's-ass chance of coming up the line. Every little pipsqueak with their own agenda regarding what made it through.

One of the reasons he tended to run lean himself. He didn't want *all* of the noise filtered out. He was the only four-star general he knew with no flag-rank staffers other than the vice-chairman.

"Then why's he here?" Barry pointed at Campos still seated beside Arkin Kavanaugh.

Drake sighed and decided to grab the bull by the horns, "Do you want me to discuss a possible court-martial in front of your people?" The three generals and assorted colonels Barry had dragged in with him all flinched before covering their shock. Most of the lower echelons remembered enough of their past to snap to attention.

"Of who?"

"You, for starters."

Barry was too old a hand to do more than offer a wry smile at the tactic. "You're just enough of a hard-ass to try that, Drake. Okay, I'll play along and hear the pitch."

He waved a hand dismissing his team. They filtered back into the waiting room doing their best to look stoic and unconcerned. Not a chance.

Barry had come up under Tadman as well, and selected the empty right-hand chair just as Drake would have.

He tapped the intercom to his assistant, "No one in. And, Ray?"

"Sir?"

"Just to keep all those jackals at bay, tell them that for the moment my reception area is a no-talking zone, and no, they don't have General Sizemore's permission to depart or use their phones."

"Sir."

Drake cut the connection, then he rocked back, kicked open the drawer, and propped his feet on it.

Barry nodded, laced his fingers over his gut, and just smiled.

Despite his own coming up through the 75th Rangers and Barry out of the USAF fighters, he'd always liked the man. He had the double arrogance of being a former jet jockey and a Texan, but it suited his competence.

"That," Drake hooked a thumb at Campos, "states that you had him issue an order in Arkin's name regarding the S-97 Raider crash site."

Barry simply steepled his fingers and tapped them a few times on his chin.

"Planning how to call him a liar and throw him under the bus?" Drake tried second guessing him.

"Trying to think of what the hell you're talking about. Care to reel that one back in a bit?"

"You know we lost an S-97 in final testing?"

"Heard," Barry's grunt wasn't a happy one. "Who do you think rousted Stimson and got him on a flight at two a.m. this morning? I love what those pilots can do at night. Even you must, despite the handicap of being Chairborne Ranger."

Of all his achievements, Drake was still most proud of his 75th Ranger scroll and the Airborne tab that he'd earned along with it. None of the other chest candy—plenty of which was for combat as Barry damn well knew—could equal the scroll and tab on his jacket's arm. Chairborne Rangers might have made the grade, but no one in their right mind let them fight anything more dangerous than a desk's inbox.

It was tough, but Drake just let that one go by. He'd be making Barry pay for it later though.

"Just might wish some that they didn't do it when I was fast asleep." Barry's grunt said that was his idea of high humor.

Well, that was something. "Then why did you order the best investigation team we've got off the site?"

"Can't say as I much recall doing that."

Drake sighed and tapped a key to bring the order in question back up on the screen.

Barry shrugged his three-starred shoulders after he read it —all of it, unlike Arkin. He was a very thorough man.

"So what's the catch?"

"The catch is that this one," Drake pointed at Campos again, "issued it under Arkin's name without Arkin ever seeing it."

"So, it's not my court-martial you're talking about, it's his," he offered his own sideways nod.

"He said you ordered him to."

Barry didn't even look at Campos. "Came up through my people. Noise about some one-star pipsqueak blocking the site."

"General Helen Thomas. I put her in place at Groom Lake after removing Harrington."

Barry only raised an eyebrow at how unusual that had been, without a single word ever surfacing as to why. Or why Harrison had voluntarily retired the next week, and moved to some godforsaken Arizona ranch and disappeared.

Drake used his flat, four-star stare to tell him he wasn't going to be finding out either.

Again, a three-star shrug. "I told them to pass down word to fix it on my authority, and not wait for anyone's fuckin' red tape. Damn S-97's a high-priority item for me. That was a final-approval flight. Still, signing your name, Arkin, gotta rein your people in. I keep them pulled in damn tight."

General Arkin Kavanaugh started to protest, but Drake cut him off and kept his attention on Barry.

"You didn't do it because you're in bed with Bell?" Bell Helicopter's 360 Invictus had been the other primary contender in the competition to replace the military's aging small-helicopter fleet. A lot of manufacturers threw serious wine-and-dine treats at generals to favor their bids and contracts...and ignore their fuckups. From hookers to gratis custom-built luxury homes. Plus the promise of a lucrative consulting slot once mandatory retirement finally swung around.

Barry snorted and held up four fingers.

"Let's see, the Raider is twenty percent faster than Invictus," he pushed down a finger with his other forefinger.

"It's already a proven technology with the X-2 demonstrator flights," another finger.

Drake half expected him to skip one and tick down his forefinger so that his last point would be telling Drake to go fuck himself.

But he didn't.

Though a mere flicker in his eyes said that he'd considered it.

"It flew four years ahead of the Invictus, *not* counting the X-2 flights. That's a lot of lessons already learned."

Last one.

"And it's about time we got the coaxial rotor running. Our technology is finally catching up with our real-world needs. It lets chaps like the Night Stalkers run SOCOM's special teams into those really tricky spots. Oh," he popped out a thumb, "and it shares engines and technology with the new SB-1 Defiant to replace Black Hawks, Hueys, Apaches, and maybe even those goddamn Marine Cobras. Save us scads on getting a common platform for training and parts. Even the fucking idiots in Congress should like that one."

Drake glared at the three men. He was missing something here, but he'd be damned if he knew what. For the moment, he'd learned all he was likely to.

"Arkin. As the Chairman of the Joint Chiefs, I have no command authority. But you damned well better put Campos on suspension pending investigation. It would look better for you if you did it before my call to the JAG Corps goes through, which will be as soon as your asses are out of my office. Get a goddamn grip on your people. Now leave."

Barry didn't show any sign of moving until the other two were gone and his office door was once again closed. Then he nodded toward the order on Drake's screen.

"Who's this Miranda Chase, anyway?"

"NTSB."

"Civvy girl. Seems I mighta heard something about that, though not her name. Little woman with major personality issues? That's how I heard it. Told them to send in the AIB. Let our boys handle it."

"The loss of nine A-10s last year. The Russian Persona satellite the NRO is busy reverse engineering. JJ's little excursion south of the border."

Barry's eyebrows raised with each one. He was one of the few who would know about even those. Drake didn't mention any of the others that Barry wouldn't know about.

"And yes, they were all her 'civvy' team with very little help from us. Even a lawn darter like you has to admit that's a serious track record."

Barry had come up during the F-16s. The early ones tended to plant themselves in the ground—hard. His grimace acknowledged the payback for the 'Chairborne Ranger' remark.

"AIB keeps trying to recruit her—lately at full specialty-hazard contractor rates—and she shuts them down flat every time."

"Shit! For that kind of money, they should damn well try to recruit me. I'd be out of this game in a heartbeat. She's nuts."

"Sure she is. But so brilliantly nuts, she makes the rest of us look like Neanderthals."

"Or squids?" Barry suggested with a smile.

"Not that bad," Drake returned the smile. Because, even to a chairborne-Ranger grunt and a lawn-darter zoomie, nobody was as low as the members of the Navy.

"Do me a favor, Barry?"

His look said he might if it suited him.

"Follow this a bit. The channel that came up to you—and how it shuffled back down?"

"Second I'm out of here," his growl said it wasn't even a question.

Drake rose and came around the desk. They traded handshakes rather than salutes.

Barry was halfway to the door when Drake became aware of the itch between his shoulder blades. That itch had been very useful in his career, even if it sometimes took him a long time to scratch it.

"And General Sizemore?"

"Sir?"

"Do it on the QT."

Barry's look was speculative, but his nod agreed before he headed out the door.

Campos had too much to lose in this. Even if it was personal, there had to be something more. Something beyond just ego and vengeance.

37

MIRANDA HAD VERY LITTLE EXPERIENCE WITH HOSPITALS.

Much like the rest of the buildings at Groom Lake, this one showed its age of construction, yet was immaculately clean. The white tile had yellowed, or perhaps it had been a faded yellow to begin with and parts of it had slowly bleached white.

The doctors had shooed them back and were hovering over Andi, the lone patient, lost in the midst of the small ward.

Perhaps this would be called an infirmary because of its size. There were just twenty beds, two operating theaters, and a pharmacy.

What were the defining lines between infirmary and hospital? Should she add sick house and clinic to her considerations? Jeremy would suggest adding sickbay from Star Trek if she were to ask. Holly would—

"What do you call a hospital?" Miranda asked her.

Holly didn't even blink. "A hospital."

"I meant in Australia." Then she noted Holly's teasing smile and held up a hand to stop her before she could repeat herself.

When Holly's smile quirked sideways—a habit Miranda had long since added to her emojis page but still couldn't react to before she fell into one of Holly's teases—she definitely knew what Miranda meant. When Holly spoke in a heavy Australian accent, that was a much better indicator that she was enjoying herself at someone else's expense.

That had warned Miranda to step well clear before Holly had kicked Colonel Stimson back into the dirt a second time.

"If you're talkin' broad-Strine, we call her a hossie."

"Okay."

Perhaps the specific naming of the structure wasn't essential. If not, then what was?

Oh, Andi.

She'd collapsed in midsentence without notice, pulling herself into a ball as small as Miranda used to strive for as a child. If she just made herself small enough, then the world left her alone. Taking no notice of her, it would just slide by.

The doctors came over to their group and began to herd them out into the waiting area. She heard them say Andi was "just fine." Which seemed unlikely given their current location.

Miranda "faded" from the group.

It had never worked on Mom or Tante Daniels. But if she imagined that she wasn't more than a soft sea breeze on the Chase's island, she could float past Dad and most of the frequent houseguests.

The members of her team might track her, but she didn't care about leaving them behind. As everyone was ushered out through the swinging doors with large wire-mesh windows set in the yellowed steel, she "breezed" (zephyred?) her way to Andi's bedside.

Is this what she had looked like when she'd been struck down by some terror? So small and helpless.

She rested a hand, firmly, on Andi's hands clenched tight against her chest.

Andi flinched in surprise, but showed no other sign she was conscious.

"It gets easier, you know."

Nothing.

"You won't believe it now. But it does."

One of Andi's pinkie fingers—the left one—slipped out and wrapped over the back of Miranda's hand. It was clenched tightly enough to pinch the tendons between Miranda's ring and pinkie fingers. Better that than a light touch.

She'd asked Mike if Andi was autistic, but he'd insisted she wasn't. If anyone would know, it would be Mike.

Andi's breathing.

"Your breathing is too fast for feigned sleep. If you wish others to leave you alone, you need to learn how to regulate that."

"I wasn't—" Andi croaked between gasps, softer than a newborn chickadee. "Where?"

Miranda tried to think of how to answer that without sounding scary. Miranda had found too much time to inspect the operating suite while the doctors had been with Andi on the empty ward. It hadn't looked at all comforting.

"In the hossie, mate," she did her best to imitate Holly's accent, and was fairly pleased with the result. It *did* sound less scary that way.

Andi cracked open one eye—again the left one. Was she left-handed as well? Miranda pictured her staking and measuring the tiny sand dunes beneath the helicopter's final flight path. Yes, left-handed.

"You aren't Holly," took five separate breaths, adding two spare syllables.

"No, I'm not."

"Your accent sucks, Miranda."

"I never tried it before."

"Special for me?"

"It sounded less scary."

"Less scary than what?" Andi opened her other eye.

"United States Air Force emergency hospital at Groom Lake Airfield."

Andi shuddered. "Okay. Hossie it is."

When Miranda went to pull her hand free, Andi didn't let it go.

"What happened?" It was the first whole phrase to fit between adjacent breaths.

Another familiar question from her own past. Tante Daniels had always convinced her to follow the threads and figure it out for herself. Mom usually broke ranks and just told her, the few times she was there.

"What's the last thing you recall?"

She clamped her eyes shut and for a moment Miranda was afraid that she'd chased Andi back into whatever dark place she'd just been.

"I was...describing their final flight. The juxtaposition of the global terrain map. I could see it so clearly—except it was wrong. It reminded me too much of being in a similar cockpit where things were equally clear, yet equally wrong."

Miranda finally extracted her hand and inspected the back of it. Despite Andi keeping her nails short, there was a distinct arc impressed into Miranda's skin. Flexing her hand didn't make it go away.

She tried differential flexing. First, alternating her ring and pinkie fingers, raised and not raised. Then stretching and unstretching the skin by making a fist and releasing it. She was about to try plucking at the impression with the finger pads on her other hand when she noticed Andi watching her intently.

Miranda folded one hand over the other so that she couldn't see the small arc that Andi had carved with her pinkie nail. It was less distracting that way. Though she did note that she couldn't feel the slight impression that she was sure still remained.

When she checked, it had filled in about halfway.

"See," she turned her hand to face Andi. "It gets better with time."

"Okay," Andi nodded in agreement.

At least Miranda assumed that's what it was, even though she still lay horizontally on the bed, so her head had technically shifted side to side with the flexion-extension spinal motion.

"What were you asking?" Andi slowly unwound from her tight ball.

"I had asked what the last thing you recalled was," she found a starting point.

"And I told you," Andi aided her in retracing the conversation, which was very helpful.

"Yes. That something was wrong. This is a crash investigation. Wrong *is* the exact thing that we're searching for."

"It is, isn't it?" Andi pushed herself upright, then closed her eyes and braced herself as if the world was still a little uncertain.

"What was wrong?"

Andi didn't open her eyes, but she spoke. "The impossible."

38

"THE TEST PROCEEDED EXACTLY AS PLANNED." GENERAL ERSIN Firat stood at attention. He still hadn't decided whether to ride on Major General Kaan's coattails...or tromp on them.

Kaan's office walls were veneered in rare mahogany, and his furniture fine-carved Madagascar ebony. Yes, this office would suit himself very well when Kaan moved up—or out.

"You trust your people?"

"I've taken precautions, General Kaan." He wasn't some newborn flea. Firat's cousin in MİT—the National Intelligence Organization—had bought the maidservant of an unimportant little noisemaker named Asli. She'd report everything Asli did, if she valued her parents' lives. Should either of his programmers misbehave, this Asli would die most painfully. He hadn't yet had cause to inform them of this, but he was prepared.

Yes, he *would* replace Kaan before this operation was over.

It was his idea, after all.

Mostly.

"Excellent!" Kaan waved him to one of the heavy chairs and

pressed the intercom to call for coffee. That was unprecedented. He must be very pleased.

Once they'd been served, Kaan asked after his wife and son. His tone was perfectly pleasant and sociable as it should be over coffee. After a time he dropped just the lightest comment about his pleasure at Firat's son's advancement to his soccer team's co-captaincy—supposedly only Firat himself and the coach knew about that. Not even his son yet.

His gonads practically shriveled into his throat.

It took everything he had to not rudely sputter his coffee.

Kaan smiled benignly, stating clearly that he too had taken precautions.

"Now, shall we speak of the next steps."

Firat thanked General Kaan for his interest in a humble servant's family before agreeing.

"My pleasure, Firat. My pleasure. I was young and proud once as well. If you practice patience," Kaan set down his cup, "we can go far."

The "we" wasn't emphasized, it didn't need to be after the prior threat. *I can kill your son just as easily.*

"That sounds excellent, General Kaan. I believe that we are ready for Final Phase on the present...endeavor." Firat recalled the private tour his cousin had once given him of the MİT's private Museum of Espionage.

Only once, seven years before, had a tiny section of the museum been opened to the public. The displayed arcanery would be of interest only to Cold War historians. His cousin had led him through the first two of the three decades of advancements since then. And they were terrifying.

Sometimes he lay awake at night staring at the back of his wife's head, wondering if one of her hairs had been replaced by a fiber optic camera. He could feel it watching him on the nights when he took her from behind.

While he did his best to shrug off what he couldn't change, it worked less well with each passing year.

"I think one more test would be in order."

Firat knew he must agree. He didn't think it was necessary, but it was not a major risk.

No one would catch them.

39

Once Andi was on her feet again, Miranda led the team, with the sole addition of Night Stalkers Colonel Stimson, back to General Helen Thomas' office.

The moment Stimson entered, Helen stopped him hard with a barked out, "Tench-hut!"

It made Miranda nearly jump out of her own skin. She noticed that Andi and Holly, who'd just sat down, both leapt back to their feet, sending their metal chairs skittering loudly across the hard floor.

Miranda covered her ears against all the noise and harsh sound splashing about the reverberant space. A linoleum tile floor and 1960s fake wood paneling didn't buffer the jarring echoes at all.

Colonel Stimson snapped to attention.

Helen stalked out from behind her desk until they were an arm's length apart.

Miranda wanted one of her tape measures to see if it was his arm-length or hers. Or did the Air Force have a regulation distance for such confrontations? Instead, she backed behind Holly, who was easing back down onto her own seat.

Miranda wasn't sure if she'd ever seen Holly's hand shake before.

Holly spotted her attention. "Old habits," she whispered, then shook it a few times and blew out a hard breath. "Bad adrenaline."

Still, Miranda would trust that she'd be safer behind Holly, with or without the shakes, than near whatever was happening with Helen. Was she now going to throw Colonel Stimson to the floor?

Helen's voice snapped out far harsher than Miranda had ever heard it. "Next goddamn time you want to countermand one of my orders, you goddamn come to me first."

"Not my doing, ma'am." Stimson stood at sharp attention and spoke quickly. "Something happened way above my pay grade. Not per my request. I was pissed at your order, and I reported it. But I'm not the one who backdoored you, ma'am, or ordered Ms. Chase's team off the site."

Helen bounced on her toes for a moment as if preparing for battle. "I'm not amused, Colonel. Not even a little."

"Nobody is, ma'am."

"I am," Holly was slouched in her chair as if she was in a pub, not moments away from a shaking hand. Miranda admired the speed of her transition, even if she had no idea how to replicate it. Instead, Miranda braced, ready to cover her ears again.

"Too bad no one cares about you," Mike teased Holly as he sat to Miranda's left.

Holly gave him the finger, but Mike's assessment appeared to be accurate. Helen and the colonel were still facing off.

"Goddamn it. At ease, Colonel," Helen returned his earlier salute before returning to her desk with a very firm step.

Miranda whispered to Mike, "Was that a walk, a stride, a—"

"It was a stalk, Miranda. A very pissed-off stalk."

"Oh." She tried to think of how to record that properly in her notebook, but couldn't.

"Let's get cracking before we all go mental."

Miranda knew Holly's proposal was already too late for her. But she didn't know if Andi's condition was long-term or an isolated event. And how was she to judge the state of everyone else's mental...

Holly wasn't looking around to inspect everyone's state of mind. Instead, she waved to Jeremy, who began loading images onto Helen's screens.

Oh. Not clinically "mental."

The first image up on the screens of General Helen Thomas' office was a close-up of the scars on the face of the rock pillar.

Miranda sat down between Holly and Mike. Andi and Stimson took seats off Mike's left, Jeremy circled around to sit beyond Holly. Helen was scowling from behind her desk.

Holly flashed a laser pointer at the center. "Mike and I saw no unusual directional scarring on the rock. If the Raider did skid to either side on impact, or up or down, it didn't leave any obvious mark to indicate that. By everything we saw, it hit—" she drove the fingers of her right hand directly into the vertical palm of her left, crumpling her fingers much as the helicopter's nose must have done, "—then it dropped." She thumped her right fist down onto the table.

"That's commensurate with what I found on the ground," Jeremy began flashing up other photos. "The debris field was spread very symmetrically. The rear pusher-propeller would have continued to drive the S-97 along the angle of impact for another eight-hundredths of a second after the nose hit—the length of the helicopter divided by its speed. It's just an approximation, but it's close enough until I can model the crash itself and integrate the likely effect of airframe collapse over time and its relation to speed of..."

He blushed for a moment, then continued hurriedly.

Miranda was unsure why he blushed. Perhaps he felt embarrassed at explaining the obvious.

"Even with the driveshaft's Mohs hardness being one below the quartzite, we still should have seen some sort of bending in the shaft material itself—unless it struck the face perfectly perpendicularly. So, the driveshaft was driven end-on into the rock. Rather than bending from a sideways force, it sheared and fractured from compression stress."

Next he put up the photograph of the bright-orange flight recorder he'd shown them before.

"The shaft turned into a rain of shrapnel surrounding a spear. That's why it utterly destroyed the flight data recorder. I tried again. There was nothing recoverable. The inner data capsule that was supposed to be able to survive thirty-four hundred g's of impact force was breached and destroyed. Did you know that's a hundred and twenty times the acceleration of the gravity on the surface of the sun?"

Miranda did the math in her head, "That's a hundred and twenty-one times, Jeremy."

"Uh," he thought for a moment. "You're right."

"Keep going."

"I had slightly better luck with the cockpit voice recorder, but only slightly." The next image revealed the *slightly* less shredded recorder.

He clicked play on an audio file, displaying the jagged lines of a spectrum analysis on another screen.

"I've only focused on the final sixty-four seconds so far. It contained just forty-one words, and many background sounds that I've only begun to analyze. I've sent everything back to the NTSB with a Top Priority, not that they have any equipment I don't for this kind of situation."

"Play that again," Andi Wu spoke softly.

Miranda listened again, but there didn't appear to be anything out of the ordinary before the final eight seconds.

Did you see that?

What?

Six seconds.

Saw that.

The recording ended abruptly two seconds later. Not even a final curse.

"Morales saw something. Christianson finally saw whatever it was, but after a long delay." Andi's voice cracked strangely and Miranda looked away from the outline of the recording and turned to inspect her.

Andi was holding the edge of the table so tightly that her fingers weren't merely bloodless white, but also shaking with the strain of it.

Mike rubbed a hand up and down her back with a surprising familiarity. Miranda had been so sure that Mike and Holly were a couple that the gesture was very confusing.

Holly had her feet up on another chair and was staring at the screen with a frown.

Miranda slipped out her personal notebook. She flipped to her new page of emoticons and tried comparing them to Holly's look. No red-enflamed cheeks, so perhaps not anger. No half-shuttered eyes of boredom or fully closed of sadness.

Perhaps frustrated? Though there weren't little steam bursts shooting from her nostrils like the emoji but perhaps the rest was correct.

Andi's expression matched sadness, except for the lack of tears.

"What's that?" Holly pointed at the screen.

Miranda snapped her notebook shut and tucked it away.

40

Mike was glad when Miranda turned away.

This was a crappy moment to smile—he could feel Andi's shuddering breath as he gave her shoulder a final squeeze. But it was really hard to keep a straight face while watching Miranda review the emoji stickers he'd given her. She hadn't appeared satisfied with her results this time.

She used it less often around the team now, so she must be stumped by Andi, Stimson, or Helen. The latter two were probably barely on her radar except as a source of information.

That meant Andi was confusing her.

"She's very sad and more than a little scared," he whispered to her.

"She is?" And Miranda turned to inspect Holly.

"No. Not her. Andi."

"What about Andi?"

"Yes, what about me?" Having overheard, Andi was now glaring at him. Perfect. Teach him to try to help.

"What's what?" Jeremy was asking Holly.

"Remove the voices, just give me the background noises for the last eight seconds." Holly was ignoring the rest of them.

Mike decided that was his only route out, and directed Miranda's attention to the screen.

All it sounded like to him was ten seconds of white noise.

"Again, louder."

This time he was able to identify the sound. The deep muffled roar of the twin rotors, overriding the higher whine of the turboshaft engine filled the room.

"Go back another ten seconds," Miranda called out when she could be heard again.

So Miranda was successfully returned to the crash investigation and Holly hadn't heard a thing.

However, Andi's glance said that this wasn't over yet.

Oh, well. Two out of three wasn't bad.

With the longer initial sound reference, Mike heard the change this time. Though Jeremy was playing it so loud that Mike's ears popped at the sudden silence at the end of the flight.

There was the tiniest confusion at the end—the recorded moments before the microphones and the recorder were destroyed—but the change had started before that.

The steady, unchanging drone of the rotors and engines had altered in the final second of the flight.

"The turbine would have already been at its set speed. So most of that sound change must be the abrupt correction of roll and pitch by Morales." Stimson signaled Jeremy to play it again. "And stop before the actual crash, it's distracting us."

For another twenty seconds, Helen's office roared with the S-97 Raider's final moments.

"Exactly as Captain Wu predicted. The strengthening of that deeper tone is probably due to additional blade loading from the abrupt rollout maneuver."

"There's also a change to the engine noise," Andi's voice was carefully firm. "I think he might have opened the throttle wider, though it was too fast for the engine to react."

"You have a good ear, Andi," Miranda turned to her.

"Thanks. I have two—"

But Miranda wasn't done and continued right over her. Just like the rest of them, Andi would get used to not interrupting Miranda.

"At one-point-eight seconds, there is a small spike on the spectrum analyzer. I suspect that will be revealed to be the sound of Morales' glove or the throttle itself as it was rotated wide open. The sudden flood of evaporating fuel would have cooled the engine momentarily—that dip at one-point-one seconds—then accelerated, that increase at zero-point-four to impact. This supports GE's insistence that the crash wasn't due to a failure of the engine."

Mike hadn't heard any of that. Nor could he really see what Miranda was talking about. But if she said it was there, then it was.

"The GE rep will be relieved to hear that," Stimson spoke up. "He's been a real pain in my ass. My prime suspect for who tried to backdoor you, General Thomas."

Helen nodded, finally mollified, at least toward the colonel.

"She only said 'supports'," Mike pointed out. "Don't let GE out of the woods yet."

"Not a chance," Stimson looked as if he might grind it into the rep's face with a boot heel instead.

Miranda turned from the screen as if it held no further interest.

"We have an indication that the aircraft was still flying and responsive to control at time of impact. Andi insists that it isn't pilot error."

Andi and Stimson were both nodding their heads.

"Their postulation is supported by the pilot's actions of advancing the throttle and changing the flight path even if it had too little effect on the final result. This leaves something that I believe Andi has already discovered."

Andi groaned.

Everyone else had twisted around to stare at her.

She did whisper, barely loud enough for even him to hear right next to her.

"The impossible."

41

ANDI WAS NOT GOING TO FOLD.

Not in front of her former commander—not a second time anyway. She took a deep breath, clasped her hands, and rested them on the edge of the table just as Miranda did, and focused on their texture.

Better to focus there than on the image inside her head.

So she watched her hands and let her voice come from some other space that wasn't quite herself. There was safety in distance.

"Remember what I said about our navigation. Four layers. Radar and the DAS Direct Aperture System are both real-time views of the terrain. Far more sensitive than mere eyesight in most cases, and obviously at night. It has many other uses actually, but none matter for this moment in the flight."

"I really want to hear about the DAS at some point," Jeremy jumped in. "I mean, I've been reading about it since the first videos came out in 2008. And—"

"What were you, twelve?" Holly snarked at him.

"Uh, yes. It was before my birthday in November," Jeremy rolled right on. "The detection of incoming fire, launch point locater, intelligent aircraft ID both friendly and foreign. I've always wanted to..."

He trailed off and looked around.

"Sorry. ...If you're willing to talk to me...about that."

He ended up staring down at the table.

Andi shrugged. "Why wouldn't I be? You have the clearance."

He looked up enough to squint at her as if he didn't believe her, but didn't speak.

"Whatever," Andi focused back on the systems. "There's one system of inertial navigation. Its main purpose is to come into play in case the GPS gets spoofed. If someone tampers with the GPS signal, it will suddenly not match the inertial nav system."

"What's the current drift rate of the S-97 Raider's MEMS chip?"

"Three meters per minute without a recalibration point," she answered before she could stop her surprise at Jeremy's question. He did know his details.

"Still? I thought they were ganging them in blocks now to fix that."

"That *is* ganged in arrays of ten. Max drift, not average."

"Still!" Jeremy looked personally offended.

Andi knew he was the team geek, but he...this whole team was operating on some other level.

"What the fuck am I doing here?"

"You're about to tell us about the fourth system's purpose," Miranda said without hesitation.

At her surety, Andi did her best to stop thinking and did.

"That pre-programmed terrain map I mentioned before does one thing no other system can do. It lets you see the future."

Of them all, only Miranda and Colonel Stimson weren't looking puzzled.

"Technically," Miranda half-nodded her head, "it's showing you a past view of your future. The map was programmed in the past, so it's actually not warping time. Rather it is showing you what *should* be around the corner. Clearly it didn't in this case. That would point to pilot error as the cause because he was hugging the cliff too tightly for *not* having a clear view of what was around that corner."

"No," Andi slapped a hand on the table. "No, it doesn't."

Mike rested a calming hand on her arm. She slapped it aside.

"Could *definitely* get to like you," Holly was snickering as Mike shook out his hand in surprise.

"Why not?" Miranda's voice was perfectly steady, as if she really didn't have any ego on the line about her statement.

It forced Andi to answer in kind—calm and precise. "Because the system would never be missing such a significant landform."

"Can you prove it?"

"Put me in a helo, pull up that map, and we'll fly the route together."

Miranda turned to General Thomas. "Helen, could you please prepare your helicopter for flight?"

Thomas just shook her head. "Nobody issued that system to me. Mine is just a transport bird for a lowly Air Force one-star general."

"There's a second S-97 Raider for eval in the hangar," Stimson pulled out his phone and called. "Prep Number Two for flight...No, that's an order. Get it done, soldier."

Andi's palms began to sweat. Except for the flight to and from the crash site, she, very purposefully, hadn't been in a rotorcraft since the one Ken had died in. And she didn't remember the return flight from the crash site at all.

Stimson must have spotted her panic. "I'm your copilot, Wu. I still know how to fly a goddamn bird after all these years."

"Sir," Andi barely managed to acknowledge.

"So," Mike was nodding. "That's what's impossible. That a piece of real terrain was missing from the map."

"No," Andi managed to answer him. "What's impossible is that the rock pillar wasn't where the GPS and inertial system would have insisted that it was. It's the only thing that fits what the two pilots said and the subsequent actions."

At her signal, Jeremy restarted the audio playback.

Did you see that?

"Morales saw something," Andi narrated. "Maybe a rock that didn't match between the terrain map and his radar or DAS view."

What?

"Christianson missed it. As pilot-in-command, his duties would *not* have included closely monitoring the navigation display though he'd certainly be aware of it. Now the long six seconds until they see it again."

Saw that.

"The error Morales observed is now confirmed by his commander. Another rock. A shape of cliff. Something wasn't right. A minor shift or they would have noted it sooner."

The sound cut out.

"He didn't start his rollout with half a second to go—the amount of time the pillar would have been visible in his 'present tense' systems. I couldn't make that work. A half second doesn't make for a sixty-degree bank correction and a four-meter climb. But—"

She ran the phantom controls under her hands once more just to be sure. It fit.

"If he began the rollout to a less aggressive mode of flight from *two* seconds before the collision, it matches. Morales began the maneuver the instant that he and Christianson both saw the second occurrence. But it wasn't enough because he was coming around that cliff too fast. The Raider was going forty-seven percent faster than the Little Bird he was used to. Something screwed up his GPS navigation. And without enough warning for him to decide to switch to the inertial guidance system." She was guessing, but it was the only scenario that fit.

One thing Andi knew for certain.

"He never stood a chance."

42

"YOU WANT ME TO WHAT?"

General Firat had escorted him, without Onur, to an empty conference room inside Siberkume. Metin hadn't even known this underground level existed. By the way the armed guards inspected him, he wondered if they'd let him leave without the general at his side. He'd just be dogshit on their bootheels.

For the length of two normal heartbeats, about ten at the moment, General Firat looked as if he might agree that it was a crazy test of his system.

Then Firat's military officiousness snapped into place.

"This aircraft," he placed a file folder on the table and opened it, but Metin couldn't manage to look down.

Firat thumped a finger on the folder's contents.

Metin did look down but couldn't make sense of what he was seeing.

"In two hours it will fly into this mountain," one more resounding finger thump that echoed off the carved stone walls. It wasn't a conference room; it was a dressed-up dungeon.

"But the people aboard. They—"

"Are not your concern."

He waited, but the general didn't add anything else.

Metin was not a soldier. He was just a programmer at Siberkume.

He'd earned his way in by unlocking a test site in only nine hours. He still held the Siberkume record by a factor of two. A detail he'd only briefly enjoyed having displayed on the main entry display screen. Few other than Onur would speak to him...even when they needed help.

Every three months, a new secure site was created and given to the Siberkume coders to crack before it was moved to the applicant testing. Those results, too, were posted prominently. He still held top place, and Onur had climbed from mid-pack to top three. Only the hard-bitten and homely Zehra stood between them, but she spoke to no one—ever.

Besides, she was more interested in *creating* security.

Metin only got seriously charged when he was *breaking* it back down.

He looked at himself in Firat's eyes.

"I...am not...your...tool." All the conviction he could muster barely reached the walls of the small underground conference room that felt as if it might become his tomb.

"Oh, but you are." Firat pulled out a second file folder.

When he opened this one, Metin managed to focus on it.

It was what the Americans would call a "rap sheet."

Not his, so he relaxed a little as he read it.

It listed meetings, contacts, protest rally attendance, and actions there. It was a long list.

Each event was documented in a style so lurid that even an innocent would be damned by the language alone. It was also incredibly detailed and in the first person. A single, tortured signature would turn it into a damning confession.

People had been "disappeared" for less.

He flipped through the pages, until he reached the final one.

Asli was looking up at him.

She was smiling, her teeth shining against her dusky, perfect skin. Her black eyes twinkled with the brightness of some prank she'd just witnessed, or more likely perpetrated.

He and Onur were clearly visible as well; close enough to either side to be pressing their cheeks to hers. Also smiling.

He rubbed a hand over his cheek. For the first time on seeing that photograph, he couldn't remember the warmth of her skin brushing his.

Firat slid the folder out from under his nerveless fingers.

"Any questions?"

"No, sir."

Firat closed the folder of the flight's information and held it out.

Metin took it.

43

Inside Groom Lake's Hangar 33B, Andi slid her hands onto the controls of the quiescent S-97 Raider.

"How's that feel, Captain?"

"I can't say, sir." She really couldn't. She had no idea what she was *supposed* to be feeling.

That Ken should be sitting beside rather than Colonel Stimson?

That something that scared her so much couldn't possibly feel as right as her hands on the controls?

That...

"It sure as shit isn't some miracle cure, sir, if that's what you're asking."

"Might have been. Even if I know better. Look, I'm sure it won't help you to know, but I have a nephew about your age. Three tours in Afghanistan. Been out half a decade and still gets the night terrors. Can't hold down a job for more than three months."

"Perfect, sir. Thanks so much for sharing."

The silence thudded into place over the intercom.

"Sorry, sir. I get that you were trying to say you understand.

Instead, what I'm hearing is that it's a long and really fucking bleak tunnel laid out in front of me."

"I suppose I can see that."

"It's not just a matter of getting back up on the bicycle, no matter how good these controls feel."

"Can you explain why it isn't?" Colonel Stimson sounded as if he really wanted to know.

For the first time she forced herself to turn and look at him. Both of their visors were still up, so she could see his face by the light filtering in from the still-sealed hangar.

"Because every single second that I'm sitting here, I keep expecting you to blow up with a grenade caught in your vest, and make a widow out of one of my few friends."

"That would be awkward."

"Yes, sir."

"Checklist?"

"Thank you, sir." And he began reading out the Engine Start checklist.

When they were done, Andi called out over the intercom.

"You two ready back there?"

There were two technician seats in the rear. An S-97 Raider could normally carry up to six troops internally. However, the Number Two bird was rigged up with enough test equipment to gag a helicopter. Miranda had chosen Jeremy to sit with her in the rear seats for the flight.

"All monitor systems are up. We're seeing feeds from your visors. Recorders running," Jeremy reported, happier than her brother winning his first big lawsuit.

Taking a deep breath as she snapped down her visor did little to help.

The helmet felt both right and wrong. It had the familiarity of the S-97 Collins Aerospace helmet that she'd become used to during testing. So much more capable than her standard rig that she'd always felt handicapped upon returning to her Little Bird.

However, it was a generic testing helmet, not the half-million-dollar version customized to her head. She wouldn't be using it for weapons targeting or enemy detection, so that shouldn't matter.

With the four-layer terrain display as a background, flight instrumentation projected down either side, and basic engine data across the bottom, she reported that she was ready.

Liar, liar, pants on fire.

Stimson called out for the hangar doors to be opened.

In between all of the meetings and planning sessions, and her hiding in the bathroom for twenty minutes trying to find enough nerve to do this after changing into a flightsuit, darkness had fallen over Groom Lake.

She might still be in that bathroom if Holly hadn't come in and kicked her ass.

PTSD is the fucking arse end of the world, Holly had declared as she'd leaned back against a sink and folded her arms.

You?

Holly had nodded. *Not your scale, but enough that I couldn't stick with SASR. Couldn't even stand to stay in Oz. Still catches me sometimes.* She raised a hand and flexed it as if she was surprised to see her own fingers.

But you've got it so together. Holly Harper was tall, beautiful, had Mike as a lover, and... *You radiate confidence like its part of your breathing.*

I did just say I'm a Sheila from Oz, right? It's a fucking birthright. Besides, I've got an image to maintain. So do you if you're going to live up to this team's standard. Now—one soldier to another—get your ass out on the line.

Then Holly had given her a friendly punch on the arm and had stridden back out like she owned the world.

And somehow...Andi had.

The hangar door cracked wide into the night.

She looked through the visor to make sure that Stimson's hands were also on the controls. He'd insisted that she fly, but he'd promised to mirror her so that she didn't kill them by having some stupid fit.

Once clear of the hangar, she eased them up off the wheels. The DAS allowed her to glance over her shoulder, through the helicopter as though it wasn't there, and watch the dark maw of the hangar doors close behind them.

At half the Raider's maximum speed, she tried to only focus on what was ahead.

44

HE AND ONUR HAD SET UP THE RUN.

They had their own soundproofed office just off the main floor. The big window let him see all of the envy, which was righteous. They had a majorly big portal into Turkey's fastest supercomputer, which was awesome.

Everything they needed to make this work had been provided, right down to a small fridge filled with Red Bull and a cupboard of all the best junk food from Clip Sesame-Sticks to Pizza Kraker, and loads of individually wrapped Pop Kek chocolate muffins. There was a McDonald's. But it was three kilometers away and he'd decided it was better to not ask for deliveries.

And Firat's threat that Asli's life was on the line was a load heavy enough to crush him.

Thankfully, the general left them alone during the prep for this run.

"This sucks, Metin. Why did you agree? Did Firat ram a lightsaber up your ass or something?"

"Can't you just quit whining?" Metin hadn't told him about the second folder and never would. Onur would freak.

Onur laughed. "Sure, that was always your role anyway. If you whined less, Asli would like you a whole lot better, you know."

And the more she liked him, the more vulnerable she'd be to Firat as a useful tool to twist him.

"Are you ready?"

"Yeah, sure." Onur took his position at his four-screen console.

Metin did the same at his. "Let's do this."

"What, no high five? No, 'That's not a moon, that's a space station'? Man, Firat really did ram a lightsaber up your ass, didn't he?"

"Initiating," Metin launched his program with a code he hadn't even given to Onur.

If Firat had done that, it would have been far less painful.

45

ANDI FOLLOWED MORALES' FINAL FLIGHT PATH. THEY HAD agreed to mirror his every motion, simply at a slower speed.

South past The Jumbles.

Over the dead tendrils of white that had once been saltwater rivers feeding the salt lake that had become Groom.

Down to Dog Bone Lake. Though they had no missiles aboard to aim at the old tank parked there, she flew them over it.

Rolling into the Pintwater Range felt like the most natural thing in the world. As if it was a flight she'd done a thousand times.

There will be times of perfect clarity, when you think it's all out of your system. Dramatic pause. *It won't be.*

Army psychs sucked.

She flew north through the canyons.

Where Morales had descended to three meters, she dropped to five.

And slowed.

By the time they reached the canyon leading toward the Tikaboo Valley, she was barely crawling.

"Everything still lining up," Stimson confirmed what she was seeing.

Andi knew she was holding on to the controls too tightly.

Loose wrist, her first instructor had repeated over and over.

And it was probably the best advice anyone ever gave her.

Except not at the moment because she couldn't ease off from full clench no matter how she tried.

She crept down the canyon.

The vertical escarpment was clear on her right. The canyon widened to her left as it curved toward the valley.

In the DAS she could see the little row of flags she and Miranda had stuck in the sand ridges.

And around the corner...

"There!"

Exactly where memory said it should be.

Through the semitransparent model of the cliff wall, around the curve, the pillar of quartzite was clear and distinct.

"No pilot could miss that."

No one spoke.

She rounded the corner and slid to a stable hover, fifty meters from the front of the pillar. All of the wreckage lay between her position and the pillar's base.

The pillar—visible in the DAS and clearly outlined by the radar—was exactly where the wire-frame model of the terrain said it would be. Because she'd come to a fixed hover, the inertial system had been able to resync and was showing zero drift.

Everything lined up for them, but it was a sure bet that it hadn't for Morales.

"Is it okay to speak now?"

"Go ahead, Miranda." Andi hadn't wanted to risk any civilian distraction while actually flying. Of course, no one probably understood the Sterile Cockpit rule of no side conversations during critical operations better than the NTSB's top investigator.

"Is the current terrain model loaded in this aircraft identical to the one loaded in the Number One test aircraft?"

"The same load at the same time," Stimson confirmed.

"And you have no control from the cockpit that could alter the calibration of that system's display?"

"I have a limited brightness control," Andi rolled it up and down, but the rock pillar didn't go anywhere. "Which we know wasn't turned down too far or Morales and Christianson wouldn't have seen the misalignment. And if not for the terrain-model system, they'd never have seen it all."

"Or they'd never have attempted to hug an unknown cliff so tightly. But in all likelihood, they were proceeding forward in full expectation of the system's accuracy—and then it wasn't. The reasons are unknown at this time but, yes, your proof appears valid, Andi. I'm done here. We can return."

And Miranda dropped out of the circuit.

No "thanks." No "well done." Though she didn't know why she was expecting one.

Andi shifted her hands to return them to base.

Or rather...she tried to.

They didn't move.

She looked down at them, but she was still seeing the DAS image on the inside of her visor.

Instead of her recalcitrant hands, all she saw ahead of her was the wreckage of the S-97 Raider. Earlier, she'd walked it until she knew where each part lay.

Is that what her wreckage would have looked like back in the Syrian desert?

If she had taken a hand from the cyclic, maybe she could have fished the grenade out of Ken's vest.

Thrown it aside.

Maybe taken the hit herself.

But a nap-of-Earth flight was the most technical flying a pilot could do. To release the controls for even an instant when passing mere meters above the ground was high-speed suicide.

Within hundredths of a second, her Little Bird would have caught a skid at a hundred and fifty miles per hour.

No, the wreckage wouldn't look like this.

They'd have been scattered across a half-thousand meters of Syrian sand.

But if she'd tried...

Would Ken still be the one sitting be—

"Captain?"

—side her?

"I have the controls." A voice. Not Ken's.

This flight—

"*Captain!*" A shout so loud that it hurt.

Ken's final plea for help that he would know could never come.

A blow slammed into her forearm.

The knife-edge slam of Stimson's hand-strike knocking her clear?

No!

The explosion!

After Ken's death, she'd kept her hands steady on the controls.

Leaned out into the wind to see around his blood smeared across the inside of windscreen.

This time, when the explosion hit, she yanked both of her hands from the controls to cover her face. To block what she'd seen the moment after landing back at al-Tanf in the DCZ.

The moment the skids were down and she'd dumped the cyclic, she'd turned to look at Ken.

Her best friend had been replaced by some kind of ghoul monster. Shattered from within, his disconnected arm lay beneath the guts that had spilled into his lap. His chest caved so hollow that his head hung down face-first into it.

Except he wasn't here.

Ken was dead.

Wasn't he?

She was sure that he was.

That meant...she was in an S-97 Raider at Groom Lake. Safe? Maybe.

Before she could find the nerve to look, the helicopter maneuvered on its own.

This time the crash would kill her.

She'd have screamed, but she didn't have a voice.

46

METIN SET THE TARGET OF THE AMERICAN 757 TRANSPORT currently descending to land at Incirlik Air Base in eastern Turkey. The one Firat had shown him in the basement along with Asli's file.

The satellites, each shaped like thick, three-by-four-meter books with two large solar wings, orbited at twenty-one thousand kilometers above the Earth.

Metin's software was loaded into the seven GPS satellites visible to the target aircraft.

Inside each satellite, the software overrode the transmitter buffers without interrupting the core code.

Metin had enhanced the control of his software. The clocked and encrypted output was redirected into a set of chained memory addresses. These weren't linked to the on-board atomic clock built into each satellite. Instead, they were driven by the clock cycle sent from the ground and time-compensated for distance of travel from the antenna farm at Gölbaşi, Turkey, twenty kilometers south of Siberkume in Ankara.

On Metin's mark, Onur cleared the hold on the queue, and

the properly coded time signals were released at incorrect times.

Once out of the queue, the twenty-nanowatt signal passed into the amplifier and was boosted to twenty-five watts. The antenna's thirteen dBi signal gain boosted the signal to five hundred watts.

The signal punched downward twenty thousand kilometers through space and the atmosphere.

The free-space path loss dropped the signal to barely a hundred nanowatts at the aircraft's GPS dual antennas mounted on the top of the fuselage.

The signal was captured, decrypted, and used to alter the information displayed to the pilot.

47

"Forty-kilometers on straight-in final. Confirm airspace clear."

Lt. Colonel Brad Whitman focused on flying the Boeing 757-200.

Colonel Abrams, a tank of a guy just like his name, was dealing with Air Traffic Control. A serious plus.

Brad tuned them out.

Thank God it was his last leg.

Air Force Two was a sweet old bird that he typically enjoyed flying. But now it had been a long damn day, night, flight, whatever. Three long legs and two stops already under his belt. It would be nighttime now back in DC, and they'd lifted before lunch. He'd hit his maximum airtime for twenty-four hours, so the next leg of the Vice President's European tour would be up to the relief crew. He looked forward to just kicking back and enjoying the flights for a while.

The sunrise was a blinding straight-in shot, forcing most of his attention inside the cockpit.

Incirlik Air Base's goddamn ILS was flaking—cutting off like a switch just as he was picking up the signal. Couldn't the

Turks keep something as basic as an Instrument Landing System operational?

He paid attention to the chatter long enough to hear the field conditions. No surprises. Should be a smooth landing. He dialed in the barometric setting announced by Air Traffic Control and Abrams confirmed it.

Incirlik's runway lay at seven hundred and eighty-seven feet. As long as he avoided Mount Medetsiz at eleven-k, standing clear and proud off to his left, he was fine.

"Cleared to descend to nine thousand."

"Roger," he confirmed Abrams' order, "descending to Flight Level Niner-zero."

After he called out reaching nine thousand, Abrams called landing gear and flaps at five. Running it all by the numbers.

A quick scan to either side of the blinding sun showed clear airspace.

When he glanced back inside, he had to blink hard several times to see the displays. Even then, he had to stare at each screen individually to see it clearly.

Everything right where it should be.

The altimeter still read nine-zero and the highest thing in the area was a mountain ridge at seven thousand. Once past the ridge, there was nothing but falling flatlands until he reached the airport.

He glanced sideways to check the central radar display placed between the two pilot positions, then returned his attention to airspeed and percentage of engine…

His gaze drifted back to the radar display.

Lieutenant Colonel Brad Whitman firewalled the pair of Pratt & Whitney turbofans to full power.

Within one-point-seven seconds, eighty-seven thousand pounds of combined thrust poured out of the twin Pratt & Whitney PW2000 engines. Nearly empty, except for passengers and a double reserve of fuel, the 757 weighed barely a hundred and fifty thousand pounds. At a hundred thousand pounds lighter than its maximum take-off weight—the 757 leapt for the skies.

The alarm began to double whoop and announce, *Terrain. Pull Up.*

"No kidding. Read me airspeed," Brad called out.

Abrams did.

Brad rode his numbers at the edge of stall speed, feeding everything he had into gaining elevation quickly. Or even at all.

Terrain. Pull Up.

They were so nose-high that his only view forward was by radar.

A broad mountain peak was becoming more detailed by the second. It was also expanding rapidly.

Terrain. Pull Up.

They weren't going to clear it.

The ridge was broad enough that there wouldn't be any rolling off to either side to get clear. Besides, he couldn't afford the loss of lift inherent in a turn.

Terrain. Pull Up.

The crest of the peak was lining up with the top edge of radar screen. Too bad his flight path was dead center of the radar.

Unless—

Terrain. Pull Up.

Praying that he wasn't about to kill them all, Brad tipped the nose down.

From very steep climb to steep climb.

From steep climb to climb.

Terrain. Pull Up.

As he nosed over, the airspeed rose.

The mountain came closer faster.

The message changed.

Too low—Terrain.

Exactly what he'd been hoping.

He'd done this in the simulator any number of times.

It had even worked once.

Once.

Too low—Terrain.

As the radar altimeter neared zero and the mountain's outline neared the center of the radar screen, he nosed over.

Too low—Terrain.

For just a moment he focused on the mechanical altimeter that had been set to the airport's barometric reading. It read over two thousand feet lower than the reading on the electronic GPS-driven altimeter.

The GPS was *wrong?*

No time now.

Too low—Terrain.

As he rolled the nose level, he was either trading a tail strike for a nose strike.

Or...

48

Twenty-seven-year-old Eylül Acar and her dog had hiked up to watch the sunrise from atop the twenty-three-hundred-meter ridge of the Central Taurus Mountains. She loved the view looking down on the tiny village of Değnek, Turkey.

She was daydreaming about whether or not she was going to sleep with her boss' son, again. He was a glorious lover, so the answer was pretty easy, despite the risks to her career.

The question was, should she cook him her grandmother's Iskender Kebab—she claimed that grandfather had first made love to her right on the kitchen table after eating that—or a chicken Perde pilavi? The latter took more time, but Eylül could make it ahead of time, leaving more time for sex.

Before she could decide, she was decapitated by the armature between the two tires of the front nose gear of a Boeing 757.

The plane was no longer traveling on the verge of an imminent stall at a hundred and nine knots. It had accelerated to a hundred and thirty-two. Traveling the length of a football field every second and a half, she never saw what hit her, though her dog did.

As the nose gear cleared the rocky peak without any damage, except blood splatter, it eased downward, lower than the rock.

But the seesaw roll from nose-up to nose-down was not sufficient to clear the main gear over the ridge.

Had the plane's flight been even a meter higher, the four tires in each set of the main landing gear would have struck the rock. All eight tires would have exploded with the force of impact, but they would have rolled on their rims.

Then the shock absorbers would have transmitted the force of that almost-landing upward with enough force to shatter the shock towers and severely distort the landing gear mounting points—the strongest point in the entire plane's structure.

The force would have driven the wings upward, warping the starboard one badly enough to severely compromise lift, and tipped the nose down past recovery. Even the steep nine-hundred-meter escarpment from the ridge down to Değnek in the valley far below wouldn't have provided sufficient time to recover with the damaged wing.

But the main gear was a meter lower when it struck the rocky ridge.

Instead of rolling and overpitching the 757, the main gear—both wheel trucks and their shock towers—were simply sheared off the plane.

The force of that impact was just sufficient to complete the desperate gamble begun by Colonel Brad Whitman.

As the nose cleared the ridge, the lower surface of the tail scraped over the rock.

But, crucially, the empennage and all of the tail's control surfaces survived intact rather than breaking off.

Other than having no main landing gear, the Boeing 757 survived the encounter intact.

The encounter had smeared the remains of Eylül Acar and her dog past any recognition.

49

"Clarissa here." She sprawled in the bed. Not having Clark home was such a luxury. No sex was a minor convenience—he was still an every-night sort of man. But no one's ego to keep an eye on was a major one. And an old t-shirt instead of sexy nightwear was an even bigger one.

She hadn't even worked late. Instead she'd come home to the Vice President's luxurious Queen Anne Victorian at One Observatory Circle. After an hour on the treadmill, she'd enjoyed a very pleasant bit of self-soothing in a bubble bath. While Clark was finally good enough in bed to no longer be disappointing, she enjoyed the perfection of the moment.

The biggest bonus, though, she had the king-size bed all to herself.

Straight up midnight. This call had better be bloody important.

"I'm alive." Clark. If this was a bootie call, she'd—

"I didn't think you were dead." He never had a good sense of time zones when he traveled, which was the only annoying aspect of Roy Cole keeping his vice president on the move.

"I just wanted you to hear it from me first."

"I'll call CNN."

"No need. I'm sure they're already covering it."

She dove for the remote. "Sorry, uh, not awake." As good an excuse as any. She'd spent a lot of time and energy cultivating Clark Winston, even marrying him of all unexpected choices. That she was mostly enjoying the experience was even more of a surprise—not something she'd ever expected.

No part of her personal path to the White House included Clark Winston turning up dead. A bad oversight that she'd have to rethink very soon. *Bereaved Wife Runs for Office to Carry on Husband's Legacy?* Too saccharine for the American voter? No, the people had long since proven that nothing was.

But first the bastard had to live long enough to create a legacy for her to carry on.

The television screen over the dresser lit up...with some lame thriller movie Clark had been watching.

The CNN shortcut button flipped her to an aerial view of a plane crash. A Boeing 757-200, painted in presidential blue-and-white, sat primly on the runway at the end of long scar.

Even as she watched, they shuffled in a replay shot from some security cam.

Coming down to land perfectly level instead of nose high.

Kissing down ever so gently.

Balancing like a kid's toy on the small stick of the nose wheel.

Then the tail settled onto the pavement.

A massive rooster tail of sparks streaming out behind it, the plane glissading a long way before it finally stopped with its nose in the air. It was immediately buried in firefighting foam. Damn but those Air Force pilots were good.

"Oh, my God, Clark." She cut off whatever he'd been rambling about.

"I know."

"You sure you're okay?"

As she let him tell her about the state of his nerves, CNN switched to a camera that showed a man standing in a cluster of Secret Service agents in sharp, black suits. He was on the phone.

"I see you, Clark. On CNN."

"Oh, hi." He waved in the wrong direction. Not even aware of what a strong moment this could be for any future campaign if he could just face the right way. *VP Survives Plane Crash.*

"Turn around, Clark! Then wave again."

He did. Still missing the camera, but at least he was close this time. The footage would play. The story would be even better if it proved to be a terrorist attack—or could even be implied that it was one.

"Any idea what happened?"

"Pilot said something about corrupted satellite feeds."

Clarissa felt a cold chill. She should have been hounding the Tweedle Twins to chase that lead they had. A detected intrusion, even through a Turkish satellite, just hadn't been *that* interesting. That would teach her. She'd just lost nine hours on these people in a game where seconds could be crucial. *Shit!*

She jumped off the bed.

How to get rid of Clark fast?

"Have you called the President yet?" She yanked off the CIA t-shirt that she wore on nights Clark wasn't around.

"No, I wanted to call you fir—"

"Well, get off the phone now. I mean, yes," Damn it! Damn it! Damn it! She didn't have time for this. She yanked open her underwear drawer and almost dropped it on her toes when it jumped off the track. "Yes, thanks for calling me first. I'm so relieved. I'd have worried. Now call the President. He'll want to know you're okay."

"Okay. Love you."

"You, too." Clarissa grimaced as she cut the call. Not the smoothest response, but hopefully it would do.

She watched the man on the screen seven time zones away. He pulled the phone away from his ear, but didn't appear to hesitate before he was dialing again.

Good. The President would distract him.

She dialed the T Twins, hit speaker, and tossed her phone on the bed as she slammed the drawer back into place and dressed.

"Uh, yeah?" Harry sounded even less awake that she had two minutes ago.

"Another attack. This time they tried to take out the VP at —" she looked at bottom scroll on the television screen "— Incirlik Air Base."

"Your husband? Is he okay? I mean—" he was wasting her time.

"Incirlik as in Turkey?" Heidi, definitely the brains of their hacker operation, came on for the first time.

Clarissa froze and looked at the CNN report again. "Yes, Incirlik, as in our military base in Turkey."

"Oh," was all that Witchy Lady came up with.

"Oh? Just oh?"

"Oh as in, Oh shit. That's really bad news. The systems that the 757s that Air Force Two uses are the same systems as Air Force One. They don't get any more secure. If Turkey can crack those..."

"Shit!" Clarissa dragged on a turtleneck and a sweater, then peeled them back off to put on her bra. "Get to the office now. Get me some answers. I'm en route."

She hung up and speed-dialed the head of the Presidential Protection Detail. She probably should have made this call first. And maybe not with her tits hanging out even if there was no video feed; she wouldn't put it past Evanston to somehow know —the guy was spooky good. She managed to get the bra yanked into place before he answered.

"This is CIA Director Clarissa Reese. We have a credible threat to VIP aviation. Cole's grounded."

"Already done. VP Clark Winston as well. We don't dare send in the Air Force Two backup bird to get him home. Not until we know what happened to them."

"Understood."

Clarissa hung up.

"Way *not* to be the one to be first with the warning. Shit! Definitely should have called them first."

Then she took off her bra, turned it right side up, and put it on again.

50

One minute, Mike had been waiting with Holly for the second S-97 Raider to land back at the test hangar.

Andi had more fallen than climbed out of the helo, but Holly somehow knew and was right there.

Before he could edge over and see if he could help, Miranda's phone had been ringing with a call from General Nason.

"Air Force Two has been involved in a crash at Incirlik Air Base in Turkey. Your team is being escalated immediately. We're arranging transport."

They'd had under thirty minutes to talk through the second S-97's test flight before "transport" arrived.

It turned out to be a Boeing 787 wide-body jet bought by an Israeli gambling software developer. It had already departed Seattle on its delivery flight to Tel Aviv when it was rerouted down to Groom Lake.

The jet was beautiful. It's brand-new paint job gleamed in the runway lights. It was red and black. Instead of an airline name, it sported a spread of four aces on the plane's tall tail.

The Groom Lake guard escort rushed the team aboard.

They clearly didn't want this plane on their runway a moment longer than necessary.

"Never thought we'd be cleared to Groom Lake," the crewman who welcomed them aboard paid far more attention to peering out the open door than looking at them.

"Holy shit! If we get a ride in this when the Vice President crashes, what do we get if the President goes down?" Holly announced as she stepped into the cabin ahead of him.

Mike was about to tell Holly to chill when he saw the setup for himself and lost his words. If he ever became a multibillionaire, he was definitely buying a plane just like this one.

Instead of three hundred passengers, it was renovated to provide luxury seating for about forty. The twenty-five hundred square feet of passenger area now included a master suite complete with showers, three smaller guest suites, even luxurious sitting areas that could also serve as a large-screen movie theater.

But the centerpiece had nothing to do with anything electronic despite the new owner's source of wealth.

A gorgeous octagonal poker table with rosewood trim dominated the middle of the main cabin. The black felt looked so darkly perfect that any card would appear to float on the surface. Safe bet that games played at this table would be seriously high stakes.

The overhead was six grand of black, Poker pendant light by Zero.

It wasn't just a poker table, it was a piece of art.

It made him remember how much he'd enjoyed convincing people that it was fun for them to give him their money. It had paid for his psych degree and launched his ad firm.

"Well, I suppose I could get used to this." Mike decided that he definitely could.

"Go ahead, say the next line. You know you ruddy well want to."

Yes, messing up the sheets with Holly in one of the plane's luxury bedrooms was a damn fine idea. They had achieved the Mile-High club using the little Mooney airplane's autopilot. This would be a very different experience, but he couldn't just give her the easy win.

"Hell of a gaming table. Who here plays poker?"

Holly's grin said she totally understood that he was messing with her. She was also the only one to raise her hand.

"I know how to play Hearts, Rummy, Go Fish…" Jeremy was the ultimate sad sack.

"Can't play a game that lame at a table as fine as this one."

One of the flight officers called over the PA. "If everyone could sit down and buckle up, we're cleared for immediate departure. The kind where they might shoot us if we don't get gone fast. We're going to be ten hours en route. There are no attendants aboard as this was just a delivery flight, but Ms. Biram said 'Welcome Aboard' and to make free use of anything in the galley, which is well stocked." He clicked off.

Because it was there, they all sat around the gorgeous table. The leather chairs were awesomely comfortable, half airplane seat and half office chair.

Mike went for the one that would place his back toward the direction of flight once they were aloft. It was a strategic choice at a poker table. Subconsciously, the other players would feel as if he was looming over them, about to fall and consume them as prey. He felt a deep kinship with the plane's designer and owner.

As soon as they were aloft, he reached into an under-table drawer and came up with a still sealed set of Bicycle cards. Not spendy KEM or even Copag plastics, but good old cardboard. He didn't know if she was thirty or ninety, but he was definitely falling in love with Ms. Biram.

He'd dealt battered Bicycle cards in the orphanage's girls' bathroom late at night, so dog-eared that it was hard *not* to read them as a marked deck. St. Bernardine had also preached against gambling, but it really wasn't with that deck. He'd dealt those cards to great advantage.

Cracking the deck, he enjoyed the snap and slide of the cheap glued-double-paper cards. They might not even last a night in any serious game, but they were always a pleasure to manipulate. He'd never liked the plastic cards for that reason.

After peeling the jokers and the instruction cards, he started with a simple overhand shuffle to break up the neatly prepackaged order. After the third or fourth riffle, they were loosening up well. He split the deck, made a pair of fans in either hand, then swung them together as neat as could be. Not a single card had doubled between another, a perfect interleave. He laced together a closed riffle, not sliding the cards together, then spread the deck along the table in a line. These too were stacked exactly every other one.

He gathered them, slipped them together, then spread the deck face up in a wide arc, all of the cards were still, actually *back* in their original order.

"Very pretty," Holly nodded toward his card manipulation. "And remind me to never play poker with you, mate, unless I'm dealing."

"Been a while, but I appear to still have it."

This time he did a real shuffle, finishing with a quick wash across the table's ebony felt, and the deck was ready.

As he flicked out a fresh fan, Holly kicked him sharply in the shin.

The cards flew from his hands and showered down on the table all higgledy-piggledy.

He rubbed one shin against the other calf as he regathered the cards.

"So, shall we play some Old Maid?" he challenged her.

Holly snorted a laugh.

"Why am I still here?" Andi spoke softly. It was the first thing she'd said since the helo flight out to the crash site.

"Why wouldn't you be?"

"I'm a rotorcraft specialist. I'm not even half through Academy training."

Once he had the deck put back together, Mike dealt five cards face down, one in front of each person. "You don't get it yet. Terence Graham sent you to Miranda Chase's team. Until things don't work out, you're a part of Miranda's team."

"I thought launch teams were assigned on the fly as needed."

"Not Miranda's."

"But I don't belong here," she waved a hand that might have included the poker table or it might have indicated the wider world.

"Talk to the lady in charge," Mike nodded toward Miranda.

"Miranda?" Andi's voice was still barely louder than the very well-insulated roar of the 787's engines as it raced east toward Turkey.

"Your insights into factors beyond the scope of the S-97 Raider itself were as useful as any Jeremy might have made."

"Hey—" Jeremy scowled, then cut himself off.

Something was definitely going on with him around Andi. Jeremy being defensive about anything or anyone, other than Taz Cortez, was unheard of. And even that had been a shocker. He simply didn't think that way.

"Additionally, your insightful management of the military hierarchy was..." Miranda pulled out her personal notebook and flipped through it for a moment before nodding and tucking it away again, "...appreciated."

Mike began laying down the next cards faceup. Five Card Stud was a good poker game to teach basics with.

"Two of hearts for Holly. Power start, not. Seven of clubs for

Miranda, not a big improvement. Jack of clubs for Jeremy, best card so far. Ten of diamonds for Andi. And—"

"Helicopters."

"What about them?"

Andi pointed at her card. "It's not a diamond, it's a helicopter."

"How do you figure that?"

"A diamond has four blade points, like a Black Hawk's main rotor. That's a ten of helicopters."

"Fine, what's this?" He flopped down the trademark Ace of Spades in front of himself. Crap! After testing his shuffling skills, no one would believe he hadn't done that on purpose.

"That's called cheating, mate," Holly spoke first.

"No, I—"

"Jet fighter!" Jeremy spoke over him. "Pointy nose. Maybe Holly's two of hearts could be bombers."

"There's a piece of truth spoken by the innocent," he muttered to her.

Holly scoffed.

"The heart shape still has a pointy end," Jeremy again sounded defensive. "With broad wings like the B-2A Spirit flying wing bomber, or the B-1B Lancer."

"Now there's a major waste of airspace," Andi muttered.

Even Mike knew there was truth in that. The Lancer program had been cancelled as an incredible boondoggle disaster until President Reagan had promised to reinvest in the military in a big way—part of which was resurrecting a plane that no one in their right mind wanted.

"Maybe it's worth negative points?" Miranda always made him laugh, especially when she didn't mean to.

"Perfect!" Mike swept the cards up once again. He ran a quick spread across the table, did a cascade flip to turn them all face up, then flipped them back. Gathering it back into a deck, he did a quick shuffle and spooled out the four aces face up.

"So, diamonds are helicopters. Spades are fighters. Hearts are bombers. What about clubs?"

"Clubs," Holly thumped down a fist, "should be bombers, because they club things."

Then the seatbelt ping sounded through the cabin. The plane was so well sound insulated that it was easy to forget they were even flying. The ping meant that they were up to cruising altitude.

Mike glanced over his shoulder toward the head of the plane. East. Toward a crash of Air Force Two. Alaska, the S-97 Raider, and now that.

He'd keep the card nonsense going as long as he could if it would give the team a little mental break.

He was just reaching for the Ace of Hearts when Holly popped her seatbelt.

"Come on, Andi. Let's rustle up some grub."

Miranda had pulled out one of her notebooks and begun making notes.

Mike sighed and turned to Jeremy. Actually, with just the two of them caring anymore, maybe he could find out what was eating at the team's youngest member.

He scooped up the aces, riffled them into the deck, then dealt Jeremy and himself ten quick cards. Then he flipped the next card and dropped it face up on the table.

"The Ace of Spades," Jeremy was watching him with narrowed eyes.

Crap!

51

"SPILL, GIRL."

"Spill what? Cornflakes?" Andi held up the cereal box she'd just found.

"We can do better than that," Holly grabbed a larger service tray and started throwing random things at it. Crackers, cheese, a couple trays of frozen beef lasagna, a pack of licorice...

Andi snagged the licorice and dug out a couple vines.

"Look," suddenly Holly was absolutely still.

Even though she was now slouched against the counter, she was so tall it gave Andi a crick in her neck.

"I don't know what you're spinning to Mike. That's not the question I'm asking. This is Spec Ops to Spec Ops." At the moment she had less trace of an Australian accent than even Nicole Kidman typically mustered.

Not trusting herself, Andi merely crossed her arms over her chest to match Holly and nodded for her to continue.

"Booted your ass?"

Andi managed a nod.

"You get blown up, or someone else?"

"The second one."

Holly closed her eyes, and Andi was surprised to see the searing pain of sympathy there.

"I don't want—"

"I know, mate. Trust me, I know. Sympathy, pity, condolences, all Mike's kindness… None of it touches the core, does it."

Since it was a truth not a question, Andi didn't bother agreeing.

Holly stared at the plane's ceiling for a while before looking back down.

"I've got one mission now."

"Plane crashes."

Holly shook her head and waited.

Oh perfect. A guessing game. She *sucked* at guessing games.

Andi had seen Holly's skills in the field. Not just scaling cliff faces, but there were items of crash-site shrapnel from the S-97 Raider's structure that Holly had been able to identify with clues that weren't even enough for Andi herself. She understood the physicality of an aircraft intimately.

"You sure you're not a pilot?"

"Been a grunt all my days, mate. All I ever knew was how to hump a pack and shoot a gun. Oh, and blowing shit up, but that's fun."

Holly's mission now was none of that? Which meant…

"You're asking if Miranda is safe around me."

"Why wouldn't I be?" Miranda showed up at their elbows as if teleported.

Even Holly jumped, which Andi found surprisingly satisfying. At least Andi herself wasn't the only Special Operations Forces personnel whose system was on the blink. Unless Miranda had some sort of stealth mode.

Andi sighed. "Just keep me away from a helicopter's controls, and Holly away from shit that blows up, and I think you'll be fine."

"Actually, I believe that Holly's issue has far more to do with *people* being blown up, but she hasn't spoken of it."

Holly steadied her.

Or perhaps steadied herself, by grabbing Andi's shoulder.

"Whoa, girl!" Holly managed a mutter.

They both took a moment and somehow kept their shit together once more. A constant struggle.

Then Holly looked infinitely sad. "'Fraid that losing people's one we've got in common."

Despite Holly's pincer grip around her upper arm, Andi felt as if she was wavering in and out of an unlikely reality. Was she *actually* forty thousand feet in the air aboard a luxury gambling casino? Or locked up in some padded room somewhere?

As unlikely as the former seemed, it was definitely behaving like reality.

Maybe she'd accept that as a premise and just see what happened from here.

Miranda had turned to Holly. "I think I've calculated the best re-indexing methodology. Diamonds are indeed helicopters as Captain Andi Wu suggested. I debated clubs with the tail section, but three-bladed rotor systems have always bothered me as if they can never be in balance despite a consistent hundred-and-twenty-degree separation."

"At least they aren't as horrifying as two-blade systems," Andi shuddered. "Mast knock still creeps me out."

"And is typically fatal," Miranda agreed completely deadpan.

Fatal and helicopter were two words Andi never wanted to hear in the same sentence ever again.

"Please check my metaphors," Miranda held her notebook open for Holly to see. "I've never understood those. But if spades are bombers as Jeremy suggested and also fighters, then clubs could be transport aircraft with their distinct tail sections. That leaves hearts, which—"

"Surely not something this girl is wasting her time having," Holly's thick Australian was back.

"—could be the misfit aircraft," Miranda continued without missing a beat.

"Perfect!" Holly laughed aloud.

"No!" Andi protested. "They're hearts. They're the old favorites."

"Ah," Holly grinned. "We've got a romantic on board, Miranda."

Andi laughed. That was so *not* her. But she wanted to kiss Miranda's feet for giving her something so ridiculous to focus on. She felt more human with each passing moment.

"Hearts would be like the Howard Hughes' Spruce Goose. Or the RAH-66 Comanche helicopter—that really should have been built *before* the Pentagon and Congress screwed it up so much."

"I like it," Holly was nodding, and began heating various dinners in the microwave.

"Hearts are favorites from any category," Miranda said slowly as if testing the idea. "I was worried about putting my F-86 in the combat category. Certainly an F/A-18F Super Hornet fighter shouldn't be excluded to make room for an aircraft like my Sabrejet, but I worry that its feelings would be hurt if I were to leave it out of the card game."

"You have an F-86 Sabrejet?" Andi didn't even know there were any still flying.

"Well, technically—"

"Don't get her started," Holly was smiling.

"—it is no longer a pure example. It has elements of the E and F, as well as the Canadair Mk 5 and 6. Oh, and the new ejection seat that the President gave me last winter."

Andi was trying to think of the last time she'd so enjoyed just talking to women. Or even *had* simply talked to a group of women. She'd been one of the very few in the Night Stalkers and had never flown with one.

Andi spotted a fold-down chair for the galley chef and dropped into it. She peeled off a couple more licorice vines before speaking.

"You're telling me that the President, the one of the United States, gave your fifty-year-old—"

"Sixty-two-year-old."

"—fucking prehistoric fighter jet a new ejection seat? What's that, a quarter of a million dollars?"

Miranda nodded. "Two hundred and forty-three thousand, actually."

"But...why?"

"Roy said it was the least he could do for my stopping the next major Asian war. All I really did was solve a series of misinterpreted crashes that appeared disconnected but ultimately weren't."

Andi glanced at Holly, whose indulgent smile said that Miranda's view was a vastly simplified one of a far more complex reality.

Fishing for what factor was most surprising, Andi's battered brain came up with, "You're on a first-name basis with the Commander-in-Chief?"

Miranda turned to Holly. "Why does that surprise everyone so much?"

"Not a clue, Miranda. Got me stonkered worse than a rabbit at a hurdle-jumping contest." Holly winked at her over Miranda's head, then went back to heating up the food she'd scrounged.

Miranda continued telling them about the aircraft she'd place on each playing card in each category.

Holly listened as if it was the most important thing she could be doing with her time.

It let Andi just sit quietly—and study Miranda in profile.

A day and a half ago, her life had been a simple reality, with no real goal beyond survival. Then Director Terence Graham had bumped her behind the top secret curtain of Groom Lake just on the chance that she *might* be of use to this woman. Now, in under thirty-six hours, she'd gotten involved in two plane crashes, one the near-death of the Vice President of the United States, and—

Just thirty-six hours?

Somehow it all centered around this woman right in front of her. The one currently debating whether to restrict the categories exclusively to American aircraft, America and her allies, or global manufacturers.

"And I don't think we should include that Comanche, even in the Old Favorites category," Holly dropped the last of the heated food dishes back on the trays. "That program *was* cancelled over fifteen years ago with only a couple of prototypes in the air."

Miranda dutifully crossed it out in her notebook.

No thanks given for Holly's suggestion. Actually, for nothing over the last thirty-six hours.

Not from Miranda.

Not *for* Miranda either. She'd helped Andi find her way back out at the hospital, and all she'd gotten for it was Andi clawing her.

Just being accepted as even a temporary part of the team was all the thanks she'd probably ever get. Maybe it was also all that was needed.

But for Miranda?

Andi pushed to her feet, wiped off the slight stickiness that the licorice had left on her palm against her pants, and then held out her hand to Miranda.

Miranda looked down at the hand, then up at her in some surprise—not quite looking at her face.

When Miranda finally took her hand, Andi shook it firmly.

"Thanks for having me on your team."

Miranda's reply sounded practiced, "You're welcome." Then she let go and turned back to her list.

Holly's quiet nod was one any Spec Ops soldier would recognize, "Well done."

52

"Why don't you trust Andi? Because she's got PTSD?" Mike had kept the conversation light through several hands until Miranda had left the table.

Jeremy looked at him strangely. "Is that what happened to her in the field at lunch?" He dropped the damned Ace of Spades onto the discard.

Mike nodded. *Crap!* He was sorry for revealing Andi's secret —he'd figured it was so damn obvious that even Jeremy would get it. Nope.

He didn't need the ace. He didn't have any other low spades, but he couldn't resist picking it up, breaking up a perfectly legitimate two-card potential straight to do so. Five hands of Gin Rummy, Jeremy was winning, and he'd been stuck with the unmatched ace every single time. At least it was only one point.

"Yeah. She's got it. Probably kinder if you don't mention it to her directly though."

"Oh, I didn't think of that." Jeremy nodded, swept up Mike's discarded eight of hearts, and announced, "Big Gin." He lay out all eleven cards.

Mike couldn't lay off even one point of his deadwood. Royally screwed. He tossed down the cards and leaned back.

He watched Jeremy as he began gathering them up. The old Jeremy he might doubt, the one before Taz Cortez. But she'd done something to change him down in that lost canyon deep in the Baja desert. Something more than just screwing his brains out.

And it bothered Mike that he had no idea what it was.

"I don't dislike her." Jeremy tried a hard riffle and shot a third of the cards across the table. "But..." He stayed very focused on the cards as he regathered them.

"But..." Mike looked around.

The plane's interior was dim with the night. The lights in the rear sections past the poker table had gone out automatically with no one occupying that area of the cabin. The only other light was from beyond the wall that masked the forward galley. Things were starting to smell good and his stomach gurgled happily in anticipation.

"But..." he played with the word and tried to imagine he was Jeremy.

Your insights into factors beyond the scope of the S-97 Raider itself were as useful as any Jeremy might have made. Miranda had said that and Jeremy had been upset.

And again, when Miranda had asked Jeremy to take photographs and samples from the sand ripples kicked up by the S-97 Raider's last flight. A pattern identified by...Andi.

He wasn't acting like the Jeremy that Mike had always thought he was.

No, like the Jeremy that he *used* to be.

His emotions, formerly limited to the two prongs of general puppy-dog excitement and utter fascination with a problem, had now been cracked open.

He must be feeling...as if Andi was sliding into his role.

Jealousy? Could it be that simple?

No. Whatever Taz Cortez had done to him that had motivated him to take a swing at Colonel Stimson was a part of it as well.

What the hell had that woman done to him?

He was no less competent, maybe more so because he was thinking about things more deeply rather than just being an insanely useful geek-gun. *There's a systems problem. Aim Jeremy. Fire!*

Whatever else he might be feeling, jealousy *was* part of it.

"You know, Jeremy," Mike scooped up the cards that Jeremy had dealt out and began rearranging his hand into groups.

Neither of them wanted the face-up card, so he drew from the stockpile but didn't pick it up yet.

"You're really growing into your team role. I mean, I've been watching you and it's like you're just settling into the traces of it —really solidly on the last few investigations." Which was absolutely the truth.

Jeremy was studying him across the pitch-black felt.

Mike slid his face-down card back and forth across the dark surface. It really did look like it was floating in space.

"I don't know if you've noticed, but Miranda now gives you whole sections of an investigation to take care of. I haven't seen her triple-check your work in a while."

"Yeah, just double-check," Jeremy grimaced.

"Remember, this is Miranda. She's never going to do less than that."

"I'm never going to do less than what?"

They both would have launched out of their seats if they weren't wearing their seatbelts.

"Yeah, what?" Holly's grin was feral and malicious. They each held a pair of airline trays. Andi carried another and a basket of sodas.

"We were just saying that you'd never—"

"—cut corners on an investigation," he cut off Jeremy.

"Okay." Miranda accepted the statement at face value. She was the only one who did.

Holly rolled her eyes.

Andi snickered.

Miranda handed him a tray with a large portion of steaming lasagna, prosciutto-wrapped asparagus, a crusty sourdough bread roll, and a side of fresh apple pie with ice cream, before sitting beside him.

"Which reminds me." Miranda began cutting up a small skirt steak. She turned to Holly, "Why wouldn't I be safe around Andi?"

Holly barely balked, "Just something Mike said. Ask him." Then she picked up a roasted Brussels sprout with her fingers and ate it.

Andi's eye roll clued him in that it had been her and Holly's conversation, not his, that Miranda had caught some part of.

He kicked Holly's shin under the table.

Jeremy squeaked in surprise.

To cover that it was his kick that had gone astray, Mike flipped over the card he'd drawn.

Ace of Spades.

Of course.

53

"Of course you had a tracer waiting for any attack this time," Clarissa breezed into the twins' office.

Because if they hadn't, she'd take them the fuck apart.

Heidi's eyeroll told her that was a real "Duh!" statement.

Fine, bitch. Have your bit of fun.

It was a good thing she'd had a driver or she might have killed somebody getting from the Vice Presidential house to the CIA New Headquarters Building.

She had no plan in place for Clark's unexpected demise. He was only twenty years older than she was, he should still have plenty of good years in him—politicians went senile long before they aged out of office. Actually, they never aged out, even if they *went* senile.

That someone would cut out that link she'd built so carefully over the years—

She didn't know what she'd do to them, but she'd start by fucking killing them, then she'd switch to lower priorities like cutting off their balls and those of every single male relation. She wasn't Jewish, but that Jewish God of the Old Testament understood a thing or two about retribution.

Heidi was on her feet, leaning forward over Harry's shoulder.

The rest of their night-shift teams would be in the cubie warren outside the office, wired up on Red Bull and pizza. Clarissa had long since learned to keep the CIA Cyber Security Center and Cyber Attack Division well stocked with both.

In the twins' shared office, there was just the two identical stations.

To her surprise, Harry's was as neat as a pin while Heidi's was the kitschy one.

A red scarf with yellow stripes was draped across the top of her monitors. An ornate wooden wand rested on a pewter stand between the pair of keyboards. A blondely perfect witch Barbie doll perched sidesaddle on her broom in a pristine *Bewitched* box. That Heidi was a brunette was obviously irrelevant. Or perhaps not as there was also a line of slowly aging boxed Hermione action figures.

"Why the boxes?"

Harry didn't even look up. "Value drops by half or more if you take them out of the boxes."

"They're worth something?"

Heidi this time, "A pristine set like that, with the Barbie, is probably about a thousand dollars."

Well, at least it was high-quality kitsch.

Clarissa moved in to lean over Harry's other shoulder.

Too bad she understood nothing of what she was looking at, but that didn't matter. She was here to motivate the shit out of Harry, not replace him.

As she watched the lines of computerese flowing through the multiple windows on every screen—some at a crawl, others so fast she could barely see any patterns—she was reminded that there was a reason she liked this place.

It wasn't her world, but she could feel the CIA's heartbeat here.

HUMINT (Human Intelligence) still had its place—barely. Agents in place, image analysts, and all the rest of their ilk.

But even in the most backward of countries, data...revealed. It could be hidden, altered, even faked. However, the underlying truth was always out there, somewhere in the data.

She needed to come down here more often, especially when all the Old School agents and former field spies were pushing a human-driven agenda. This was both the present and the future. Here is where shit happened.

That was definitely food for thought. If only she could trust the Tweedle Twins, they'd be useful assets in ensuring her path to the White House.

But she glanced at Heidi's station with its too cutesy paraphernalia, and Harry's with just a wedding photo—in full Harry Potter regalia. Even the minister had no compunction, dressed in a long beard and equally ornate gray robes.

They probably lived by some bizarre code of wizard's honor, despite being the two top cyber-guns at the CIA.

No, she couldn't trust them with her personal plans. But with national security...

"We're through a three-satellite jump," Heidi told her without turning from the screen. "The signal didn't hand off to the Russians, or the Chinese for that matter. It appears to have come to ground at an antenna farm in Gölbaşi, south of Ankara."

Clarissa stood up. "That means that—"

She spoke slowly enough one of the twins would feel obliged to cut her off before she was forced to turn it into a question. Exposing her own ignorance was never a good thing.

"Right," Harry did it for her, so pup-dog pleased to know the answer. "Siberkume. The Turkey Cyber Security Cluster. They're running a five-year-old SVR supercomputer, not even a petaflop machine. It was out of the TOP500 before they even turned it on."

Heidi stood and leaned back against her desk, idly picking up the vine-covered wooden wand, and fooled with it for a moment before speaking.

Clarissa stood up as well so that she kept her clear height advantage—except she'd pulled on sneakers instead of heels. It would have made them the same height if Heidi wasn't slouching.

"You're right, Clarissa. Up until now, they've only had two targets. Disrupting Greece—which is such a disaster anyway, I don't know why they're wasting the effort—and internal Turkish security. They're spending most of their resources tracking and arresting their own citizens. They've managed to climb their rank of prison population per capita from nineteenth worldwide to third, behind only us and Russia. They're roughly tied with Ukraine now."

She swished her wand as if sweeping all those people aside. Maybe Heidi wasn't as pushover as Harry appeared. But why had she chosen to lead the security division and Harry chosen attack division?

"I did a little digging around last night, just in case it actually was them." Heidi flicked the wand to point over her shoulder. "*They* have a laughably small foreign attack division. Twenty, twenty-five at most. The majority of the code that comes out of there... Meh!" Again a flick of the wand, brushing it aside as garbage. "Except—" She tapped her wand on Harry's head as if snapping him from his coding reverie.

"This guy's code is tight," Harry turned on like a piece of clockwork. "He doesn't know about blocking any tracers, or even having alarms to tell him that we're peeking. But the primary code itself is world-class. Heavy enough that it probably takes two guys to run it properly."

"Trash it." Then maybe she could get back to sleep. Or move on to the problem of what to do about accelerating Clark's ascendancy.

"Not that simple," Heidi waggled that damn wand at her. "Besides, our trace was a generic tracker. It reached the Siberkume firewall, then purposely degraded without giving any sign it had been there. We need him to open the door from the inside one more time," she did a swish-and-flick motion, "if we want to get all the way in."

She must have read how close Clarissa was to grabbing it and jamming it through one of the gibberish-filled computer screens. She hung it carefully back on its pewter stand.

"Besides, they're after something. If we just shut them down, we'll never know what and they'll come after it again, maybe from some angle we don't catch next time."

"All the more reason to crush them first." Then Clarissa thought about some of the other possible targets that would fit Turkey's agenda, such as the complete destabilization of NATO. "How much more important than crashing Clark's plane?"

"Two attacks would indicate—"

"Three," Harry spoke up as he rattled at the keys. "I've been rolling back through the satellite logs. Historically, the GPS satellites get just a few hundred hack attacks each week."

A graph resolved on his screen.

There was a sharp curve upward. "Here it jumped to a thousand a week, then a thousand per *day*. That rolled along for three months."

Just over a week ago, it cliffed back down to previous levels.

"What happened there?"

"The first successful hack. He—"

"Or she," Heidi put in.

"—or she," he acknowledged with one of those mushy smiles from sitcoms and people with brains made of primordial ooze, "found her *or his* way in. No need for more testing. That same signature occurs just three times: the initial success, the one we told you about yesterday, and the Vice President tonight, morning there in Turkey."

"The question is, what's coming next?"

54

"WHY CAN'T I HAVE A SPITFIRE? SHE GETS HER SABREJET." Jeremy was back to dealing Gin Rummy.

Miranda found the game a little too predictable. With four players, by the third time around the table, she'd know what everyone was collecting. And then it was over before an accurate proof of count could be attained. It was an unsatisfying game in two ways.

Poker was a game of skill, but calculating odds was only a narrow slice of it. The game also included the need to read and manipulate others' emotions. The latter left her out of that game.

A game needed an arbitrary variable, perhaps more than one in order to function properly and avoid the pitfalls of over-simplicity or being dependent upon a specific skill.

"You mean other than the Messerschmitt Bf 109?" Andi zinged back along with a four of hearts. She had a spade straight and probable eights.

"The Me 109, as the Allies called it, did record the most aircraft kills in WWII, including many Spitfires," Miranda appreciated

Andi's clear knowledge of aircraft history. It showed that she hadn't merely flown for the military, but had loved doing so enough to really understand its history. At least its aviation history.

"Besides, if you put in the Spitfire, what's to stop us debating some of the truly groundbreaking aircraft like the JN-4 Jenny biplane that reshaped World War I and post-war aviation? Or the VS-300."

"What's that one?" Mike picked up an eight, not seeing the conflict with Andi, and laid off a three that Jeremy snatched up quickly.

"First practical helicopter," Miranda and Andi said in unison.

Would the rapidity of Jeremy's selection indicate an emotion? Speed correlated to intensity of emotion much the way an aircraft's speed capability corresponded to the thrust-to-weight ratio of its engines. If humans were aircraft...

Miranda looked down at her lists of aircraft.

Mike would be...like her Mooney M20V Ultra that he typically flew. Very fast, but only within the confines of its category. He was truly brilliant in his category of people, though weak in technical areas that might be represented by a more sophisticated aircraft. Not that Mike was unsophisticated, but...

The whole thing began to break down in her head, so she moved on before it dissolved completely into random neuron firings.

Captain Andi Wu flew rotorcraft. Top military rotorcraft. Again, as she'd shown in the field, extremely good in her one specific helicopter. Only time would tell how she did in other areas. It was as if she was a helicopter herself, Miranda smiled, one a little bit prone to crashing.

She herself? Miranda put little tick marks next to the F-86 Sabrejet and the Cessna Citation M2. Most comfortable alone might be the Sabrejet part of her. The Citation might be…efficiency?

Miranda inspected her notes with some surprise.

Metaphors. These were metaphors. But she sucked at metaphors.

Maybe she finally understood them. Like a coded cipher, one symbol standing in for another…

If Holly was an aircraft? Or Jeremy?

She scanned her whole working list of over seventy-nine aircraft she'd listed as being potentially useful for the game. Cargo planes like the Condor that Holly had ridden across Russia? A gunship like the one that had almost killed Jeremy?

Maybe if she tried switching them: Holly the gunship, and Jeremy the cargo plane.

No. She just didn't understand how they aligned either way.

She tried adding basic parameters to each of the aircraft: speed, passenger and cargo capacities, combat and ferry distances. Then she rescanned the list, with little more insight.

They…

She looked up from her notes.

The dirty dishes were gone and all of the plane's cabin lights were turned down except one spreading a soft light over the black table.

The seats were empty except for Mike sitting two over. He had a beer bottle. By the lack of any condensation on it, and the way the rippled bottom of the once-damp label crinkled as he idly twisted it back and forth, she'd estimate that it had been empty long enough to dry even from the inevitable condensation.

"Where is everyone?" Then she could see them, stretched out on the couches, blankets pulled over them. "Why didn't they use the bedrooms?"

"Didn't want to mess up someone else's sheets? Maybe. What are you working on so hard?"

Miranda had to look down to remember. "I'm not sure. It's either the new card game or else I'm working on metaphors."

Mike slouched deeper and crossed his feet on one of the other chairs.

"Okay, I'll bite. Give me door number two."

"I," Miranda looked around. "The only doors I see are to the bedrooms in back and the wing emergency exits. None of which have the number two on them that I can see. At least not from here."

Mike smiled at something. The light was low enough that his eyes were in shadow. She was comfortable with him like this. "Tell me about your metaphors."

So she did.

He nodded in easy agreement at his pairing with the Mooney. "Makes sense. Fast at what it does. Good with people. A nice team plane. And I like that it moves fast but not too fast. Not overly complex like your new jet. A simple pilot's plane. That's a good fit for me. Who's next?"

She hadn't seen most of those parallels. But Mike did move fast, but not too fast. He was always there when she needed him to be, but he never left her feeling overwhelmed the way Holly or Jon did. Talking to Jeremy was like...talking to an extension of herself. He appeared to bother others at times, but she never minded him.

Mike nodded. "Holly as an AC-130 Gunship is intriguing."

"But?" Miranda could actually hear his hesitation.

"Since I'm sleeping with one and have ridden through a battle in the other... Actually, I've sort of battled both of them. But I think there's a better match for her."

Miranda studied her list, but didn't know what it might be.

Mike pointed, "The Warthog. A-10 Thunderbolt."

Miranda squinted at him. "I thought Holly was beautiful?"

"She's gorgeous, though don't tell her I said that. But a Warthog is the loveliest sight in the world to a soldier on the ground needing close air support. The A-10 may be lethal from on high, but its true role is getting down and dirty close-up. And both craft are tough as hell."

She liked that. She wished it was a prettier plane, but everything else fit. Miranda noted that down.

Mike glanced over at the couch where Jeremy had gone to sleep. "Jeremy is like, I don't know, the Condor or a C-5 Galaxy that he flew that time. He carries a massive load around in his pack, and his brain. And it's as if he's never quite sure what to do with it."

"It's not a very reliable aircraft. Even with the C-5M Super Galaxy upgrade, it barely maintains a sixty-two percent average mission-capable availability rate."

"Good point. Well done on the metaphor front, Miranda. Hmm..." He stared up at the ceiling.

She looked aloft to see what was written there before she could stop herself.

"How about the MH-47G Chinook? A high-capacity workhorse. Fast—the fastest military helicopter out there before the S-97 Raider. Not a lot of personal defenses—which absolutely fits, though I think he's learning. Yet for all that, it's smooth handling, and does incredible things under the protection of others—like this team."

Miranda made note of that pairing as well.

"And Major Jon Swift..." Mike stared up into the darkness.

She'd forgotten about Jon.

Mike opened his mouth, closed it, then just shook his head.

"What?"

"I was going to say that he's like Jeremy's Spitfire, but I think that's unfair to him."

"Why?"

55

He couldn't have shut his mouth one sentence sooner, could he? *Crap!*

Mike finally satisfied Miranda's need to complete things with the explanation that Jon Swift and the Spitfire were both superior fighter craft in any era.

During the game of Rummy, Jeremy had regaled them about it being one of the few planes that was used throughout the Second World War and beyond. It had gone through many modifications, but it was still one of the few planes to span the whole war without becoming obsolete. As had its adversary, the Me 109.

Miranda finally headed for bed and Mike turned out the light, but found himself reluctant to leave the beautiful table.

Instead, he sat there, slowly shuffling and reshuffling the card deck. Other than flashes of palest white, reflections of the emergency egress lights off the card faces, the darkness in the cabin was complete.

Once Miranda had settled, the rest of the team were little more than soft shapes stretched out on the long couches.

The 787's windows were oval and larger than most other

aircraft. No shades, the dimming was controlled by some electronic process he was sure Jeremy would be glad to explain.

For now they were undimmed, letting flashes spill in from the anti-collision strobe atop the fuselage, blinked across the outer wings. They must be in some sort of thin cloud, as he could see the red and green of the outward-facing wingtip lights scattering off water droplets along with the pulse of the wingtip strobes. The plane's heartbeat across the sky.

There's a metaphor for you, Miranda. Gods but she cracked him up sometimes.

As his eyes adapted, he could make out the fronts of the cards, though it was all in the monotone of semidarkness.

He dealt the cards of Miranda's metaphor.

Miranda the Queen of Spades—the big kahuna thirteen-pointer of a Hearts game. Flying high in her jets.

Jeremy the Jack, following in his workhorse Chinook.

Holly the King? No, the Ace of Clubs—the bludgeon of the A-10 but also a fine-honed weapon.

Andi.

He half wondered if he should fetch the Joker. The unknown, the wild card. He finally tossed her down as another Queen. Terence Graham had ridden his own ass hard all through the Academy, yet he'd sent Andi to Miranda filled with praise.

No, Mike twisted the card sideways, like the second card in a tarot Celtic Cross—the junior queen. Still not right, but righter.

For Jon, he tossed out an eight. Not low enough to be caught repainting roses during *Alice's Adventures in Wonderland.* Those gardener cards had been named for their spots: Seven, Five, and the lowly Two.

But like the Spitfire that Mike had suggested without thinking first, Jon was old-fashioned, even outdated. He didn't quite make sense with Miranda the jet queen, not that Mike had any clue who could be better for her.

Jon's kindness ran deep. Mike switched out his eight for a nine.

Unlike the two of diamonds for Arturo Campos. There was a useless piece of crap, trying to sabotage Miranda because she'd refused to sleep with him. Despite what he'd told Miranda, he'd bet that was the real reason Campos had dumped on them.

Mike was half tempted to call Drake to find out what had been done about him. But he didn't quite have the balls to call the Chairman of the Joint Chiefs of Staff except on Miranda's behalf.

For himself?

He shuffled through the cards, considering Andi's question.

What am I doing here?

He twisted his chair enough to prop his feet on the next one over.

Yet Miranda kept him around. That was something.

He tossed down Jack, Queen, King. Here to deal with all of the face cards, all the people she didn't want to. He was useful for that anyway.

He threw down a second Ace beside Holly's, diamonds for Jeremy's Chinook helicopterishness? No. He swept it back up and dropped the Ace of Hearts because he was just such a good kid.

Side by side, Jeremy and Holly were definitely aces in Miranda's tool vest.

Mike re-drew the Ace of Helicopters, and hesitated before tossing it down with the other two. Would Andi turn into an ace, too, or would she disappear back into the NTSB system?

He flicked the card with a fingernail a few times still not setting it down to float on the midnight table.

Holly had said that the Night Stalkers were the best helo pilots in the world.

And Colonel Stimson had assigned Andi to his most critical testing program. Which meant underneath whatever mess she was, she was insanely competent and driven.

But would she fold?

He wasn't thinking about another PTSD attack—those didn't magically stop.

Rather, would Miranda start to depend on her, and then find that crutch had suddenly been kicked out?

The day, a year-ago now, that he'd joined the team, before he even knew who Miranda was or that she was on the autism spectrum, he'd seen the devastation she'd suffered when losing her team.

Her prior team had disappeared from under her in a single blow that she hadn't seen coming. She'd been told about their leaving but still not absorbed it—no big surprise now that he knew her. A coincident retirement and maternity leave should have given her plenty of notice; she simply hadn't heard it as being relevant until it happened.

Still, that "desertion" had thrown her minimal judgment so far out of balance that she'd charged a one-star general despite his sidearm pointed at her face. He still wondered how she'd managed not be shot dead on the spot.

He couldn't imagine Holly or Jeremy ever walking away from Miranda.

Captain Andrea Wu formerly of the 160th Night Stalkers though?

He glanced over toward the couch she'd chosen but couldn't see to read anything there.

Holly had said the Night Stalkers unit motto was just four letters long, NSDQ—Night Stalkers Don't Quit.

If she was one of their top pilots, he'd wager it went beyond that. Not that she wouldn't choose to quit, rather she probably didn't know how. Not on others. Not on herself (though he suspected that concept might surprise her at the moment). After what she'd been through, losing her copilot in such a shocking fashion, she was still in the aircraft game. Had even flown the S-97 Raider in a test.

Stimson had pulled him aside and warned him about her freak-out over the wreckage, especially when a wind gust had slithered through the canyon and bounced the helo hard.

Yeah, the S-97 Raider was a good aircraft for Miranda's metaphor list. When Captain Andi Wu was banging on all four cylinders, she was probably formidable. And stealthy, because it was the last thing even modern perceptions would expect from such a petite and pretty woman.

He set the Ace of Helicopters on the table beside Jeremy's and Holly's cards.

Andi was definitely pushing on Jeremy's confidence about his role on Miranda's team. The Raider Ace was perfect for her in more ways than one.

Mike gathered up the other extraneous cards until there was only Miranda the Queen of Spades underlined by the three Aces of Holly, Jeremy, and Andi. He'd removed one too many, so he reselected the nine and tossed it down for Jon—Mr. Spitfire.

Then he drew the last card.

Ace of Spades.

Mike knew he was...useful.

He'd spent a lot of effort over the last year trying to find ways to be precisely that. Everything from flying around the team to giving Miranda a set of emoji stickers—that he'd purposely printed on a sticky label just the right size for her to paste into her notebook.

His Mooney-ness was *useful,* but did she really *need* him?

Mike was on the verge of burying his card back into the

deck when it struck him that perhaps he was asking the question backward.

Did *they* need Miranda?

Jeremy aspired to be her. He was a better man for having that goal in front of him every day.

Miranda gave Holly someone to protect with all of that heart she hid so carefully behind her brash Clubishness, even from—no, *especially* from herself.

Not yet, but he'd bet that Andi would soon see Miranda as a sign of hope that she too could overcome her past.

And him?

He flipped the card behind his hand, then drew it out of his opposite cuff.

Still the same damn card.

Without Miranda, he'd be a dismissed FBI stooge, searching for a con because it was clear being a decent human wasn't paying off.

He didn't really know this kind, considerate guy who helped Miranda, encouraged Jeremy, and got to sleep with a seriously hot Australian blonde. Even walked a damaged pilot around the edges of a PTSD sinkhole to hell.

But he could certainly get to like being the new him, or at least pretending he was like that. He had little doubt that it would all collapse soon enough, but it was a wave he definitely should ride—probably would until long after it no longer made sense. He'd never learned that last key step of when to just cut and run.

He slapped the Ace of Spades down beside Holly's club.

Yeah, that was a stupid place to be. Holly had made it all too clear that this relationship had zero chance of going anywhere. Which actually was the only reason he wasn't already long gone in search of other targets.

Was it his old self who only felt safe with one foot out the exit door?

What about his new self?

He picked up the four aces, blind-shuffled them, then spread them back out.

Andi and Jeremy, Holly and himself. Nope. Breaking it off right now just didn't look to be in the cards.

Once more just to test the fates.

Andi, Holly, himself, and Jeremy.

Fine. He lined them up neatly just below the Queen. Jon's nine still floating off to the side.

Leaving them set that way, he pushed to his feet.

Holly had tossed a blanket down on the couch next to the one she'd chosen.

Grateful, and careful not to wake her unexpectedly, he sat on the couch. The leather was cool, softer than a Ferrari seat, and smelled of its newness. Even the blanket smelled of its packaging rather than the detergent of its first wash.

Now that he'd stopped, he couldn't find the energy to shift from sitting to lying down. Though this couch couldn't help but be more comfortable than the one in Jeremy's room at Groom Lake... He was exhausted past any hope of sleep.

Instead he stared down at the suggestion of the carpet's Persian design in the plane's dim lighting.

The team might fit together—much to his surprise—but something else definitely was off-kilter.

That poker player's itch that said someone, or maybe something, was bluffing.

The cards were right as he'd laid them on the table.

Weren't they?

Even when the plane started catching up with the sunrise, and he got to watch the pilot remote dimming all of the windows, he still couldn't see what he was missing.

56

SHE MOVED SO SILENTLY, MIKE NEVER HEARD HER COMING.

One moment he was staring at the Persian carpet and wondering at quite what it was doing on an Israeli's poker plane. He assumed Jeremy would already have analyzed how it had been woven as a single piece to perfectly fit the entire plane from wall to wall.

The next moment he was staring down at the dim outline of Holly's socks. No big toe sticking out, though they still didn't match. When he looked up, she was holding out a hand. Her gold-blonde hair caught enough light to see her tip her head toward the back of the plane.

Toward the bedrooms.

He tried to push to his feet, but not even her offer could get him moving. She reached down and took his hand, hauling him up.

Still holding his hand, she guided them aft. When he shifted his hand to interlace their fingers, she didn't pull away.

The master suite wasn't vast, but it was luxurious. Unlike the crisply modern poker room, the bedroom was a journey to the tropics. The sheets were wave-motif satin. The carpet, sandy beach. The walls, tropical island beneath a shining blue sky. The mahogany tiki mini bar with two stools had a curving eave above that just might have been real thatch.

Too numb to help much, he mostly nuzzled Holly's hair as she undressed them both.

"I—"

"Keep your kisser shut, mate." No more than a whisper, but definitely a command.

She pushed against the center of his chest and he tumbled back onto the satin waves.

Their sex was typically a very active engagement.

Tonight, this morning, whatever, perhaps realizing that he was barely functional, Holly took complete control.

Her soft skin and smooth curves were the best anodyne possible for his doubts. It was impossible to focus on anything else when she was in his arms. All that remained was the brush of her hair across his chest, her strong hands as they dug into his shoulders, and the powerful heat of her when she straddled him.

As she rocked them on the satin sea, he floated free of all sensation except the two of them.

And when they rode over the top together, it wasn't some steep plunge, but a long, smooth glide to the softest imaginable landing.

If his complaisance surprised her as much as it surprised him, Holly gave no sign.

They always slept apart. Not by much. She might have a leg draped over one of his. Sometimes he'd wake to discover her arm over one of his.

Close but not too close worked for both of them.

Tonight, he lay flat on his back in the satin ocean, so blissfully sated he couldn't have moved for the entire world.

Holly curled against him as she sometimes did before they began making love. Her head on his shoulder, an arm across his chest, and a leg over his hips. She *never* did that after sex.

A line from a Passover Seder he'd once attended drifted through his thoughts: Why is this night different from all other nights?

She'd been intimate. Kind. Loving?

The last word was sufficiently startling that he roused his drifting thoughts enough to wonder if this was really the Holly Harper he knew. Just this morning, yesterday morning maybe, she'd made it clear that there was nothing between them but sex.

So what had this just been?

She traced a light finger over the line of prints where she'd nearly crushed his windpipe.

Oh. This was makeup sex—the best kind of apology in the world. That he understood. That wasn't quite the Holly he knew, but it made more sense than any of the other thoughts drifting through his head.

"You okay, Mike?" Her whisper was so soft that her words seemed to drift in from far away.

In answer, he wrapped an arm around her back and held her tighter.

Yes, they were okay.

He nuzzled his face into her lovely soft hair. If they woke up this way, that would be something very hard to reconcile with the Holly he thought he knew.

Or the Mike.

57

"THIS 'DOESN'T *FEEL* LIKE AN ATTACK'?" CLARISSA SPUTTERED and nearly choked on the slice of pepperoni pizza they'd offered her as breakfast.

She'd have to go double on the treadmill today to just clear the grease out of her system, never mind the calories. Not willing to face a Red Bull, she had a can of Diet Coke they'd scrounged up at three in the morning.

Some breakfast.

"How does taking down the Vice President's plane not feel like an attack?"

Harry grabbed a pair of pizza slices, sprinkled them with red peppers from a shaker on Heidi's desk shaped like some lumpy golden ball with filigree wings. Then he folded the two slices face-to-face and began eating them. Heidi tossed a couple of paper towels into his lap.

"Well," he managed to speak clearly despite the mouthful, "his first successful hack was ten days ago. Then there was a long gap."

"Oh," Heidi had a single slice, no red peppers. "*She* found which slice of *her* code worked after months of trying. So she spent a week stripping away all the stuff that didn't. Shouldn't take nearly that long..."

"Maybe if *he* then took the time to optimize it."

"Oh, right. So, *she*—"

Clarissa stopped herself from reaching for another piece. "I swear to God, I'm going to kill you both if you keep that up. It's Turkey. What chances are there for a woman to get ahead there?"

Heidi's grimace was sufficient answer. "Okay, so *he* takes a week to isolate his code—which shouldn't have taken more than a few hours. That means he wasn't in a mad rush to use it again, probably spending the time optimizing it. That fits. Then he takes it out for a second run to prove he's got it right."

"Then twenty-four hours later, *whap!*" Harry slammed his palm down on the corner of Heidi's desk hard enough to make all of her junk jostle and rattle. The scarf slithered off the monitor but Heidi snagged it midfall and flipped it around her neck.

"Exactly. The attack on the Vice President wasn't premeditated. More a target of opportunity. A definitive test before the big play."

Clarissa had to admit that was a relief. They might have targeted Clark's plane, but it wasn't some premeditated attack on the Vice President. He should be safe while they set up whatever the real target was. Still, she'd definitely be accelerating her plans because he was vulnerable to other attacks.

"That means that their end play is something much more drastic."

The twins looked very unhappy. Heidi even lost interest in her pizza. Neither one was arguing.

"Where were the first two attacks?"

"Well, an airplane has to be able to see at least four satellites at once for the system to work. More typically, they can see seven to eight, sometimes ten. The hacks appear to have hit clusters of six to seven, so it's hard to pin down. All northern hemisphere. North Pacific somewhere for the first. Then Western US. Now the VP's plane in Turkey."

Clarissa hadn't heard of any recent aircraft losses other than Clark's, but it wasn't the sort of thing that normally came to her attention.

Though she knew whose attention it *would* come to.

Suddenly the pizza sat less comfortably.

Screw it!

If she was going to make this phone call, she'd need some fortification. She pulled another slice onto her paper plate and waved a hand for Harry to pass over the golden flying ball thing.

Careful not to let any grease drip onto her blouse, she didn't bother waiting until she was done chewing.

"Once he pokes his nose out again, can you really shut down this bloody Turk?"

"Shut him down soft or shut him down hard?"

"What's the difference?"

The twins exchanged a glance, and oddly enough it was Harry who set aside his pizza, before leaning forward with his elbows on his knees.

"We drive a worm so far up his system that it eats everything. Their entire Siberkume will know its been hit. Nothing will boot or work after that. They'll probably have to reload every single thing from scratch like their fancy supercomputer is a piece of scrap iron."

"Okay, so what does soft look like?"

"That was soft." Harry smiled and tipped his head to Heidi. "If you want hard, we unleash—her."

Heidi didn't look happy, but acknowledged that she could do much worse with a grim nod.

"Now that I like the sound of."

58

"Have there been any plane crashes lately?"

Miranda had clawed her way up out of a dream of planes turning into numeric arrays of failure probability curves before raining down out of the sky and landing like tumbling dice on perfectly geometric fields of glacier and desert. Squares, triangles, heptagons, all mating together seamlessly on an infinitely flat plane worthy of Edwin Abbott Abbott's seminal work *Flatland.*

She pulled the phone away from her ear to stare at it groggily. The plane had excellent wi-fi. She supposed that it was a good thing that she'd logged in, so that the call came through. Though at the moment, sleep still tempted.

Andi was an upright silhouette in the dark.

In moments, Holly and Mike hurried up from somewhere.

Where was—

The soft hum of the 787's two Rolls Royce Trent 1000 engines gave her place.

The windows were pitch black. She pressed the controls on one to reduce the electrical flow through the sandwiched gel between the two glass panes. Just enough to turn it from blackout to a semi-transparent dark blue. There was a hint of dawn dusting the far horizon off the right wing. Astern was an icy landscape. Ahead a darkness dotted with white, not of city lights, but of moonlight reflected off the ocean.

They'd left Groom Lake at midnight local time. They'd eaten and played around with the cards until two a.m. by which time it was three a.m. in Mountain Time.

Now?

The trans-polar route from Nevada to Turkey would take them over Hudson Bay, Greenland, and southern Scandinavia.

She peeked again out the window before darkening it.

Another line of white lay ahead. Hudson Bay.

They were now three hours into the eleven-hour flight, which meant she'd had less than an hour's sleep.

At least now she knew where she was.

A tinny voice sounded from the phone.

She'd forgotten about the phone.

The display listed it as Clarissa Reese.

"Clarissa?" she held the phone back up to her ear.

Mike and Holly both twitched as if they'd been electrocuted. They crowded close to either side of her as soon as she sat up.

Miranda set the phone to speaker. Clarissa wasn't the most comfortable person to speak with, maybe Mike could help with that.

"Could you just answer the question, Miranda?"

Miranda had to think a moment, but couldn't quite be sure what the question was. She made a guess.

"The probability of a C-17 Globemaster III suffering a GEnx engine failure at sixty thousand feet..." No, that didn't seem likely. For one thing, that was fifteen thousand feet over the aircraft's service ceiling. For another, the C-17 flew with a Pratt & Whitney PW-100 turbofan, not the GE. That was the alternate engine choice for the 787 they were on right now.

"What?"

"What?" Miranda definitely no longer knew what the question was.

"Miranda!"

The three of them were huddled in the dark over the phone like it was a campfire. Was that an appropriate metaphor?

"Are we three huddled together like the phone is a campfire?" Miranda turned to Mike.

"What?" Clarissa sounded less daunting coming from a phone's speaker than she did in person.

Miranda ignored her and looked up at Mike's phone-lit features.

"Yes. Good one."

"Despite the fact that the light is electronic rather than a heat release caused by the rapid consumption of organic combustibles? And the light's intensity is invariant by any human senses?"

"It still works," he reassured her.

"Oh good."

"Mir-an-da!"

She hated that tone. It always made her ears buzz like the hard beat of mismatched engine speeds on one of the old De Havilland Dash 8 regional turboprops before they were replaced by the Bombardier Q400 series. Actually, the beat of mismatched speeds was little better in that class either.

"Could you repeat the question?" Thankfully Mike took over.

"Have. There. Been. Any. Plane. Crashes. *Lately?*"

"Yes." Mike was smiling at his one-word answer.

"What were they?"

"Several of them are still classified and it isn't in the habit of the NTSB to discuss on-going investigations."

"Goddamn it, Mike. That's who this is, isn't it? Get the fuck off the phone. I'm talking to Miranda."

Mike reached for the hang-up button, but Holly blocked him.

"Hello, Clarissa."

"Shit." Clarissa's groan was deeply resigned. "Hello, Holly."

"So, why don't you lay out what you've got, and we'll tell you if you're even playing footy."

"Footy? Never mind. Forget I asked."

"Football, mate. And we're not talking Australian Rules here; we're talking Association Football. No, wait, you're a crass Yank, so soccer to you. I'll send you a Matildas' ball cap—they're the very best women's footy teams in all Oz. You'll be a better woman just for wearing it atop your head thatch. Seriously, Clarissa, what's chapping your ass?"

"Other than you?"

"Other than me." Holly was smiling as she leaned toward the phone. She looked like some kind of hunting animal ready to pounce. Would that be a metaphor if she could think of which one? Maybe.

Miranda studied Holly, even tried squinting her eyes. But she just looked...like Holly.

That still didn't tell her what was going on in this conversation.

"Have you had any crashes recently? Incidents? Events? Whatever you people call them. North Pacific area. Or Western US."

"Or Turkey?" Miranda finally knew where she was in the conversation.

"Fuck!" Was Clarissa's sole comment.

Because neither Mike nor Holly hung up the phone on her behalf, Miranda felt safe assuming that it was a generalized curse rather than one targeting her.

Miranda saw no reason to withhold details from the CIA Director as none of the three crashes had been classified as secret.

"We have an unexplained civilian collision in Alaska nine days ago. A military crash during testing in Nevada less than thirty hours ago. And now the incident with your husband's plane in Turkey. Is that why you're calling? I would think you would know more about Vice President Winston's condition than we would. We were assured that he was alive."

"He's fine. Grounded at Incirlik." Clarissa didn't sound interested in dwelling on that, which was a relief.

Miranda would far prefer to talk about planes.

"We have a trace on a possible hack of the third generation of GPS satellites."

"Including the M-Code? They would have to hack that in order to affect two of those three incidents." Miranda knew that it had been touted as "hack proof" not that there was such a thing.

A new voice came on the phone. "Is Jeremy there?"

"He—"

"Hey, Harry." Miranda jumped in surprise. Jeremy had come up behind her couch.

"How did they override the encryption?"

"They didn't. Never actually touched the core code. Instead they forced each satellite's clock to loop a couple extra million or so cycles through the transmitter's processer before it was sent. Still encrypted, just differentially delayed at each satellite's transmitter, based on how many backloops they pushed it through. That's how they did the first two. They got a little more sophisticated on the third one, but same effect."

Jeremy circled around the couch to get nearer the phone. "Kind of brute force, but smart for all of that."

"Wait," Mike held up his hands.

Miranda looked at him.

"Am I getting this right? There was a GPS interference event in the north Pacific region ten days ago?"

"Yes."

Mike jabbed a finger toward Holly, then Jeremy. "Hot damn! I don't want to say I told you so but, 'Nyah! Nyah! Nyah! I told you so!' There. Now I feel better."

"What are you yabbering about, mate?"

"If their GPS got mangled, it wasn't the Alaskan pilots' fault. Just like I said."

"Oh," Jeremy had the decency to look chagrined.

Holly nodded as if conceding a minor defeat. "I still think you were guessing and just got lucky."

Though Miranda had kept her silence during the debate in the Tacoma Narrows Airport Office yesterday, she'd been inclined to agree with Holly and Jeremy. In her experience with midair collisions, pilot error was a significantly common factor —sufficient to be commonly deemed a most-likely cause. She would have to be vigilant to avoid accepting that bias in the future.

"Am I the only one who's lost here?" Andi came to stand beside Holly. "What crash are you talking about and who is that on the phone?"

"The CIA Director and one of her top IT folks."

"I'm here too," a female voice sounded from the phone.

"Oh, hi there, Heidi." Jeremy was happy-smiling.

As far as Miranda knew, Jeremy had never been to the CIA.

"How's the honeymoon?"

"Three months in and I still haven't had to kill Harry. So, I'm thinking we're good to go for the long haul."

"That's great. Though I didn't have any doubts about you two. I mean—"

"Will you four shut the fuck up?" Clarissa snarled. "Adults are speaking here."

"Jeremy is an adult," Miranda pointed out, "as is Mike. And by the sound of their voices and the fact that they work with you and were recently married, I suspect that neither Harry nor Heidi are adolescents."

"You have no idea, Miranda. No idea at all. Trust me on that."

Mike tapped her knee to get her attention, then mouthed, "Metaphor."

Oh, no wonder she didn't understand. Too bad. After last night, she'd thought she might finally be getting better at those.

59

Clarissa looked at the twins.

So goddamn smug.

How *did* they know Miranda's little geek?

Because he'd helped them utterly destroy her project to discredit the A-10 Thunderbolt fighter jet. It had taken her months to be sure that she wasn't caught up by the aftermath of that train wreck. It had also required more drastic personal action in the field than she'd taken in a long, long time.

Perhaps Jeremy had also been instrumental in the twins' cracking the security on her own past.

That, at least, made sense.

Nothing she could do about it now. The twins had made it clear that if anything untoward happened to them, her past would be splashed out for all to see.

Was Jeremy their safety? The one holding that information just in case?

Maybe, but only maybe. Not sure enough to bet on.

She sighed and refocused on the fact that Miranda's team once again knew more than she did.

"Where are you people now?"

There was a pause. Miranda was probably going to reel off some GPS coordinates along with temperature, elevation, humidi—

"It's difficult to be precise, but I'd estimate we're just north of Southampton."

"What are you doing in England?"

"Southampton Island, Nunavut Territory, Canada. We'll be crossing into the Arctic in the next twenty minutes."

Harry brought up a map on his display and pointed to somewhere white with ice.

"What the hell are you doing up there?"

"We were escalated to proceed to Turkey to investigate your husband's plane crash. We're on a polar circle route."

"Oh. Let me know what you find. Clark's pilot said something had gone wonky."

"Is that the technical term for it, Clarissa?" Holly snickered.

"Eat hot shit, Holly."

"You first, mate," she offered in her sweetest tone.

"Just tell your goddamn pilot to be sure to make a visual landing, not an instrument one."

"Oh, right. I'll go tell the pilots not to trust their instruments," Jeremy's voice faded as he rushed away from the phone.

"And Holly?"

"Yeah?"

God she hated being nice to them when she'd rather see the whole planeload of them plummet into the Arctic Ocean. No, too fast. Crash land on the Greenland ice sheet with no hope of rescue, that sounded much better.

"The CIA has reason to believe that the first three events were tests. That they're building up to a separate major event."

"Like Twin Towers major?" No smarm in Holly's voice now.

"We...just don't know."

She nearly hung up, an awkward place to leave the conversation.

"Uh, when you see Clark, tell him I said, 'Hi'. Okay?"

"Okay," Miranda assured her. Then *she* hung up.

Apparently the conversation was over from her view.

Clarissa toyed with her now silent phone as she contemplated Holly's last question.

It was 9/11 that had vastly increased the CIA's need for agents willing to do whatever was needed. Afghanistan black sites had opened a lot of doors for her, ones she'd leveraged all the way to the directorship in under twenty years.

Was this going to be some equally significant opportunity?

Perhaps this was her shot at the White House.

Now wasn't that an interesting idea.

60

"MORNING, BARRY."

Barry just grunted.

When a three-star like Barry Sizemore was playing it cagey, Drake knew it meant bad news. Worse, he was being cagey right at the crack of dawn.

The August weather hadn't yet broken the back of the DC summer. The five-acre park that was the center of the Pentagon would soon be baking like an oven. Despite the trees, by ten a.m. the air trapped inside the four-story pentagon that surrounded the park would be stultifying.

At this early hour, it was still pleasant under the maple trees.

They met at the Dunkin' Donuts in the center of the courtyard.

"I still miss when you could get a goddamn hotdog here," Barry growled in greeting.

"Christ you must be old." Drake remembered the Cafe Ground Zero fondly. As far as he was concerned, everything since the old hotdog stand closed back in 2006 had been a downhill slide: Au Bon Pain, Sbarro, and now Dunkin' Donuts.

They both ordered black coffee and a bagel with cream cheese before going to sit at a table under one of the trees.

Within moments of sitting, the tables to either side cleared.

"Privilege of rank," Barry slathered his bagel and crunched down.

"You found something." The ginkgo tree they sat under was the loudest tree in the park. The post-dawn breeze shuffling the leaves loudly together would mask their conversation even if anyone still sat near them.

"I found a fucking shitstorm. There's so much CYA going on that we should install adhesive toilet paper in the bathroom, because they sure aren't wiping any of their shit off."

Drake tipped his coffee toward Barry in a toast before drinking. He couldn't agree more on that point.

"Okay," Barry looked down, rubbing his forehead.

Bad sign.

"I've got a pair of two stars in cahoots with your Campos... except Campos is probably too much raw meat to know he's being used. Though going after your girl, Chase whatever, was his idea alone. As you guessed, one of my generals is *deep* in bed with Bell. And Airbus. And anyone else who'd buy him." Then Barry waved a hand to indicate a table off to his left.

About a minute later, a pair of JAG officers, accompanied by two massive sergeants, approached a table under a nearby maple. By the time the scene had played out, the general there was in cuffs and being escorted out.

A distant circle of majors and colonels watched the show. Any flag officer who'd been in the park for their early morning caffeine fix had long since bolted for the moderate security of being *non es in loco.* By getting themselves gone, they'd think they had plausible deniability about one of their own being taken down, achieved by hiding in their Pentagon offices. Probably under their damned desks.

"Judge Advocate General's office has enough shit on him to

send him to Leavenworth for life. Bet you a twenty he gets minimum security for two and then a consulting gig that nets him his salary times ten for life."

"No bet." Drake didn't like the odds.

"You tell your buddy Roy Cole that if he pardons that piece of pig-fodder, I just might send him a B-52, fully loaded. I hate this. I groomed that bastard. Thank God I didn't listen to him as much as he'd have liked."

Drake's coffee was suddenly bitter.

"Too bad he's not the real problem."

Drake looked around the nearly empty park. Even the lower ranks had cleared out for the moment.

One look at Barry's expression and Drake wished he hadn't even had what little coffee he'd managed to swallow.

61

The phone ripped her awake again.

Again, the first thing she saw was Andi's silhouette as she sat up and turned to look at her.

Miranda answered the phone, and again Mike and Holly were soon seated to either side.

"Hello, Drake."

This time she noticed when Andi also came close.

Jeremy hadn't so much as wiggled.

The clock said she'd slept seven hours. Or at least had been lying down that long. It felt as if she hadn't slept more than two.

"Good morning, Miranda."

Was it morning? At least wherever Drake was.

No, it hadn't been seven hours of sleep. Because she'd synchronized her phone to the plane's wi-fi, it was updating its clock as they flew. They were several time zones from Clarissa's phone call. And because they were above the Arctic Circle, the time zones were significantly narrower and the plane passed through them faster.

She decided that her inability to calculate precisely what

that implied meant that she'd had far closer to two hours sleep than seven.

"Are you alone?"

Miranda considered.

Only her team sat around her: Mike, Holly, and Andi.

She'd spent so much of her life alone. Sometimes, even with her parents and Tante Daniels close by, she'd still been very alone in one sense.

Inside herself.

Closed in.

"You still there, Miranda?"

"Yes."

Was she alone, despite the team sitting around her?

In the worst way. Actually, that wasn't accurate. She'd been in the worst way enough times in her life to know that this wasn't the worst. But to have three unresolved crashes—

And then to be told by Clarissa that they weren't *really* crashes and she had to solve a future crash? *Before* it happened!

An unsolved crash that didn't actually exist yet?

It was worse than sitting and watching the S-97 Raider test flight before it impacted the Eureka Quartzite stone pillar.

"Are you alone?"

"Yes..." a whisper was all she could manage.

There was an audible click of her teeth as Holly, on the verge of speaking, snapped her jaw shut.

Mike looked at her a little strangely.

"We've detected an internal security breach here at the Pentagon."

"I'm busy now, Drake. You know that. You are the one who sent us to Turkey to investigate the crash of Air Force Two. I can't come to the Pentagon. What do I know about security? I don't even know where we are. Besides, we have reason to believe that it's unsafe to fly."

"But you're flying now, aren't you?"

Jeremy came hurrying over, "You know, if you look out the starboard windows right now, you can just glimpse Iceland. I've never been to Iceland."

"I thought you said you were alone," Drake sounded...

"Angry?" she whispered to Mike, who nodded.

"I am alone. There's only me inside me, Drake, and that's a very lonely place to be sometimes. Mike says you sound angry. Why is that?"

There was a long pause, then a deep sigh. "I should really know better."

"Better than what?"

"Never mind."

"You know I'm not very good at that, Drake."

Again, another sigh.

62

"You've got to fight for what you believe in."

"It's not that simple, Asli."

Metin had needed to get away from General Firat, Siberkume, and even Onur. Asli had replied to his text to please meet him in Tepe Prime Mall with a: *Love to!*

It gave him both hope and dismay. They were so screwed and it was his fault. Instead of his options expanding, they were shrinking at an alarming rate.

The open-air mall curved around the base of three towering buildings. The ground floors were pharmacy, bank, dry cleaners, and a dozen restaurants, all opening beneath broad awnings that blocked the summer sun or trapped its warmth in the winter.

Because he couldn't think of anything else, he texted back to meet at Waffle In Love. It was a food truck separate from the buildings. Permanently parked at one side of a brilliant orange canopy covering fifteen small tables, it always looked like a good place for a cool date.

It might have been.

Except at the peak of an overly hot August afternoon, it was more like being hung out to dry.

Great move, Metin. Worst date place ever. Which fit perfectly, because seeing Asli, letting Firat and his spies know that he cared about her, only put her in more danger. That made he himself the worst *date* ever.

Even with the tent's floppy plastic windows rolled up, no breeze wound between the buildings. In a few hours, the evening would be lovely. And when night arrived, the windows would be lowered, making it cozy; then they'd slap occasionally and perhaps it would have made it harder to monitor their conversation.

Now it mostly just sucked.

Nobody else except the cook was here at the moment, but he didn't fool himself that they were unmonitored. Two blocks from Siberkume was only three blocks from the main government offices—every restaurant in the area would be heavily monitored. Perhaps even looking up into the tent's structure to see if he could spot the bugs would be bad.

He did look up anyway, but the strings of twinkle lights, which were always on day and night, were a little too bright to see past. Not that it mattered anymore. He was in it too deep and he'd now dragged her down with him.

"You have to be more careful, Asli."

She dug her fingers deep into that liquid brown hair he longed to touch, then leaned onto her elbow, propping her head as she slouched across from him. She continued to eat her waffle with her right hand, but she was paying attention to him.

"You get more beautiful every day." Even in the sullen midday glare reflecting off the grocer's windows, she was the most amazing woman he'd ever seen. If it was evening and there were just the twinkle lights, she'd be... He didn't know what, but it would be really, really nice if he was the one sitting across from her when it happened.

"Wow! A compliment from the silent Metin," her smile just added to her dazzle. "Something must be really bothering you for you to finally ask me out without Onur hovering. We've been wondering how long that was going to take you."

"We? Onur, too?"

"Uh-huh. Though I told him I'd beat him up if he mentioned it."

Onur was twice her size, but he didn't think that would stop someone like Asli.

"But you're nearly as traditional as your parents. I kind of like that about you, so I told him not to push. I was willing to wait a while longer for you to notice me."

"Why do you think I come to your house with Onur every chance I get? Even if he is my best friend." Metin mushed a tiny square of waffle into syrupy oblivion on his plate.

Her smile said she knew that. "So, I'm betting that you can't talk about work."

Metin could only shake his head. General Firat, rather than being upset about the Vice President's survival, had been ecstatic. Very unnerving and he didn't begin to understand what was happening.

"And...you probably wouldn't have gotten up the nerve to call me unless something *at work* was really stressing you."

"How do you figure that?" It was dangerously accurate. Firat had said all of this, even the Vice President's plane, had only been a test. So what could possibly come next? Whatever it was, it was going to be bad. He *never* should have involved her even this tiny amount.

"You mean other than my not seeing you or my brother for the last week or so? Or what you're doing to that poor waffle?"

Metin stopped himself halfway through mushing the latest tiny waffle square that he'd segmented off. "That obvious?"

"Duh."

"We've been...busy. It's a big project."

"Meaning more governmental top secret madness. You know that all that crap you do is another tool of suppression by The Regime."

Never the President or the Government with Asli, it was always The Regime, complete with capital letters. As if they were suddenly becoming the Turkish Reich in Germany's image instead of having sided with the Allies in World War II. Asli knew way more than he did about those kinds of things. So maybe Turkey was becoming what she said.

"Don't you ever think about what you and Onur do in there?"

"All the time." *Now.* That was the problem.

When he'd signed on, there'd been no need to think. He'd been recruited straight out of the university computer lab with promises of the world—and they'd delivered. Souped-up machines. Access to the real Internet, not just the slice of it authorized to mere civilians and governmental grunts. Code like he'd never get to work with anywhere else. And now a general, an actual general, had jumped to get him a slot on the most powerful computer in the country. And a private office for him and Onur.

But just last night he'd started thinking about who might have had that office before he came along.

And who might have it after, if he screwed this up.

Then this morning, mere thoughts had turned to raw terror when General Firat had threatened to have Asli disappeared and tortured until she'd confess to anything they asked of her. That image had sent him from that meeting to the toilet, where he'd barfed his guts out.

The agony had built throughout the day until he didn't know what to do.

Somehow he'd thought that calling Asli was a good idea. Too late for it to be either good or bad now. Her fate was—Metin couldn't bear to think it.

"I don't know what to do. If I try to stop..." he shrugged and began killing off more waffle squares.

"They've really got something over you, haven't they?"

He tried not to look up at her. Tried to stay focused on his waffle. But he couldn't.

As he watched her, Asli sat up very slowly and set her fork down.

"What do they have on you?"

But he could see that she already knew the answer.

She reached across the table and took his hand. Her fingers were just as warm and her touch just as kind as he'd always thought it would be.

For a long time he stared down at her fine fingers. So much more graceful than his own. He finally brushed a thumb over them.

"What are you going to do?"

He shrugged. "I don't think I have a lot of choice." Maybe if he memorized the shape of her fingers, the sharp curve of her narrow nails, the sticky spot where she'd splotted a bit of honey without noticing. Maybe if he could hold that image perfectly, it would somehow be okay.

"Isn't there any way through this, that— Ow!"

A colonel he didn't recognize had come into the tent, and he'd crushed down on her fingers.

Wings.

The colonel had wings.

A pilot.

A wife came in close behind him with two excited children. An early dinner with his family.

That was too elaborate a setup to just watch him and Asli hold hands over cold, mushed waffles.

Metin forced himself to relax slowly.

Asli didn't miss where his attention had gone.

"Okay, Metin. Are you listening?"

He managed a nod.

"The answer is that you must do what's right or you'll become just like whoever threatened you." She didn't add "with hurting me" but she did swallow hard.

"But how will I know what *is* right?"

"Simple," Asli clamped down on his hand hard enough to hurt. Maybe she actually could beat up Onur. "Ask yourself, if you *were* allowed to tell me what you did, would you be *willing* to?"

The answer right now was a big fat no. *I just came within meters of killing the American Vice President and I have no idea why.* All he really knew about the man was that he'd gotten to marry a tall blonde built like a one-woman porn movie. And that the thirty-year-old governmental plane he flew in was three times older and far less luxurious than any plane in the Turkish executive fleet.

"No matter the cost," Asli squeezed even a little harder, forcing his attention back to her face.

"No matter the cost?" *Like your torture and death?* "But—"

She raised a hand to silence him.

"You must do what you know is right. No. Matter. The. Cost."

She knew exactly what she was saying.

He held on for all he was worth, sticky spot and all.

"You're the bravest woman there ever was."

"You can tell me that afterward." Then she retrieved her hand and began eating again with a smile that he almost believed. "Until then I plan on hiding under the covers and shaking like a leaf."

He ate his own first bite as the owner delivered the colonel's meals.

The tent still felt brutally hot and exposed.

63

"We have no concrete evidence yet but—"

"Drake, that isn't how I learned to conduct investigations," Miranda felt bad about cutting him off, but this was one thing she simply couldn't give ground on. "We start with evidence of the crash, tracking and tower records, and eyewitness accounts. We gather evidence to—"

"I don't need all of the details."

She couldn't read his emotion over the phone. And being on speakerphone made that even harder.

A glance at Mike, and he made a circling sign that she took to mean she should keep going, which she was going to do anyway.

"—identify potential and likely issues. We base our investigations on evidence, not hearsay."

Mike's grimace said he might have meant something else.

Oh, like she should wrap up what she'd been saying? But that's exactly what she'd done. Wasn't it?

"Well," Drake jumped back in. "This *hearsay* is coming to you from the Chairman of the Joint Chiefs of Staff, so please don't think that I'm saying any of this lightly. Think of it as just another goddamn piece of evidence if you—"

"But you said it wasn't evidence."

"And now who is interrupting who?" Drake actually sounded like a snarling dog.

But he did have a point, so she remained silent and waited.

The pause stretched long enough for her to push to her feet and return to the poker table. The others followed and sat in the same seats they had last...night?

Earlier this morning?

What was it they said of the Pony Express riders? It was a new day when you saw the dawn whether you'd slept twelve hours or none of the last twenty-four.

Ever since her father had told her that story, dawn had made significantly more sense than the arbitrariness of starting a new day when the sun shone directly on the opposite side of the planet.

Besides, midnight was only solar midnight for a half of a degree within each time zone that encompassed fifteen degrees. Or if one used the centerline of the sun, as would be more appropriate, then it was only true for a theoretically infinitely thin line on the opposite side of the Earth.

Besides *that*, time zones were such a senseless hodgepodge. How likely was it that Western Canada, Greenland, and China each claimed a single time zone though they geographically spanned four of them. Russia spanned twelve time zones yet only used eight, one of those completely overlapped by another. Yes, dawn was a much more sensible metric for measuring a new day.

It was midafternoon where the airplane presently flew, which meant the sun was rising over Groom Lake soon. By either measure it was a new day.

She hung up her phone and tucked it in her pocket.

"Did you just hang up on Drake?" Mike's eyes were wide.

"Did I? I suppose I did." She pulled out the phone and called him back.

"What's going on, Miranda?"

She recognized anger again.

Holly spoke first. "We've slept two hours of the last twenty-four, mate. Chill a piece."

"Technically, two of the last twenty-seven hours. Personally, with the five hours I slept at Groom Lake, their guest beds are not very comfortable by the way, I've slept seven hours since our last night in Alaska, so I've slept seven of the last seventy-nine hours. Why is any of that relevant?"

No one offered her a good answer.

"I don't sleep well when there's an unsolved plane crash."

"Oh," Andi nodded vigorously. "That makes perfect sense to me. Even when I'm not on the mission, I can't sleep until the others of my company are safely back and debriefed."

Miranda agreed. That too made perfect sense.

"Look, all of you. Gods," Drake groaned, "how many am I talking to? No, don't tell me, I don't want to know. Just know that this is top secret. In fact, Miranda, code word classified Androcles."

"Understood, Drake. Androcles who pulled the thorn from the lion's paw."

"Actually, the name one of my grandnieces gave to a stuffed lion she bought for me. He wears a terrycloth bathrobe."

There was laughter around the table, so she joined in. Though the earliest versions of the tale stated the hero's name as Androclus, and in no version had he given his own name to the lion. In fact, she couldn't recall any name ever being attributed to the lion, which was rather stingy.

"It was kind of Drake's grandniece to rectify the oversight."

"What oversight?"

By the time she was done explaining it, she finally understood the old aphorism, "if you must explain a joke, it's no longer funny." She had to consult the index to locate that in her personal notebook—it had been an outstanding issue for years—but she was finally able to cross it out as understood.

Drake was speaking again. "A former commander of Incirlik Air Base, where you'll be landing in a few hours—"

"Four hours and thirty-six minutes based on our current flight speed."

Mike had begun fiddling with a queen, four aces, and a nine, as if he too was working on the new game.

She wanted to ask him about that but—

"I'm sorry, Drake. What were you saying? I didn't mean to interrupt you again."

"Goddamn it, Miranda! Focus! I'm telling you that I may have a rogue two-star general here who might be in cahoots with the Turks. We don't know how, but until we do, you'd better be goddamn careful."

"Oh. Careful of what exactly?"

Drake either didn't hear her or didn't know as he continued right on speaking.

"And Harper? Anything happens to Miranda, it's your goddamn ass."

Miranda looked at Holly. "What does your ass have to do with anything?"

"Well," Mike tapped a finger on the Ace of Clubs, "it's a very nice ass."

"Clubs?" Holly looked at him.

Mike just rubbed his throat.

Holly shrugged a maybe.

Miranda had no idea what was going on.

At least that much was familiar.

64

ANDI HAD FLOWN THROUGH INCIRLIK ANY NUMBER OF TIMES. IN the past her layovers had been brief and always happened in the middle of the night.

Which it might as well be. Ten p.m. local on minimal sleep certainly felt like the middle of the night. The entire team had spent the last four hours and thirty-six minutes of the flight modeling, in precise detail, exactly what GPS aberrations would have been necessary to cause the collision of the two planes in Alaska.

Miranda wasn't merely thorough; she was practically terrifying. By the time they were done, Andi felt as if she'd flown every inch of both flights herself.

Once they'd done the first round of calcs, they'd settled in the plane's luxurious movie theater. Keeping the windows dark as they flew through the rest of the day and into night, it felt as if they were in a cocoon formed by deep leather lounge chairs and a screen nearly as big as the cabin itself.

Between Jeremy and Miranda, they worked miracles on the computer that she could barely follow. They flew simulated planes with simulated cockpits beyond anything she'd ever seen outside of a military training center.

When they shifted from the Alaskan plane crash to analyzing the S-97's impact with the rock pillar, they'd asked her to take over the helo simulation's controls.

Mike had asked if she was okay with that when Miranda simply handed her the control elements. The first was a simple fat wand that would detect any shifts in her hand motion to simulate the movement of the cyclic joystick control that normally came up between her knees—Miranda and Jeremy had been using it to simulate the control column of the two airplanes.

The plastic's surface was rippled enough that it felt coarse and grainy, yet kept nearly falling from her uncertain grasp. Another wand would be the collective for controlling the bite of the rotor blades. The Velcro of a pair of motion detectors were stuck to her boot laces to allow her to simulate rudder pedal motion. A few controls were put on the tablet in her lap.

At her uncertain response, Mike had offered sympathy.

But, much to Andi's surprise, Holly simply looked around Miranda at her...and nodded. As if she trusted Andi to have this.

Oh. To have this—and *not* let Miranda down.

No pressure. It was a damn good thing she was a Night Stalker. Had been.

So she flew the simulation against the rock pillar until she knew, simply...knew, that she'd precisely recreated Morales' final flight. Every detail right down to the amount of GPS aberration that would have made him speak precisely when he did, as he did.

When she was finished, the exhaustion had slammed into her. She hadn't even been able to raise a hand or lift a foot to help Jeremy retrieve the simulation gear.

As they disembarked from the 787 onto the runway at

Incirlik, the night air was fresh and helped wake her up. Andi hadn't been through here in two years, but the look and smell of Incirlik Air Base hadn't changed.

The south side was held by the Turkish Air Force, which still boasted mostly American aircraft. The control tower stood tall at midfield on that side.

To the north was the American compound. Inside the heavy perimeter fence were small hangars, each just big enough for a pair of F-15E Strike Eagle fighter jets. Outside the fence were base housing, and the main American compound to the west.

Back then, she'd still been Captain Andrea Wu, newly named to the S-97 program. Little knowing she had less than eighteen months of clear flying left ahead of her. Two years ago it had felt like a lifetime.

Now?

She was just Andi.

But she still knew that smell.

Heavy metal.

Eight C-5M Super Galaxy transport jets were lined up outside of the US fence line.

That many big planes meant a lot of support. Thousands of flights through here, a lot of them seriously hot fighter jets, had left their permanent mark on the air: scorched rubber of a hundred thousand tires screeched a black line down either end of the runway on landing. The sting of kerosene from the jet fuel. The stench of tens of thousands of grunts who had spent their entire tour here—the long hours of sweat, boredom, and blood. A lot of wounded had come through here on their way to the hospitals at Ramstein in Germany.

Eight C-5s implied an immense amount about everything else that had to also be here. An aircraft carrier didn't move alone, it moved with a massive support team of destroyers, supply ships, submarines, and aircraft.

A C-5M Super Galaxy did not exist in a vacuum either.

And eight of them?

The brass was expecting some serious shit for that many to be parked here at once.

It was more Galaxies than she'd ever seen gathered together other than Travis Air Force Base in California. More than Dover or Lackland. More than Bagram for certain, even at the height of the war, because you didn't leave the largest airplane in the entire fleet sitting in a hostile zone for one second longer than necessary.

There were only fifty-two of them still in service, and one seventh of all the ones in the world were lined up right here. That spoke clearly of just one thing: the ability to empty the entire base fast.

Send in a flight of fighters from a handy aircraft carrier—and she'd bet there always was one nearby—and launch every fighter that was in the thirty-odd hardened hangars inside the American compound. Then even the twenty-five hundred personnel here could be evacuated in just a single flight of the eight monstrous Galaxies. A second flight for all of the essential equipment, and a base dating back to when the US Army Corps of Engineers built it in the 1950s could be abandoned in under twenty-four hours. Probably under twelve.

Since 9/11, massive amounts of personnel had moved in and out of Southwest Asia through Incirlik. It was a place for a warm cot, food, and entertainment—all without getting shot at. The warm cot being about all she'd seen of it in her late-night passages.

Of course, that was before 2016. Post the Turkish coup attempt in 2016, Incirlik had become a veritable ghost town. Instead of ten thousand personnel poised at a far-forward staging area, it had become an "unknown"—a dangerous place to be on foreign soil. Even the Germans, specialists in not giving a shit about what others thought, had pulled their troops and gear in 2017.

The British were no longer giving the US permission to use their sovereign rights bases in Cyprus; they were barely hanging on there themselves. They only had a few hundred personnel here at Incirlik with the Americans.

The base in southern Syria, as Ken's death had only emphasized, was a barely defensible stretch of desert.

If Incirlik really went down hard, there wouldn't be any bases worth mentioning between Italy and Qatar on the far side of the Arabian Peninsula.

This time, instead of landing in the darkness and feeling as if she'd escaped a war zone, Andi felt as if she was flying into one.

The pilots of their borrowed 787 poker plane had certainly felt it. They'd taken on the minimum required fuel and boosted aloft practically before the team's feet touched the ground. They sure hadn't waited around long enough for a custom's official to catch up with them.

Then she looked at the other four who had deplaned with her.

A nerd. A Mr. Nice Guy who felt as if he was maybe just a bit of con man as well. An autistic air-crash genius. And one other soldier—a twitchy ex-SASR operator. Just what you wanted close beside you. Being with a twitchy SASR operator was like carrying around a grenade that tended to shed its pin without any notice.

And then, speaking of detonating without any notice, there was her.

She turned to look at the blue-and-white 757 that had been dragged onto the marginally grassy median. What the hell did she know about Vice Presidential aircraft?

Not only did this mission feel dangerous, her being here was going to be so utterly pointless.

65

"WHY ARE THEY SO ON EDGE?" MIKE FOLLOWED THE OTHERS TO the screwed-up Air Force Two. Miranda, Holly, and Jeremy were practically racing each other. He and Andi brought up the laggard rear echelon.

The guards around the plane were *very* twitchy.

Now Mike was glad he'd hung back. The vanguard had been surrounded by an imposing number of guards.

"Five military. I don't know who the guys in black suits are," Andi spoke up.

"Secret Service. I recognize the type."

"Oh. I never had anything to do with those guys. What are they like?"

Mike had to think about the few he'd met. "Quieter and steadier than most military. And probably just about as lethal. Think Special Operations without all the armor."

Even the base commander, a Colonel West, coming to smooth the way didn't help much. At least it kept them from being arrested, but every guard stood with their rifle unslung and their finger alongside the trigger guard. Mike wasn't going to guess on the position of their safeties because he didn't want to know.

"Man, they're in a bad mood."

"That's not just any 757," Andi reminded him.

"Yeah, it's a symbol of the American leadership."

"No, Mike. Look at it again."

The 757 looked both cheerful and very sad.

Because its tail rested on the ground but the forward landing gear was still intact, it looked as if it was soaring aloft free as, well, a very powerful jet.

That's where the illusion broke.

The tail rested on the ground, perhaps "sat" was more appropriate; the back of the plane had clearly been reshaped to the angle of the ground.

The lower third of the engines must have been ground off as they were scraped down the long runway. It looked as if the plane was trying to fly up from underground, with the lower parts of the engines and the tail yet to emerge from the soil.

He let his eyes follow the heavy tracks in the dirt where they'd dragged the plane off the runway. The pilot had held the centerline the entire way. By how far they were down the long field, that must have been some fine landing of an unflyable aircraft.

"Okay," he sighed, "what am I not seeing?"

"Two things," Andi pointed up at the open cabin door.

An aircraft stair was roughly lined up with the canted opening. On the exposed inside of the door itself was the Vice President's seal of office.

"The seal?"

"There's a communications room in that aircraft that can be used to control the entire government in case something has happened to the President. It may be smaller than Air Force One, but anything from negotiating peace to launching everything we've got can be done from a small comm center right there."

"Okay, I get the guards now. What else am I missing?"

This time she didn't point. "Notice the two guys standing just in the shadow of the nose wheels?"

"They, uh, look different." They still wore camo gear, helmet and all. But their rifles were slung, and two large packs sat on the ground close beside them. They were the only ones who didn't look as if they were seeking a target.

"EOD—Explosive Ordnance Disposal. They're also very, very good at blowing things up."

Mike looked at the rest of the team now ducked under the wing to inspect where the main landing gear should be, but for some reason wasn't. Then he looked at the plane hanging over their heads.

Then back at the team.

"Uh, at blowing up things like 757s?"

"Well, they aren't acting like its something unfamiliar to them, are they? You can't have any of the technology aboard be captured."

She was right. They looked bored out of their skulls. Just as he would be if he had to spend an entire night staring at broken landing gear parts.

"Let's go find the pilots."

66

IT WAS ELEVEN P.M. LOCAL TIME WHEN THEY TRACKED THE 757'S pilots down.

The crash had been at seven a.m., while Andi had been flying the test of the second S-97 Raider last night in Nevada. Except now it was noon there.

No wonder she was too tired to stand.

The two pilots looked little better than Andi felt herself. They weren't bunked down; they were sitting in the back corner of the mostly shuttered DFAC. Only one cook was needed to serve all the needs of the overnight shifts, and none of them were in the dining facility at the moment.

The poor airman who'd pulled the graveyard line duty was thrilled to make them a quick sandwich. Mike split his turkey on rye with her but he got them both their own oatmeal cookies and hot chocolates.

At their introduction, the two pilots barely blinked. They each had coffee mugs that had been empty long enough to have dried rings at the bottom. No sign of having eaten, not even a crumpled napkin.

"Not the AIB?"

"NTSB."

"It's in the report."

"We haven't seen it. Care to fill us in? We're both cleared to top secret, if that's of any concern."

Mike started them out but Andi took it out of his hands pretty smoothly and began asking all the pertinent questions. They opened up more quickly to her. Maybe it was Air Force colonels to Army captain. Or they were just too relieved to be alive and wanted to talk it out. Even if they were just Neanderthals trying to impress a seriously cute woman, it didn't matter. They were talking more easily to her than they typically would have to him, so he settled in to listen.

One thing that quickly became clear was that piloting the Vice President's plane was yet another step on the pilot spectrum.

There were plenty of private pilots everywhere tooling around in their little Cessnas and Pipers. Flying IFR in the Mooney, he was at the heavy side of that tier of pilots.

The next tier were all of the commercial aviation group, from the two poor shmucks in Alaska who'd just been going about their flight-tour and salmon-delivery days, right through to the cargo and passenger airliner fliers. Miranda flew somewhere in that group. Well, she did fly a Sabrejet, so perhaps she too was on the heavy side of her tier.

Then there were the military fliers, trained to combat. Combat in aircraft over enemy territory when he was barely comfortable flying Alaska to Washington at night along a civilian flight corridor. Andi was the heavy end of that crowd in Special Operations Forces like the Night Stalkers.

Then way out there in a country of their own were these two guys. Top Air Force pilots who then trained to fly the President and Vice President of the United States of America.

He might not have calibration on what that really meant, but he saw that Andi quickly did. The more at ease they became talking with her, the more impressive she became—and the less he understood.

Shit! Was he even replaceable on his one identified skill, that he was good with interviewing people?

Any part of the conversation he could have followed was soon dusted off the table, onto the linoleum floors, and ground under all of their military boot heels.

Unable to tolerate it anymore, he pushed to his feet, "If you'll excuse me? I don't want to interrupt, but I did want to thank both of you for your help. And I just pray that I never need that nose-over maneuver you pulled off, Brad. Not a chance I'd get it even close to that right. Andi, I'll catch up with you later."

And he turned and left.

Nowhere to go.

He might as well go back to his normal role of being a Jeremy-and-Holly servant.

Can you fetch that tool for me, Mike?

You're not doing anything, Mike, go walk the debris perimeter.

Go suck an egg, Mike.

He was as useful as a Handi Wipe.

Maybe.

He stopped just inside the main gate and watched the team going over the 757. Small floodlights were focused up under the aircraft—carefully aimed so that they wouldn't be visible to an aircraft on the runway or taxiways.

It was clear that he might need Miranda's team but that they sure didn't need him.

"Sorry about that."

Mike nearly leapt out of his skin. He'd made it all the way back to the main gate of the American compound and never heard Andi come up behind him.

"Why did you leave them? Was the interview done?" He wished he had a jacket. He wasn't cold, but it would be nice to have something to wrap around himself like…protective armor or something.

"Weren't you listening?" The excitement was bubbling off Andi as she looked up at him, so he stared steadfastly at the gate.

"Sure. Doesn't mean I understood a single thing."

"That's why I was apologizing."

"Still don't get it." Mike forced himself to look at her. So that's what his replacement looked like? Miranda had certainly taken her PTSD right in stride. He liked the fighter in Andi. Too bad he wouldn't be around to enjoy even that.

"I didn't mean to take over your interview."

"Like I said. Didn't understand the tech stuff anyway." He went to walk away to nowhere, but she stopped him with a hand on his arm.

"We're looping here, Mike. The reason you didn't get that stuff is because guys at that level just don't talk to people like me under normal conditions. Under *any* conditions. I might have been a Night Stalker, but I would have been just an Army captain to them without you. You set me up to play the NTSB-nerd card."

"Jeremy's role."

"Yeah, it's where I got the idea—the *four* Aces you lined up below the Miranda Queen. I sooo don't belong in your row, but Ace of Diamonds, that was me, wasn't it?"

He nodded even though she didn't stop for a breath.

"Weird. I don't get it, but if you do…" she shrugged like his opinion actually meant something. "Anyway, Spec Ops plus nerd plus NTSB plus you playing the top secret card meant they'd talk to me. The tech those guys have on tap aboard a big airliner, instead of a tiny helo where I have to account for the weight of an extra hundred rounds of ammo, is simply awesome. The stuff we were talking about toward the end was just pilot chatter shit. Nothing to do with the crash. I've missed that *sooo* much since I was thrown out." She did a little shuffle dance of unbridled happiness.

Mike couldn't doubt the sincerity of it.

Until this moment, no, until this interview, he'd only seen Eggshell Andi. Walking so carefully and gently around herself that it was a surprise she *didn't* crack or explode with each step. Now her face was lit by far more than the base's security lights.

That she was effusing right in front of an Air Force blue semi-truck trailer with full-height yellow letters down the whole side, "Crash Recovery," was pretty appropriate.

Could she see in this moment that she had found even a brief glimpse back to who she'd once been? He didn't point it out because he didn't want to spoil it for her by making her think.

"What's next?"

Like he had a clue.

"Maybe the Control Tower?"

He looked across the field. The square tower rose ten stories directly opposite the main gate.

67

"Metin, my dear boy. It's a pleasure to meet you at last."

"Hello, sir." Firat, as usual, had given him no warning. At least this time he'd been led up to an above-ground office for the midnight meeting, not down into a subbasement interrogation room.

Two-star General Kaan didn't face him across the big desk. Instead, he led them to a deep, leather sectional sofa. Even perching on the edge of it, Metin felt he was slouching. Kaan leaned back and draped a casual arm over the back cushion. At least Firat looked as uncomfortable—also perched as if on a precipice—as he felt.

They were high in the curving facade of the AFAD Emergency Services Headquarters. AFAD was supposed to be about preparing for disasters like earthquakes and floods.

Yet it was clearly more than that—Firat had been sweating in the elevator that took them from the underground Siberkume location up to General Kaan's office.

The building was creepily quiet at this hour.

He'd sent Onur home hours ago, hoping Asli would feel a little safer with her favorite brother around.

But he hadn't been able to walk away himself. He'd needed to think, but the more he thought, the less he could find a way out.

If he refused to act, Asli's freedom would end —permanently.

Sabotaging his software program, even undetectably, would make him suddenly useless to them. He and Onur would probably be permanently disappeared as security risks for what they already knew.

...and he hadn't come up with a third option by the time General Firat had come by and said, "Oh good. You're still here. Let's go." And led him into the vast stillness of the AFAD building in the middle of the night.

Metin tried focusing on the bright-lit parade ground at the center of the government complex. But all he could see was Asli standing there in front of a firing squad, about to die in terror over trumped-up charges all because he liked her. Because he liked her and worked for a couple of ruthless bastards.

"Yes, a lovely view, isn't it?"

"Yes sir." Metin managed against a dry throat. He resisted fussing with his tie and blue jacket. Next to the generals' sharp uniforms, his jacket probably looked as cheap as it actually was.

"If I can have your full attention..."

"Yes sir. Sorry, sir."

Metin cursed himself eight different ways and focused on Kaan's face. It was the "benevolent father" face. The face his own father wore like a mask when everything wasn't exactly as he wanted. A face that barely approved of Onur and would never approve of Asli as a reasonable prospect for his eldest son.

Kaan's gentle smile didn't fool him for a second.

Unlike Father's smile—which never signaled more than the onset of pleasure or, more typically, displeasure—Kaan's, he suspected, could wield undreamed of rewards or death without varying in the slightest.

"I'm sorry I wasn't able to...fully disable the plane as you requested." Thank God for the pilot.

"No, my boy. I'm pleased. Very pleased. That you were able to fool the very best of the American planes at all was the purpose of that test. You exceeded expectations."

Which by his tone meant that, if the plane had escaped with one tiny bit less damage, this would be a very different meeting in a very deep basement.

"The tests are now behind you."

No matter what Asli told him to do, to deny General Kaan would be a death sentence.

"I'm glad that you're pleased, General."

"I am, Metin. I truly am." And his smile agreed with his words. "From this point forward, we need you to be ready to act on short notice."

"Even using the SVR computer, I still need over fifteen minutes' warning before I can act, sir."

"That should be more than sufficient. Yes, very good." This time the smile and nod said if he didn't halve that time within a week, the punishment could be severe.

"Yes sir," he gave his word to achieving the impossible.

"Your task will be simple. Syria is a problem."

"Syria?" He knew there was a war there, not that he'd paid it much attention. Now he wished he'd listened more when Asli was on one of her rants about it. Instead, he typically sat near the back of the group and simply marveled at the way she'd convince others of the rightness of what she was saying. Barely nineteen, her intelligence and passion made her a natural leader in any group.

Syria?

He really should have listened more.

68

"General Tomas Yazar, thank you for joining us."

"My pleasure, General Sizemore, General Nason," his salute was sharp. More correct than most two-stars bothered with anymore. "How may I be of service?"

Barry waved the man to a seat across his Pentagon desk, beside Drake.

He wasn't sure if he'd met Yazar before, though he now knew a great deal about him from the file Barry had provided about his assistant.

Drake had never been in Barry's office.

This end of it wasn't all that different from his own: big desk, a few chairs, and little adornment other than the USAF and US flags behind him. Rather than a conference table and a lounge area, he had a vast, waist-high worksurface. It was divided into areas by branches of the military, and each of those were subdivided into sections regarding types of weapon systems.

Clearly most of General Barry Sizemore's meetings were done on your feet.

Drake barely had time to glance at it before Yazar's arrival. A person could walk to that table, choose a topic, and immediately have everything at their fingertips. He'd glanced at Army / Future Vertical Lift and it already had an initial one-sheet report from Colonel Stimson on the S-97 Raider's crash atop one stack. It had already included an initial assessment from Miranda that it had been neither an aircraft fault nor pilot error.

Damn but he liked having her around.

He'd have to come by and spend some time going over that table with Barry.

"You served at Incirlik," Barry opened the conversation with Yazar. Well, he'd never been known for his subtlety.

"Yes sir. Two tours. The first was two years as the Wing Vice Commander, the second pair as Wing Commander."

"And you worked closely with your Turkish counterparts at the time."

"Yes sir. We're guests at their Air Base, each of us running roughly half the field. We worked very closely together—a much more cooperative environment than now exists. At times we had ten or fifteen thousand personnel on hand, not the twenty-five hundred of today. I was there for the initial planning of the nuclear perimeter upgrade, though it was implemented after my time."

"The nuclear perimeter upgrade?" Drake didn't know about the upgrade. He just knew there were fifty B61 bombs there that he really wished weren't. They were causing a great deal of concern with the rapidly deteriorating American-Turkey relations.

"New perimeter road, no-man's-land between double fences, full lighting, cameras, dogs, the whole nine yards, sir."

They were still stuck in the ground because the Turkish President didn't want to lose face with NATO by having the nukes removed from his territory. He'd already blocked three separate attempts to extract them.

Drake nodded to Barry to keep it moving.

The bombs were still stuck on the ground.

69

"NUKES?" MIKE'S SKIN CRAWLED AS IF HE COULD FEEL IT BEING bombarded by radiation this instant.

"Sure," Andi said it matter-of-factly, like a nuke was an old friend. Was that the way Holly would react? Probably. Military people were so incomprehensible at times.

All he'd done was ask why so much of the American part of the base was outside the security perimeter.

"This fenced area is mostly just to keep the nukes safe. They sit in underground vaults beneath all these hangars you see. Each one is about seven hundred pounds, a foot across, and a dozen feet long. They don't need a B-29 like the *Enola Gay* to deliver them anymore. They can jack them up out of the vaults, bolt them in pairs onto the F-16s in the hangars, and zoom! They're in play in minutes." Her smile and tone said that she was teasing him a bit, but he couldn't help his reaction.

"Nukes?" Was all Mike could manage as he stared aghast at the hangars scattered across the grassy area in humps.

"Three- to four-hundred-kiloton yield—twenty or so Hiroshimas—neatly packed in a much more convenient to-go package."

"Shit!"

"You don't swear much," Andi sounded perfectly calm.

"Only when I'm about to crap my pants."

"Need a bathroom?"

"Go take a flying leap, Captain Wu."

Her smile faded a little. "Sorry, Mike. I wasn't trying to spook you. It's just part of the reality of what we do. These nukes, being here at Incirlik, are a real problem." She began leading them through the main gate and over to the crashed 757.

"Why?"

"Well, despite all of these pretty C-5M Galaxies lined up here, we actually don't dare evacuate this base. Aside from the fact that this is a really useful base that we don't want to lose, the Turks don't want the nukes to go away. They'd love it if we all fell over dead, but not the nukes."

"So that they can use them?"

"They can't. We can permanently disable them all in minutes. Even if we don't, without the right codes, they aren't doing anything. But being one of the six places in the whole world, off US soil and ships, that we have a nuclear sharing program—meaning we store weapons there—has a lot of political pull. Turkey doesn't want to give up that pull. Once when we tried to evac some of the nukes, they shut down the airfield and wouldn't let us fly."

They passed through the gate and reached the 757.

The guards were as twitchy as ever.

Under the wing, the only sign of the team was a pair of boots hanging down from inside the head of the wheel well. They were too big to be attached to Miranda or Jeremy.

"What did you find, Holly?" He called up to warn her they were there.

She slithered down and landed lightly before moving out from under the plane's wing. "Hey, you two. Been having fun?"

"You know they have nukes here?"

"Fifty B61s. Yeah, helluva bang, mate."

Mike sighed.

Holly looked back toward the wing. "I just know that someone needs to write a majorly nice goodonya to Boeing. The degree of metal deformation caused by the gear impact should have snapped off any self-respecting wing. Not only did they hang on, but they didn't even break while dragging the jet engines down a thousand meters of concrete. Damned sweet!"

"Can it be fixed?"

"Sure, with a cutting torch," she made a slicing motion at the base of the wing. "Fuselage might fly again, but with different wings and tail. Easy-peasy, right chaps?" she called over to the two bored bomb techs.

"Sure Holly. Just tell us when." "Anything to get this mother out of here." And then they went back to looking bored.

"Where are Jeremy and Miranda?"

Holly pointed up at the fuselage.

"Let's see what Miranda wants to do next." He led the way up the metal stairs. Inside, he circled around the heavily guarded communication room and the Vice President's office. Downslope, they found Jeremy and Miranda sitting at the six-person conference table with their laptops open.

Mike knew what they were like in this mode. Without preamble, he told them everything he'd learned from the pilots.

When he signaled Andi to continue, she just shrugged. "Only a few minor details to add."

Much to his surprise, the details were indeed minor. Nuances that he'd heard, but not really registered. He really had understood everything that wasn't "pilot chatter," which was something of a shock.

"It all fits," Miranda acknowledged. "The Turkish hacker altered the GPS-supplied reading drastically, this time vertically rather than horizontally. Remember, that the GPS gives us positioning in three dimensional space, height as well as location. I couldn't make sense of why the pilot didn't notice, but the glaring sunrise shining directly into the cockpit was the missing element. With the airport's ILS on the blink—"

"Or intentionally switched off?" Mike wondered who had ordered that.

"Wow! Would people do that?" Young naive Jeremy was firmly back in place.

Mike nodded.

Holly and Andi voiced their agreement.

"That's nasty!"

Miranda fooled around with her pen for a moment. "There are only two outstanding questions. First, should he have noticed the discrepancy between the altimeter and the GPS-driven readout? And, second, should he have noticed the radar terrain indication sooner?"

"The fact that he did notice one, and saved the plane when he saw the other—despite all of the instrumentation telling him he was on the proper glidepath—counts strongly in his favor."

"And this." Jeremy twisted his screen around for everyone to see.

The critical part of the flight in the moments before impact with the mountain ridge were playing out. Even Mike could see what an incredible maneuver that was to save the plane.

"That's sooo good," Andi moaned. "This guy deserves a medal, not censure. Just for that move alone."

Miranda made some notes and Jeremy saved the file and closed his machine.

"So," Mike finally noticed the soft luxury of the seat. Maybe not quite like the 787's poker table seats, but deep, cushy, business class felt awfully good. His body was thrumming with lack of sleep.

"What's next?"

70

"SYRIA?" METIN STILL DIDN'T KNOW WHAT TO MAKE OF THAT.

Kaan finally leaned forward.

Now he felt pinned between Kaan and Firat.

"Our President is getting very tired of our longest border being under constant threat. ISIS, the Kurds, the Syrian government, refugees, and now the Americans and Russians sparring in the skies."

"Okay."

"And we're going to fix it for him."

"How?"

"The Americans have been playing their own cautious game there. 'As long as you don't make us too angry, we'll let our diplomatic corps do all the complaining.' It's time we forced their hand and *you* now allow us to do that."

"How?" Metin felt a little like a parrot repeating himself. Actually, in this room, more like a parakeet sitting between two very hungry cats. Metin the Coyote had long since run away to hide.

"Two ways. Every time the American jets are coming close to the border, you will spoof them over the border into Syrian airspace. And every time the American jets get too close to the Russian jets, you will drive them closer by altering their GPS. We don't expect it to work often, but a few close calls leading to a shootdown, or an actual collision..."

Kaan clapped his hands together as if crushing the aircraft himself.

"Those will drive the Americans crazy. And while they spend their fury driving out the Russians and finally taking down the Syrians, we can once again capture and properly cleanse Syria. It will be ours again, just as it was for over four centuries until it was ripped from our grasp after World War I."

Kaan sat back, very pleased with himself.

"You, Metin, will have the honor of restoring a major piece of the Ottoman Empire to modern-day Turkey. You will be very well rewarded."

"Yes sir. Thank you, sir." Metin hoped he was keeping a straight face. Screaming in abject fear didn't seem like the right way to show his patriotic acceptance of his new role.

They wanted him to start a war. A war that would kill hundreds of thousands by the time Turkey had wrested Syria under control.

He definitely couldn't tell Asli such a thing.

And he finally understood what she'd meant.

Neither could Metin ever *do* such a thing.

Even if he had no choice.

71

"YOU'RE WORKING WITH TURKEY TO DRIVE US INTO A WAR WITH Russia over Syrian soil?"

"I never said that. I didn't say that." But General Yazar's sweaty brow and rapidly shifting gaze, from Drake over to Barry and back, told a different story.

"All I said was that the Russians recently redeployed their Su-57 Felon fifth-generation fighters to Syria for combat testing. It's our chance to trial our own newest systems. A real-world test of our F-22 Raptor and F-35 Lightning II fighters. We should be doing the same against China's Chengdu J-20 and the Shenyang J-31 in the South China Sea. We've got to put these people in their places."

Barry's look didn't change in the slightest, but Drake could read him. He sat bolt upright in his chair, his fingers interlaced, except his forefingers, which he tapped lightly together.

He was thinking.

Then his fingers went still.

"So, you fed information to the Turks about how to hack our aircraft."

"Never, sir. I wouldn't do that."

And that's when Drake saw it. If they weren't hacking the aircraft... "Oh shit."

Both Barry and Yazar turned to look at him.

He didn't have all of the pieces yet. Far from it.

But he'd just figured out where a couple of them definitely lay.

72

Miranda's phone rang loudly. She didn't recognize the number, but the 703 area code told her it was probably the Pentagon.

"Miranda Chase. This is actually her, not a recording." So many people paused and then were surprised that she wasn't a recording of herself that she'd begun to say what she was up front.

There was a pause, then a brief chuckle.

That wasn't a sufficient result to make it a permanent change in her phone answering technique.

"Hello, Miranda-actual. This is Drake-actual. What's your status?"

"I'm sitting down." Then she considered that might be an insufficient answer. "In the main conference area." Probably still not enough. "As the Vice President is not aboard, this isn't technically Air Force Two."

Again the pause before he continued in a different tone. "What did you learn about your present crash?"

"That Boeing builds an exceptionally tough plane. That the USAF pilot assigned to fly the Vice President is remarkably skilled, despite having missed two possible clues revealing the hacker's interference prior to the actual crash. That this plane will not be flying out of here under its own power."

"Well, we can't leave that plane there. It has millions of dollars of highly classified electronics."

"There are EOD technicians standing by, sir," Mike informed him.

"We're not blowing up an eighty-million-dollar airplane. Can't we get some helicopters to carry it out?"

Miranda didn't know if that was meant to be a joke or not. She considered trying a laugh, but no one else was, so perhaps not. Instead, she answered it seriously.

"It weighs a hundred and thirty thousand pounds, Drake. An MH-47G Chinook can barely lift twenty thousand. The Russians have the Mi-26, which can lift forty-four thousand."

"I definitely don't want to have the Russians involved in this."

"Even if three could fly in such close formation, which they can't, it would only be marginally possible."

"I said no Russians. Let it go, Miranda."

She tried considering various Y-harnesses, but nothing was going to work without adding significant weight to the total load. The 757 was a hundred and fifty-five feet long and an Mi-26's rotors were a hundred and five in diameter. Two could theoretically be attached to either end of the fuselage, but there was no position to safely place the third. She'd have to agree with Drake that it was an idea not worth pursuing.

"We need to get it out of there now."

"Why the big rush?" Mike leaned closer to the phone.

73

DRAKE HADN'T KNOWN WHY THERE WAS A REASON TO RUSH. BUT all those years kicking in doors for the 75th Rangers had taught him to not question the instinct.

Now he had to back it up with reason.

"Because…" he looked at Barry, who just raised his eyebrows in question. Then Yazar, who just sat there sweating and doing his best to look innocent.

What if he actually was innocent? Nervous, but not in cahoots with the Turks.

Or…not knowingly in cahoots with them.

There it was.

"The Turks have been feeding really bad ideas to one of our more hawkish generals. Between that and the hacker's actions, I think they're trying to create a war."

"Where?" Miranda asked.

"Syria!" Yazar gasped out.

Barry's desk phone was still on speaker.

"I swear to God I didn't know. My old friends there, we'd just be chatting about the world at large and they'd talk about Syria. And how it could be a testing ground, a good place to show the Russians just who was who. I never would have—"

"Shut up, Yazar." Barry didn't even raise his voice, but was nodding. "It passes the piss test, Drake."

Drake turned back to the phone.

"I believe that you may be in great and immediate danger there, Miranda. You need to leave immediately."

"It isn't safe to fly at the moment."

"Find a way and get clear. And bring my Vice President with you."

He hung up the phone. Miranda was suddenly the least of his problems.

Barry finally broke the silence. "You need Yazar for anything else?"

Drake shook his head.

Barry dismissed him with admonishment to talk to no one about anything, especially not any of his Turkish friends.

Then the two sat in silence.

Barry kicked open a drawer, thunked a bottle and two glasses on the table. He poured a single finger of scotch for both of them—twelve-year-old, good scotch—then put the bottle away.

"It's almost five," Barry shoved one glass across the table.

Drake smiled at the memory. When Tadman had been the Chairman of the Joint Chiefs, he'd done that sometimes.

He picked up the glass and rolled it back and forth between his palms, slow enough that the amber liquid barely swirled. The still pool before the storm.

"They're trying to yank us into a goddamn war."

Barry nodded, but he didn't drink yet either. "That gives us two big problems at Incirlik."

"Air Force Two along with the Vice President."

"That's one," Barry agreed and picked up his glass.

"And fifty B61 nuclear bombs."

"That's the other."

They toasted each other and knocked back the alcohol.

Drake set his glass on the desk. Just as he was about to push it back, he realized what was next. Maybe having a drink hadn't been the best idea.

Well, he wasn't going to go this alone.

"Get your goddamn coat, Barry."

Sizemore tucked away the glasses, but didn't ask why.

"I'm not going to the President alone with this one."

Barry sighed, but didn't argue.

74

"It's not as if there are any civilian flights out of here. This is a military base." Jeremy was tapping away on his computer.

Something was niggling at the back of Mike's mind.

He slouched in the chair and closed his eyes. He'd either think of it or get some sleep. And if he woke up dead, well, stranger things had happened. Waking up all wrapped up in Holly being a prime candidate.

Shoving his hands in his jacket pockets, he ended up holding the deck of cards from the 787. It wasn't like the new owner would want a used deck.

Not really thinking about it, he began peeling off the cards as he'd left them, without pulling his hand out of his pocket.

Miranda, the Queen. Still taking notes.

Jeremy, the systems Ace. Convinced that if he looked hard enough, flights would magically appear from Incirlik Air Base in Turkey to Tacoma Narrows Airport in Gig Harbor, Washington.

Andi, the flying Raider Ace. The Spec Ops lady who could talk about nukes without triggering her own fragile PTSD.

Holly, the structural Ace. Who'd said they could fix a 757 by cutting off its wings...

"Holy shit!"

He yanked out the cards and spun the queen and three aces down onto the table.

"What?" Everyone was looking at him.

He held the fourth ace, Mike the Ace of Spades, aloft but facing away from the others.

"He's lost his mind," Holly scoffed, but she wasn't looking away.

"I don't know," Andi still trusted him, even when he wasn't smart enough to trust himself.

"What does it look like to lose Mike's mind?" Miranda actually looked around, even under the table.

There was a long second of silence around the table while everyone wondered if she was seriously asking something that ridiculous.

Then Jeremy burst out laughing, and Miranda smiled at her joke.

Hysteria would be a kind word for the laughter that followed.

They were barely half recovered, when she spoke again.

"I mean, we know what the team looks like when one of the rest of us loses our mind. But Mike's? I don't know what that looks like."

"Oh Christ. If I'm the steady one in this group, we're all in trouble."

They all raised a high five and Mike slapped them around the table because he didn't know what else to do.

"Serious trouble," Andi finally declared. "So what's your idea?"

He began tapping the cards.

"Miranda solved the crashes. Andi thinks the nukes are a

big issue here at Incirlik. Jeremy wants a flight out. And Holly thinks the only way to fix this plane is to chop of its wings."

"There are nukes here?" Jeremy looked suddenly interested.

Mike ignored him and whapped down the Ace of Spades.

"And here's what we're gonna do."

When he was done laying out his plan, Holly snagged him around the back of the neck with the same iron-hard clench she'd used on his throat.

Dragging him half out of his chair, she kissed him even harder.

Mike figured that meant she liked the idea.

Now they just had to survive it.

75

LAST NIGHT'S SHORT SLEEP WAS TAKING ITS TOLL, AND THE silence from the Tweedle Twins was testing Clarissa's patience.

When she strode into their office, they were just sitting at their computers doing nothing. Exactly like the three other times she'd checked in on them through the day. Except now it was night.

Nine p.m. last night, she'd been sliding into a hot bath and an empty bed.

Tonight she was doing neither.

"Well?"

"Well, nothing," Heidi snarled without looking up. It was hard to tell if she was snarling at the screen or at Clarissa herself.

"She gets like that," Harry looked far more relaxed. "She hates waiting. We only had tracers in place when he attacked Air Force Two. Not knowing where he'd be, we couldn't have a full counterattack in place."

"You have one now, I assume?"

"The moment that little shit sticks out his neck, I'm going to cut off his dick." Heidi's ire was definitely aimed at the screen.

"Any chance of it happening soon?"

Harry shrugged as if he hadn't a care and took a slice from a half-empty pizza box she hadn't even noticed.

He wandered to a microwave, zapped it, and set it down beside Heidi, who ignored it.

"Want one?"

"Sure, what the hell."

He did the same for her and himself before lounging back in his chair.

"Soon-ness depends. Anything interesting happening at Incirlik tonight?"

Not that she knew of.

Of course it was now probably five in the morning there.

She sank down into a chair and bit into her pizza before noticing it was Canadian bacon and pineapple. Who thought these things up? Probably some West Coast weirdo.

76

MIKE STOOD BACK AND LOOKED AT HIS MASTERPIECE. IT HAD taken five exhausting hours, three calls to Drake in the Situation Room with the President, and a lot of local assistance from the base commander and the Vice President.

Once they'd laid it out, VP Clark Winston had been glad to play his role.

On Mike's signal, three completely separate tasks had kicked into gear at once.

Clark's whirlwind tour of Incirlik Air Base was Mike's priority.

It began with a personal tour of the Control Tower.

Then an unscheduled meeting with the Turkish base commander and a tour of their side of the field.

He traveled to visit base housing units, bringing the Turkish leadership with him.

Together, they all laughed their way through an impromptu late-night talent show held at a party that magically materialized in the base gym. The crews coming off the noon-to-midnight shift had been game.

Everywhere he went, all attention focused on the Vice President and his growing entourage of distraction.

Stars and Stripes had a reporter and camera crew following him everywhere, offering a through-the-night live news feed.

In the quiet of the Vice-Presidential backwash, one very small area of the base was intensely busy.

That was Jeremy and Miranda's task.

Their first step had been dragging the broken 757 inside the secure compound and rolling it into the very biggest hangar. So big that there was also room there for a C-5M Super Galaxy that had just completed getting a new set of tires and a brake job.

Exactly as Holly suggested, they cut the wings and tail off the Vice President's 757.

The C-5's cargo bay was only twenty-five feet shorter than a 757 and it was over a foot wider. With the tail removed, the 757's fuselage had slid neatly into the cargo bay.

Andi and Holly had taken on the third task.

Together they'd shepherded the base's emergency team running surprise fire drills. Part of those drills included towing the big, blue-and-yellow Crash Recovery trailer to hangar after hangar.

At each one, the B61 nuclear bombs stored there were cranked up out of their secure underground vaults and loaded into the trailer.

When it finally reached the main hangar, it was groaning under thirty-five thousand pounds of Armageddon.

These were hand-loaded into the 757's cargo hold that was now installed inside the C-5. The Galaxy's loadmasters ordered the bombs' placement, and the mechanics did whatever was necessary to the 757's hull to anchor the bombs against any movement.

By five a.m., just five hours from when he'd had the idea, his phone rang.

Which was good, as he'd completely run out of ideas on how to keep the Vice President razzle-dazzling an entire air base.

Now was the tricky moment.

77

MIKE AND CLARK DID A FINAL "THANK! YOU! ALL!" FOLLOWED BY a hasty fade and retreat.

The C-5M Galaxy was already spinning to life by the time they reached the hangar.

They actually had to run—stagger arm-in-arm with exhaustion—to make it up the rear ramp before it folded upward and the clamshell doors closed around it. Clark's Secret Service team was hot on their heels, and not in much better shape after the long night of whirlwind activity.

Inside the C-5M's cargo bay, they were faced by a sawed-off end-view of the 757. A giant donut of ragged steel. Great bundles of wires, air, water, and hydraulic conduits, and only Jeremy or Miranda would know what all, stuck out like a thorny thatch from the edges of the truncated fuselage. The amputation had been crude, but effective.

A third of the way up the donut, the slab of the cabin's floor cut across the twelve-foot diameter. Below, in the baggage area, long lines of bombs were attached to the hull's frames.

"They don't look as scary as I expected," Clark had squatted down for a clearer view.

Each bomb was twelve feet long and a foot across. The tip was black, and the stern had four little fins; the rest was Air Force gray. It looked like any kid's drawing of a science fiction rocket. The exceptional thing about them was how unexceptional they looked.

"They look about ten times scarier than I expected," and Mike never wanted to see one up-close again...ever.

Clark's brief bark of laughter acknowledged that might also be the truth.

Several technicians were watching him and Clark closely. Mike assumed that in addition to tending the bombs, their job was to trust no one who came near them.

"Let's get out of their way." Clark led them to a short ladder up into the 757's cabin as the C-5M started to roll.

They hurried up the aisle to join the others at the forward conference table. The Secret Service team dropped off into their familiar seats in the part of the rear section that was still attached to the plane. Only the press seats had been excised along with the tail.

The Press Corps were probably all still asleep in their hotel. No matter how angry they were when they found out what they missed, Mike knew they wouldn't want to be aboard.

Now, Mike knew, was when it got interesting.

78

"C-5's IN THE OPEN," ONE OF THE ROOM'S MARINE CORPS attendees announced.

Drake watched the Situation Room screen. He wanted to shed his jacket, but Barry hadn't, so he resisted.

In fact, Barry hadn't shown any nerves except for the silent tapping together of his forefingers.

The clearance-to-depart request echoed through the room.

"This is Incirlik Tower. Cleared for immediate midfield departure Runway Zero-Five."

"Midfield?" President Roy Cole asked. He'd been in and out through the night.

"Miranda Chase's idea, sir. The 757 shed half its weight when we chopped off the wings and tail section. Even with the bombs aboard, it's mostly empty air, barely a hundred thousand pounds. The C-5M can lift half a million. Rather than wasting time taxiing to the end of the runway, they're just going to perform a short-field takeoff and fly away. Still have plenty of room for a safe abort if they need it."

"Rolling," the invisible Marine announced.

They had both the feed from the Tower and a satellite view

as the plane crossed the thousand feet from the compound's main gate to the runway.

As the C-5M turned onto the runway and opened its throttles wide, a new voice cut across the airwaves.

"This is Turkish Air Control. Flight on active Incirlik runway, abort departure. I repeat—"

"And now," Drake said softly.

On cue, it was already done. Power for the entire base flickered briefly, then blacked out.

The emergency generators in the American section kicked in and the lights came back on.

Drake knew that the emergency generator for the Control Tower had been sabotaged by the simple expedient of a pair of Vise-grip pliers, of Russian manufacture, being clamped on the rubber fuel line. The generator coughed once but never produced any power.

The C-5M, now visible only by its navigation lights, could be seen accelerating down the runway. The Control Tower camera, conveniently still hooked to battery power, showed the C-5M rotate and lift off.

"Have done a good job, guys. Have done a good job." Barry was repeating it over and over like a prayer. His stress was finally showing.

There were times Drake was glad he didn't know the full implications of someone else's job.

Barry would know exactly what it meant if the loadmasters had screwed up.

If the 757's fuselage was more than a meter out of perfect balance inside the plane, it would be uncontrollable. It could dive or climb beyond the ability of the plane's control surfaces to correct. The fifty-ton load might weigh less than an Abrams Main Battle Tank, but there were so many unknowns in a chopped-up chunk of 757 that it would be much harder to balance it fore-to-aft.

Dozens of Boeing engineers back in Seattle had worked with them over the last four hours to make this happen.

They continued the climb cleanly.

"Two engine starts," the Marine set another screen back to the Incirlik field and circled bright spots on the darkened field. "Three. All in the Turkish compound."

"How long?" President Cole called out.

Barry answered him. "She's not a speed demon, Mr. President. The Galaxy makes about five hundred miles an hour. Fifty miles to international waters. Six minutes to clear."

"Those are F-16 Falcons they're firing up?"

"Yes, sir. They can fly at fifteen hundred miles an hour. Three minutes from alert to flight. They can overtake us before we reach the coast."

"What the hell are you—"

Drake held up a hand, then pointed.

With seeming coincidence, two flights of two F-15 Strike Eagles were returning from a Syrian patrol...freshly refueled out over the Mediterranean by a C-130 out of Italy.

"They're faster and more maneuverable."

79

"METIN!"

"What?"

He slapped the screen clear. For half a second he was afraid he'd actually hit the Purge command.

A hundred times in the five hours since meeting General Kaan he'd reached out to delete his program. And a hundred times he hadn't dared.

If he could be sure there was no backup, he might do it—no matter the cost *to himself.* But he couldn't be sure.

General Firat was standing over his desk, shouting...something.

It took him shaking his head to clear it enough to unscramble his words into meaning. He really should have slept.

"Now! The plane! Departing Incirlik! It must be stopped! Turned! We need it! Safe!"

Well, that sounded okay. Not a life-or-death moral question.

He opened the launch screen.

While he'd been thinking last night, he had come up with a

way to accelerate his program. It had been easy to knock together.

The first question the program now asked on launch was, "Ludicrous Speed?"

Spaceballs had made him and Onur laugh their asses off when they'd found it on a pirate site.

He punched the Y key.

Every other user was immediately dropped from the SVR supercomputer and the login file blocked. His program now owned the entire machine's two hundred and ninety servers and five thousand cores.

It *was* Ludicrous Speed.

He launched into the American's GPS system like it was döner kebab and he was the sharp knife filling a pita bread with shavings of American code.

80

"THERE!" HEIDI'S SHOUT JOLTED CLARISSA OUT OF HER REVERIE.

She'd been trying to think of how to leverage this to make Clark's star really shine, and frankly coming up with very little. He had all the marketing savvy of a city councilman.

"He's faster than before," Harry had jumped onto his console as well.

"Not even close to fast enough." Heidi's hands were moving so quickly that Clarissa could barely see them. "Cut me another slice."

Why would she choose this moment to ask for more pizza when she'd spent the last hour ignoring the one by her elbow?

"Oak Ridge? Italy?"

"Japan!"

"Oooo," Harry turned his head just enough for Clarissa to know that he was now talking to her even though his hands were moving as fast as Heidi's. "She's *really* pissed at this guy. Japan means Fugaku, the world's fastest supercomputer. There!" He punched a final command. "I cut you a fifty-thousand-core slice."

Heidi barely grunted in acknowledgement.

"Hope Los Alamos doesn't mind," Harry was actually chortling with hacker delight. "Their Summit and Sierra machines are going to be running kinda slow here for a few minutes. Right now? The biggest supercomputer in the world is sitting in that chair and going after our pal."

81

LIEUTENANT COLONEL BRAD WHITMAN SAT IN THE JUMP SEAT close behind the C-5M Super Galaxy's pilots.

"Remember, ignore everything except visual and radar."

"You've told us that a few times, Brad."

He grinned, "Gonna tell you guys a few more times, I'm sure. But I'll try to restrain myself."

"How about the pair of fast movers hustling up on our asses?"

"I'm thinking they're going to have a few issues any moment now."

82

"Flight leader. Target is two-five miles ahead. I'm on your seven o'clock a little low. I'll—"

Captain Tamar's instruments went nuts.

Half of them said he was headed west in a steep dive. But he'd been flying southeast in a shallow climb a moment before.

His instincts said to correct.

He pulled up, and the dive got steeper.

He checked the artificial horizon—but he wasn't inverted.

Banking right didn't get him back to southeast. Now one instrument said he was going north and the other south.

One climbing, one diving.

He looked up just a moment too late.

83

MAJOR GÜR FELT THE HARD JAR AS CAPTAIN TAMAR'S F-16'S TAIL clipped the underside of his left wing.

A warning light flickered on for the Number Three hardpoint's AIM-9 Sidewinder missile. The rear mount broke loose, but the front one held. The partially severed wiring harness sparked once, twice, then the missile launched.

The bent rear nozzle and fins—also damaged by the collision with Captain Tamar's Falcon—aimed the dangling Sidewinder up and to the right.

It launched directly into Major Gür's cockpit.

Major Gür could only stare down at the long gap bisecting his leg for an instant before the Sidewinder ignition circuit fired and utterly destroyed his plane.

84

Captain Tamar saw the complete destruction of his flight leader's plane. The guy was an asshole, but he was a good pilot.

And Tamar knew that unless he did something amazing, he was going to be thrown out or jailed for what they'd call an "irresponsible loss of control."

At least his own plane was still flyable.

Intercept and escort them back to base?

Like hell.

They'd unleashed some kind of jamming signal he'd never seen.

He was going to kick their asses.

He ignored everything other than the radar signal, now out at thirty miles. They were at the coast. In twelve miles they'd be safe in international waters.

His missiles could only reach twenty.

He slammed the throttle into afterburner territory and punched after them.

They were seventy seconds to international waters.

He couldn't catch them that fast, but he could get well

inside the missile's range in that time, then it could burn them wherever it wanted to.

As Tamar blew through Mach 1, a pair of F-15E Strike Eagles flew up alongside him.

There was just enough light to see the American markings and each pilot silhouetted against the glowing predawn sky.

One signaled him to turn around with an upward twirling gesture.

Tamar gave him the finger and focused on the C-5M Super Galaxy lumbering along ahead of them.

Ten more seconds to range. Twenty to make sure there was fuel to spare in the missile's engine.

He was pushing the limits of the Never Exceed Speed of the aircraft. No drastic maneuvers at this speed. He wasn't planning to make any.

Then the two Strike Eagles jolted ahead.

They dipped, then shot aloft in an X pattern not fifty meters off his nose.

When he hit the turbulence of their jet wash, he might as well have hit a brick wall.

He tumbled.

And the very moment he overcorrected, he knew it.

He reached for the ejection handles just as the right wing separated from the aircraft.

If he ejected and survived, they were going to take him out and kill him for his failure.

If he rode it down, the propaganda machine of the government might declare him a fallen hero. Then his wife and little girl would have an easier life.

No. He'd take his chances. As he reached for the ejection handle, the decision was taken out of his hands. The left wing folded as the F-16 performed a backflip.

The wing's edge sheared the cockpit and the top half of his body away from the plane.

85

METIN HAD NEVER SEEN ANYTHING LIKE WHAT SLID INTO HIS computer. All three screens slipped out of his control.

On the left-hand screen, a very sexy green monster—like if Zoe Saldana from *Guardians of the Galaxy* had a love child with a *Tyrannosaurus rex*—grabbed the edges of screen, peeled his code away from the edges, and read it for a moment. Then crumpled it up in its tiny hands before stomping the shit out of what was left.

"Why are you playing video games, Metin?" General Firat asked from somewhere beside him.

"I'm not." Metin tapped the keyboard, but nothing happened. "I'm not in control."

"What do you mean you're—"

Metin ignored him.

His middle screen, which had been showing the plane flights and how the GPS was being locally altered, went pure white—like pristine snow.

The right-hand screen had been monitoring the status of the SVR computer. A sexy blonde witch on a broom flew into the middle of the screen, pulled out a wand, winked at him, then appeared to tap it against the middle of the screen.

A thousand beams of light shot out in every direction.

The witch remained, watching as the beams began returning.

With flicks of her wand, she swept things this way and that.

For a second he saw his own face flash up behind her. Her wand sucked that up. Then Onur's. There was a longer pause when Asli's file opened.

With Asli's photo still on the screen, the witch looked over at him for a moment so steadily he'd swear that she could see him, though his consoles had no cameras. No, but she'd know he was watching.

More files gathered.

General Firat popped up. And General Kaan.

"What the hell is going on?" Firat demanded.

"I don't know."

She flipped through them for a moment and appeared to be shaking her head sadly.

Then there was another wink as the witch dropped their two files, and a third general he didn't recognize, into a mail slot that had magically appeared entitled, *The New York Times.* She repeated the action twice more for *Pravda* and *Al Jazeera.*

Then the slot blinked and was gone.

Next came a network diagram. He recognized their small section of Siberkume, but the rest was new. He never knew how extensive the network really was.

A giant red button appeared on the screen.

The witch moved to press it, then stopped and turned as if to look at him.

When he hesitated, she began tapping her wand against her other palm as if counting seconds.

He'd wager she wasn't going to count past ten.

A glance aside. Firat was on the phone, yelling for Kaan to pay attention.

Metin turned back, thought of Asli—

No matter the costs.

—and punched the Enter key.

The witch smiled brilliantly.

An email address flashed up too briefly for him to fully see, but he'd bet it was hers.

She wrapped it like a present, in layer after layer of code.

Then she made a show of dropping it into a private e-mail inbox that no one anywhere was supposed to know was his.

The message was obvious. *Once you're good enough to crack this code, you'll be able to contact me.*

She pointed her wand upward.

Along the top of the screen, three satellites showed impossible little rockets—fire didn't burn in space. But the brilliant orange exhaust fumes were spitting out the word "Deorbit" from each sat. The three Turkish spy satellites were coming down.

Then he watched the nodes on the Siberkume network map go dark, starting with the SVR supercomputer.

One by one they blinked out.

Through the open office door, he heard angry exclamations out on the main floor as their machines were being wiped.

Onur's station beside him dazzled for a moment, then the screens went dark.

The witch hopped back on her broom, waved cheerily, and zipped across all three screens, which was a good trick as they were three completely separate computers.

All three screens dazzled white.

Then a raw BIOS boot prompt flashed onto his screen.

He'd bet the computers, all of them throughout the complex, had been scrubbed back to factory-fresh bare drives.

Metin rose very slowly from his chair, then tucked it neatly back under the desk.

He stepped up beside General Firat, who was just standing there. Very still.

Firat slowly turned his phone toward Metin. “What does it mean?”

The Cataclysm. No Extra Life.

Firat tapped the screen, but it wouldn’t clear.

“Just what it says, sir.” Metin pulled out his Siberkume pass card and tucked it into Firat’s pocket before leaving.

“The Cataclysm” had been the ultimate weapon at the end of the *Ready Player One* gamer movie. And the hero, the entire world that mattered, had been saved by an “Extra Life” token—that Firat hadn’t been given.

Metin knew he hadn’t won the game. But he hadn’t lost it either. He’d survived it. For this game, that was all he needed to do.

Once he was out in the sunrise, he sent a text to Asli.

Did the right thing.

She sent back a heart emoji.

86

"We made it?"

"Yes, Clark, it would appear we did." Miranda had expected more than a straight-and-level flight to escape Turkey, but no additional maneuvering had been necessary.

They had kept the fuel load light to escape Incirlik. But now they'd refueled over Italy and would cruise straight through to Washington, DC, to drop off Clark. Then on to Groom Lake. There, Miranda could retrieve her Citation M2 jet. The 757 might be stripped there or sent back to Seattle to be rebuilt. Someone else would make that decision.

"Before I go and call my wife to let her know I'll be home for dinner, I wanted to thank you all again. You've got a hot team here, Miranda. It's one your parents would be proud of. Don't let any of them go. Especially this one." He grabbed Mike's hand and shook it solidly. "Anything any of you need, just ask."

"Some sleep might help, mate." Holly said cheerily.

"Whoa!" he held up his hands. "I'm only Vice President. That's out of my jurisdiction."

He was still laughing as he dialed his phone and walked toward his office at the front of the 757.

"I like him," Andi said softly.

"He knew my parents." And she still didn't know if she wanted more of the stories he might be able to tell about them. He knew them back when they were all in the CIA. A whole part of their lives that they had never shared with her.

Maybe someday, but not today.

"What the hell are you doing, Jeremy?" Holly nudged his arm hard enough to send his hand skittering across the keyboard. He'd been typing on his laptop since the moment they'd boarded at Incirlik.

"I'm...just... There!" He tapped a final key and then closed the machine. "I was just finishing the reports on all three crashes. I just sent the drafts to you for review, Miranda."

"Yes, he's always like this," Holly whispered loudly to Andi.

"I wish I could stick around to find out," Andi's voice was even quieter.

"Where you off to?"

Andi shrugged. "How often do you investigate helicopters? You don't need me."

"Oh, right," Mike nodded.

Something in his tone had Miranda looking up.

Holly was glaring at him but he was facing Andi.

"Because you were absolutely no help at Incirlik. You didn't know anything useful. You didn't find out things from the pilots that none of us could understand. You didn't solve that the GPS satellite was a prime suspect. None of that."

"No, wait." Miranda actually pulled out her notebook to review what she'd written there. "No, Mike, you're wrong. She did every one of those things."

"Not according to her," Mike shrugged as if he didn't care. "Who am I supposed to believe, the woman herself or that bit of nonsense called reality?"

Miranda looked down at her notes again. She might not understand Mike at times, but her notes were real. She'd had seventeen years of practice, solving crashes based on these kinds of notes.

"No. She's wrong. These are real," she tapped her notes.

"Oh," Mike said, still in the kidding voice.

Kidding voice. She recognized it now. There was some elaborate joke going on that she was completely missing.

Mike's wink confirmed it before he turned back to Andi.

"Seems you're wrong, Captain Andrea Wu. You actually *are* useful. Guess you're stuck with us. Unless you have somewhere better to go?"

As Andi looked around the table but she was smiling. "Somewhere better to be? Not a chance." Her voice caught hard as a single tear slipped down her cheek, but her smile grew.

Miranda decided that people were going to continue being a constant mystery for a long time to come.

"Good." Mike reached into his pocket, pulled out a deck of cards, shuffled, and began dealing them around.

"Gin Rummy. Aces wild."

That got a laugh around the table that she joined in with but didn't understand.

"And trump is Queen of Spades," Mike announced.

Miranda knew *that* was wrong. "But there is no trump in Gin Rummy."

"Exactly," Mike agreed as he plonked the deck face-down in the middle of the table and gathered up his cards.

Miranda looked around at her team.

Her team.

Could she count them as friends? Maybe.

But one thing was absolutely certain, it was impossible for them to have achieved what they did tonight without every single one bringing their own unique skills.

More importantly, for the first time in her life, she knew

that she could rely on each one of them no matter what. She hadn't known that about anyone since...she'd been a child.

Mike's raised eyebrow reminded her to pick up her cards. She looked them over, arranging possible groupings in her mind. What she was supposed to do with the Queen of Spades she'd been dealt, she had no idea.

Apparently, there was a new game to learn.

Keep reading to explore and excerpt from
Miranda Chase #6
Chinook

CHINOOK (EXCERPT)

IF YOU ENJOYED THAT, BE SURE YOU DON'T MISS THE NEXT TITLE IN THE MIRANDA CHASE SERIES!

CHINOOK (EXCERPT)

SIX MONTHS AGO

OUTSIDE THE CRIPPLED AC-130J GHOSTRIDER GUNSHIP, TWO MEN wearing the only two parachutes were falling through the midnight darkness toward life.

Inside there was only death.

US Air Force Colonel Vicki "Taser" Cortez stared at the inside of the jump door she had just closed, blocking her own chance of survival.

Except she wasn't any of those labels anymore.

If she set foot back on US soil, she'd be stripped of rank and court-martialed along with every other person on this plane. Too guilty to ever plea bargain a lesser sentence. Leavenworth for life. For what this crew had done, they might bring back the firing squad.

The sick joke was, she wasn't even Vicki Cortez. That was just the name on the identity papers her mother had bought when they'd slipped across the Mexican border a lifetime ago. A name she'd since associated with bank accounts, pensions, and security clearances that properly would belong to a dead girl.

With the two civilians off the plane and parachuting to

safety, and the Ghostrider yawing drunkenly through the last of its death throes, there was nothing left to do.

No one left to be.

For nineteen years she'd followed General JJ Martinez on his quest. A man of perfect integrity.

He had fought for what was best for their country—his country, not technically hers.

And when blocked one too many times despite their combined efforts, the three-star general had taken on the battle himself.

Had it been a failure?

The shuddering of the deck through her boots would argue for that. The highly modified C-130J Ghostrider was damaged past any ability to land. Two hundred million dollars of stolen aircraft was in its last minutes of life.

The main gun mounted in the middle of the cargo bay, the 105 mm howitzer, had exploded and was still on fire. Through the small round view-glass in the jump door, she could see that both portside engines were also now burning. Fuel pouring from the shrapnel-punctured wings caught fire even as it streamed out.

Yet tonight they had destroyed four major drug cartel strongholds along the south side of the Mexican border. Hundreds had died beneath the barrage of this gunship. Millions, perhaps billions of dollars of drugs had burned as well. It wouldn't stop the flow, but it would cripple it while each cartel fought an internal battle to establish new leaders now that so many had been executed.

Perhaps it would finally force the United States and Mexico to do something useful together.

Perhaps not.

But all that was over.

All that was left to do was to die.

There would be no landing in Arizona's Sonoran Desert—

impact with the terrain was imminent.

A day ago, even a few hours ago, she'd have gone to sit by the general and await her fate.

But Jeremy Trahn had shown her something before she'd strapped him into the last parachute and shoved him out the jump door to safety. Against his sweet nature, he'd helped her. He hadn't killed. But he'd shown her how to, and she'd done it without compunction.

While being her prisoner, he'd also improvised a weapon that would have blinded her, would have stopped the general—but hadn't used it. The unused weapon and a final kiss were the last things he'd given to her.

Yet he'd given her more.

An anger.

A fury!

The plane slid hard across a pocket of turbulence, slamming her against the closed bulkhead door. She could *feel* the plane's will to survive as the damaged wings caught air and stabilized despite all the damage done to it.

Why couldn't *that* have been her life?

Instead, for nineteen years she'd been the general's weapon, unleashing all the blackness coiled within her chest at his command.

His Taser.

Go find out what's really happening at Lockheed on this project and fix it.

Track down whoever is blocking this initiative and have them court-martialed for being an idiot.

She had done everything except kill for him.

Until the cartels' headquarters tonight.

Taz didn't know if it was funny or sad. For the nineteen years she'd been in the military, she'd never killed anyone.

During her youth in the ghettos of Mexico City and later as a teen in San Diego, she'd been lethal with a knife. She'd never hesitated to serve justice as executioner—wasting no time with judge and jury. All that had ended the day she'd walked up to the Air Force recruiter to escape that life.

And now, she was again *not* military—for the act of stealing this brand-new plane and eradicating with prejudice the leadership of four Mexican drug cartels. Those very acts had severed her from her decades of dedicated service.

Now? She wasn't even the general's Taser anymore.

The only thing that remained truly hers was the nickname "Taz."

If Jeremy had done anything, it was to offer her a glimpse of an alternate life.

Taz glanced around for the general. He'd gone back up to the C-130J's cockpit. She could see his back as he sat rigidly upright in the jump seat behind the pilots, watching them fight the already lost battle to retain some control of the landing. The AC-130J Ghostrider was going down hard no matter what they did.

Only now did she understand that the general had taken her life as surely and carelessly as she'd given it to his service. He'd never abused her, but he'd *used* her without mercy or a second thought.

She flexed her wrist and felt the Benchmade Phaeton drop-blade tactical knife she always wore there.

No.

Another hard yaw threw her to the deck hard enough to knock some sense into her. The hull's metal groaned as forces torqued the airframe one way and then another. There was no need to take the general's life; the plane would do that for her.

The weapons console was useless now. All of the Ghostrider's bombs had been dropped—all of the ammunition fired. The explosion of the very last round had killed both the big howitzer and the wing. Only the HEL-A laser remained, but its aiming cameras had been burned away. Nothing left to shoot at anyway.

Two of the gun crew members who'd survived the initial explosion of the M102 howitzer stared blankly at the shattered weapon. The three others were dead or dying on the narrow walkway around the gun.

Jeremy's lesson.

Of them all, that's the one that counted.

And it was so simple...

Live!

And the safest place in a plane crash?

Aft.

Taz sprinted for the tail, racing upslope against the steep dive of the C-130.

An inch under five feet, she was small enough to slip through a gap under the Bofors 40mm autocannon.

The pair of surviving gunners still hung on beside the ruined howitzer, taking no action to save themselves.

Squeezing between them and the big gun, the hot metal of the breech burned a line along her shoulder, but she ignored the pain.

The AC-130J's rear ramp had been fitted with vertical bomb launch tubes. No seats back here. Maybe, if she braced herself against the tubes and the tail broke away on impact, she'd have a chance.

The gunners had been snapped out of their lethargy by her passage. In moments they'd squeezed in to either side of her as the dying plane flailed and twisted toward the hard earth. The g-force pressed the three of them more tightly together than if they were having a threesome.

It was dark back here. Almost safe. The red night-fighting lights by the gun barely reached the launch tubes. Just enough that she could see the wide eyes of the man pressed chest-to-chest against her.

A sickening lurch.

"There goes the wing," the one behind her gasped out.

She'd helped recruit them to this final mission, but now couldn't even recall their names.

In a death spiral now, inevitable with only one wing. Not even being in the tail would offer any safety.

General Martinez would welcome death come to find the warrior at last.

Well to *hell* with him.

Before the first spiral was complete, before the twisting momentum became unsurvivable, the plane slammed into the ground.

***

Taz remembered only flashes of what came next.

The impact.

The curious soundlessness of the fuselage ripping away from the tail—the hull skin shredding, the cross-connecting beams shearing.

A clear view as the fuel in the remaining wing exploded, pulverizing the main fuselage—too loud to be called a sound.

The gaping mouth of her chest-to-chest companion as he was burned alive by the flash of fire blasted into the now open-ended tail section. She was small enough, or he big enough, that she remained tucked safely in his heat shadow—saved from the worst burns by yanking her flight jacket over her hair and face.

The final shudders of the man behind her as his neck was broken when slammed against the launch tubes.

No more slide and tumble, the tail came to rest in a shallow arroyo filled with sand and tumbleweeds.

Claw her way out from between two corpses.

Tumble onto the night-cool sand.

No longer a US Air Force colonel.

Crawling.

No longer the general's feared right-hand Taser.

Crawling with no thought but...away.

No longer Vicki Cortez.

All of her past selves dead in the flaming wreckage.

Another hard explosion behind her—she didn't bother turning to see—assured her that her body wouldn't be missed.

She was north of Nogales.

In the Sonoran Desert of Arizona.

Once more in *los Estados Unidos*—north of the border.

Once more an illegal with no identity.

Just as she had at eleven years old, she set her guide by the North Star and kept moving.

Clear of the wreckage, clear of the likely search perimeter, she buried herself in the cool night sand and slept.

When she woke, it was...again? ...still? night.

She continued north.

Taz hadn't expected to survive this operation, hadn't expected to want to, or she'd have emptied her bank accounts. Now all she had was the emergency fund that was never off her person.

In Tucson, she bought a new identity. Colonel Vicki "Taser" Cortez of the United States Air Force became US citizen Tanya Roberts.

The clean social security number and identity came from a crooked mortician and a corrupt medical examiner who took most of her funds between them for *not* reporting Tanya's recent death. Tanya was buried as Jane Doe—death by mugger.

No family.

Nothing in "her" apartment worth keeping or pawning when Taz checked it out, except for a phone with no contacts or recent calls other than work, and a set of car keys. Tanya had been a true loner, and perhaps even welcomed death. Perfect.

Taz replenished her funds by emptying out Tanya's meager bank accounts, and she was done.

As Tanya, she was now legally five years younger—which was closer to her true age. She'd actually joined the Air Force at fifteen straight out of high school after her first name change had aged her three years. Now, her ID declared she was thirty-two instead of Vicki's thirty-seven, or the thirty-four she actually was in some half-forgotten reality.

With her size and looks, she could have safely dropped ten years instead of just the five.

A week and a hundred miles later, she filed for a legal name change in Phoenix. Somehow, having the same name as a tall, redheaded, 1980s Hollywood sex-kitten actress just seemed too unlikely. She also wanted as clean a break as possible from anyone seeking the dead Tanya Roberts.

Flores was her original family name, left south of the border when she was eleven. She took that back for her mother's memory.

Her birth name was meaningless. In the Air Force she was always Taz or Cortez. But Jeremy had called her Vicki when they'd made love.

Made love.

She'd had sex when she cared to, but there was little question that mere sex wasn't something Jeremy Trahn understood.

And he'd proven the difference to her, much to her surprise.

She wasn't Vicki to anyone except Jeremy. So, she kept both her family name and nickname, and, for luck, the name that Jeremy had called her.

The Motor Vehicle Department clerk hadn't even looked at the picture on Tanya Roberts' old driver's license before issuing her one under her new/old name, which had saved the five hundred dollars she'd had folded tight and ready. They'd switched over the vehicle registration at the same time. Social Security had accepted the name change with the court order and new ID; they gave her a fresh card just as painlessly.

With no plan beyond survival, Tasia Vicki Flores pocketed her new identity, climbed into "her" rusted-but-running 1997 Toyota Corolla, and left Phoenix to follow wherever the North Star led.

"You've got to be kidding me." Jeremy looked at the card he'd just drawn.

"Your poker face sucks. You know that, right?"

"So helpful, Mike." The game's rules kept evolving, but there was no question that the B-1B Lancer bomber was the greatest suck of an airplane card—and truly appropriate for such a sad aircraft. When he'd taken Miranda's list of aircraft and remade them into a card deck, he'd arranged them by coolness factor. Actually, by how he guessed Miranda would grade each one before making a few adjustments of his own.

What he hadn't planned on was how often he drew the deuce of combat planes. This definitely required some rethinking.

"Whatever," he laid down the card and rolled his dice. He needed at least a four to keep the plane aloft.

A one.

He augered in. Too many total crashes, and he was out of the game before it had really begun.

Chinook
Miranda Chase #7
Coming in March, 2021

ABOUT THE AUTHOR

USA Today and Amazon #1 Bestseller M. L. "Matt" Buchman started writing on a flight south from Japan to ride his bicycle across the Australian Outback. Just part of a solo around-the-world trip that ultimately launched his writing career.

From the very beginning, his powerful female heroines insisted on putting character first, *then* a great adventure. He's since written over 60 action-adventure thrillers and military romantic suspense novels. And just for the fun of it: 100 short stories, and a fast-growing pile of read-by-author audiobooks.

Booklist says: "3X Top 10 of the Year." PW says: "Tom Clancy fans open to a strong female lead will clamor for more." His fans say: "I want more now...of everything." That his characters are even more insistent than his fans is a hoot.

As a 30-year project manager with a geophysics degree who has designed and built houses, flown and jumped out of planes, and solo-sailed a 50' ketch, he is awed by what is possible. More at: www.mlbuchman.com.

Other works by M. L. Buchman: *(* - also in audio)*

Action-Adventure Thrillers

Dead Chef

One Chef!
Two Chef!

Miranda Chase

*Drone**
*Thunderbolt**
*Condor**
*Ghostrider**
*Raider**
*Chinook**
*Havoc**
*White Top**

Romantic Suspense

Delta Force

*Target Engaged**
*Heart Strike**
*Wild Justice**
*Midnight Trust**

Firehawks

MAIN FLIGHT

Pure Heat
Full Blaze
*Hot Point**
*Flash of Fire**
Wild Fire

SMOKEJUMPERS

*Wildfire at Dawn**
*Wildfire at Larch Creek**
*Wildfire on the Skagit**

The Night Stalkers

MAIN FLIGHT

The Night Is Mine
I Own the Dawn
Wait Until Dark
Take Over at Midnight
Light Up the Night
Bring On the Dusk
By Break of Day

AND THE NAVY

Christmas at Steel Beach
Christmas at Peleliu Cove

WHITE HOUSE HOLIDAY

*Daniel's Christmas**
*Frank's Independence Day**
*Peter's Christmas**
*Zachary's Christmas**
*Roy's Independence Day**
*Damien's Christmas**

5E

Target of the Heart
Target Lock on Love
Target of Mine
Target of One's Own

Shadow Force: Psi

*At the Slightest Sound**
*At the Quietest Word**
*At the Merest Glance**
*At the Clearest Sensation**

White House Protection Force

*Off the Leash**
*On Your Mark**
*In the Weeds**

Contemporary Romance

Eagle Cove

Return to Eagle Cove
Recipe for Eagle Cove
Longing for Eagle Cove
Keepsake for Eagle Cove

Henderson's Ranch

*Nathan's Big Sky**
*Big Sky, Loyal Heart**
*Big Sky Dog Whisperer**

Other works by M. L. Buchman:

Contemporary Romance (cont)

Love Abroad

Heart of the Cotswolds: England
Path of Love: Cinque Terre, Italy

Where Dreams

Where Dreams are Born
Where Dreams Reside
*Where Dreams Are of Christmas**
Where Dreams Unfold
Where Dreams Are Written

Science Fiction / Fantasy

Deities Anonymous

Cookbook from Hell: Reheated
Saviors 101

Single Titles

The Nara Reaction
Monk's Maze
the Me and Elsie Chronicles

Non-Fiction

Strategies for Success

Managing Your Inner Artist/Writer
*Estate Planning for Authors**
Character Voice
*Narrate and Record Your Own Audiobook**

Short Story Series by M. L. Buchman:

Romantic Suspense

Delta Force

Th Delta Force Shooters
The Delta Force Warriors

Firehawks

The Firehawks Lookouts
The Firehawks Hotshots
The Firebirds

The Night Stalkers

The Night Stalkers 5D Stories
The Night Stalkers 5E Stories
The Night Stalkers CSAR
The Night Stalkers Wedding Stories

US Coast Guard

White House Protection Force

Contemporary Romance

Eagle Cove

Henderson's Ranch*

Where Dreams

Action-Adventure Thrillers

Dead Chef

Miranda Chase Origin Stories

Science Fiction / Fantasy

Deities Anonymous

Other

The Future Night Stalkers
Single Titles

SIGN UP FOR M. L. BUCHMAN'S NEWSLETTER TODAY

and receive:
Release News
Free Short Stories
a Free Book

Get your free book today. Do it now.
free-book.mlbuchman.com

CPSIA information can be obtained
at www.ICGtesting.com
Printed in the USA
LVHW032105080421
683868LV00001B/108